Taylor Blake
SEIZES THE DAY

Books by Laura Jane Williams

Taylor Blake Is a Legend
Taylor Blake Seizes the Day

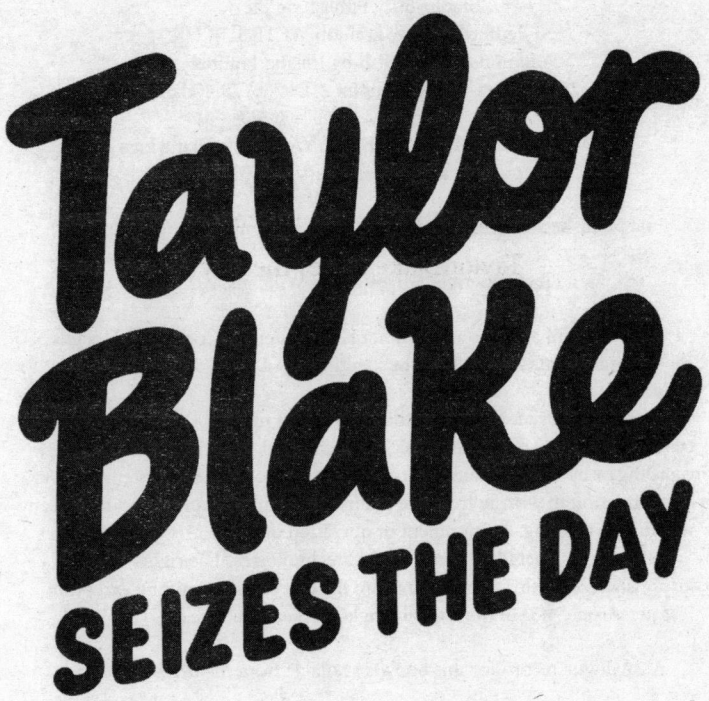

Taylor Blake Seizes the Day

LAURA JANE WILLIAMS

BLOOMSBURY
LONDON OXFORD NEW YORK NEW DELHI SYDNEY

BLOOMSBURY YA
Bloomsbury Publishing Plc
50 Bedford Square, London WC1B 3DP, UK
Bloomsbury Publishing Ireland Limited
29 Earlsfort Terrace, Dublin 2, D02 AY28, Ireland

BLOOMSBURY, BLOOMSBURY YA and the Diana logo
are trademarks of Bloomsbury Publishing Plc

First published in Great Britain in 2025 by Bloomsbury Publishing Plc

Text copyright © Laura Jane Williams, 2025

Laura Jane Williams has asserted her right under the Copyright, Designs
and Patents Act, 1988, to be identified as Author of this work

All rights reserved. No part of this publication may be: i) reproduced or
transmitted in any form, electronic or mechanical, including photocopying,
recording or by means of any information storage or retrieval system without
prior permission in writing from the publishers; or ii) used or reproduced in any
way for the training, development or operation of artificial intelligence (AI)
technologies, including generative AI technologies. The rights holders
expressly reserve this publication from the text and data mining exception
as per Article 4(3) of the Digital Single Market Directive (EU) 2019/790

A catalogue record for this book is available from the British Library

ISBN: PB: 978-1-5266-6820-2; eBook: 978-1-5266-6809-7;
ePDF: 978-1-5266-6808-0

2 4 6 8 10 9 7 5 3 1

Typeset by RefineCatch Limited, Bungay, Suffolk
Printed and bound in Great Britain by CPI Group (UK) Ltd, Croydon CR0 4YY

To find out more about our authors and books visit www.bloomsbury.com
and sign up for our newsletters
For product safety related questions contact productsafety@bloomsbury.com

For Carla Hutchinson, for loving Taylor as much as I do, and Alex Antscherl, for taking over with such enthusiasm

1

The girls squeal so loudly, and for so long, that I honestly think I might go deaf.

'THIS! IS! AMAZING!' yells Lucy, leaping up to her feet and launching at me so that I fall over backwards on to the carpet, her arms around my neck and my eyes staring at the clouds painted on Star's bedroom ceiling.

'Pile on!' trills Star, leaping off her bed to clamber on to me as well, so that my vision gets blurred by a mass of hair and body parts. I push them off and roll away, grabbing a pillow to use as a shield from further attack.

'Stoooooppppp!' I say, giggling because I don't really mean it. I've just told them about last night, about kissing Duncan. My first-ever kiss! And to be honest, I could talk about it all night and all tomorrow and probably the day after too, if they let me.

It's a big deal. HUGE. *Massive.* Taylor Blake is no longer the only girl in the world not to have been kissed! Alert the press!

'Taylor and Duncan, sitting in a tree ...' Star starts to sing, and Lucy quickly joins in.

'K-I-S-S-I-N-G!' they bellow together, like some sort of bonkers cabaret act, all jazz hands and wide-open mouths. Then they cackle like witches around a cauldron.

I throw the pillow I'm holding at them.

... And I miss.

'Oh, Taylor, I fancy you so, *so* much, come here for a massive snog!' says Lucy, putting on a deep voice and pretending to be Duncan.

Star sniggers and says in a stupid, high-pitched sing-song, 'Oh, Duncan, I think you're hubba-hubba-hot! Let's be havin' ya, handsome!'

They collapse into each other and pretend to smooch – as everyone's favourite couple it's an act they've perfected in real life, so taking the mick out of me and Duncan is very convincing. They're a silly Taylor-and-Duncan tribute act, running their hands up and down each other's backs and making noises of delight.

'Oi!' Star's dad, Bo, barks from downstairs. 'Stop jumping up and down! The whole bloomin' house is shaking. Have fun more quietly, please!'

Star gives Lucy a quick peck on the cheek and then they

pull apart. 'Sorry, Dad!' Star shouts, and then she lowers her voice to add, 'It's just that Taylor has been sucking face with Duncan Higginbottom and she can't stop talking about it!'

'You asked!' I shriek.

Lucy rolls her eyes jokingly. 'We're just *teasing*,' she says. 'Because we're so happy for you. Plus, I still can't get over how he was all, *I've never kissed anybody and you've kissed loads of people so now I'm nervous.*'

'I know,' I say. 'I've been so worried about being a kiss virgin that I just assumed I walked around with a humongous neon sign above my head that flashes *Never been kissed!* and everyone secretly laughed about it behind my back.'

'Noooo,' insists Star. 'There's loads of people who still haven't been kissed yet.'

'Although you're not one of them ... not any more!' adds Lucy, genuinely thrilled for me.

I grin again, so hard my lips might fall off my face as my cheeks explode with delight.

'Gah!' I exclaim. 'It was so nice! I know you thought I was mad for being so obsessed with getting my first kiss, but it was perfect and totally worth the wait ...' I sigh dreamily.

'So what now?' asks Lucy, ripping open a sharing bag of Monster Munch. She takes one, pops it in her mouth, and then offers me one, totally casually, like *so what now?* isn't the biggest question in the entire world.

'What do you mean?' I ask, helping myself to a crisp. It's weird, but I feel cold all over suddenly, like my body knows what she's getting at before my brain can catch up. I swallow hard. What now? *Quelle question*, as my French exchange partner, Axel, would say! I don't know what happens now!

'Do you want to kiss him again? Or kiss somebody new?' Lucy presses, taking another crisp. She sits on Star's desk chair the wrong way, so she can lean her chin on the back as she waits for me to answer.

From the bottom of the bed Star crinkles up her face, confused, and says, 'Aren't you going to be dating now? Exclusively?'

I look between my two friends: Lucy, with those big eyes and that floppy blonde fringe, like butter wouldn't melt, and Star, short dark hair and almond-shaped gaze, serious and solemn.

'Urm …' I falter.

'Nooooo. They're not boyfriend and girlfriend,' Lucy says to Star. 'Not after just one kiss.'

Star bats back: 'But they like each other and they've been on a date and kissed and want to kiss again. That's pretty serious.' She looks at me. 'Duncan wants to kiss again, right?'

I blink, processing the question. I've been so caught up in thinking about how I feel, I actually haven't considered what Duncan wants. He texted me this morning, a smiley face, and I sent a smiley face back. But that's it. Neither of us have said we should do it again sometime. And to be fair, I asked him out last time so I think that means the ball is in his court now. Or is that not feminist? Maybe I shouldn't put rules on it. Hmmmm. This particular conundrum isn't mentioned in my Bible, aka *How to Be Parisian When You're Not from Paris*. I wonder if they ever wrote a sequel? I take a breath, trying to channel my inner chic French girl to see what she'd do, but decide it's pointless. French girls don't have to worry about love, do they? Everyone just fancies them and then they take their pick. Oh, to be French!

Lucy sighs theatrically and grabs her phone. 'I'm going to google it,' she announces, jabbing at her screen and narrating what she types. 'Is … he … my … boyfriend … now … we've … kissed?'

Star and I await the verdict of the search engine gods. I feel quite nervous, actually. If I thought a first kiss was somehow the end of my problems of being a kiss virgin, I've not realised it was actually only the beginning of a whole *new* set of worries!

Lucy squints, the light of the answers illuminating her face as she purses her lips and her eyes move back and forth as she reads. I don't know what I want her to say, that Duncan is my boyfriend now, or that he isn't. I like him! But now I'm worried he might not want to kiss me again. Not that I did it wrong or it wasn't nice, because I'm 99 per cent sure it was as good for him as it was for me, but … well. You just never know, do you? Perhaps we *are* a couple now, and I just didn't get the memo yet? THIS IS ALL SO UNKNOWN TO ME!

'This says,' Lucy begins, Star and me holding our breath, 'that he's not.' She puts on a fancy voice to read out: *'Most people do not define their relationship without talking about it first. So if you want the person you kissed to be your boyfriend or girlfriend, ask!'*

'Oh sure!' I say, mortified at the very idea. 'I'll just walk up to him and say, oh, hello, Duncan, do you want to be my boyfriend?'

Star pulls a face, amused by me.

'That's what Lucy did to me,' she says nonchalantly. 'She asked me one day, after RE.'

I look at Lucy. She shrugs. 'I like clarity,' she says. 'And I knew Star was too much of a scaredy-cat to bring it up herself.'

'Hey!' Star says, wrinkling up her nose.

Lucy blows her a kiss. 'Just kidding.'

My head is overwhelmed with thoughts, loads of them coming at once. 'Right,' I say, scratching my chin like an ancient philosopher with a beard. 'So, let me just check I understand. At some point, if I want him to be my boyfriend, we'll need to talk about it?'

'Yes ...' says Lucy, like I'm a bit slow and she's waiting for me to catch up. She'd roll her eyes if she could get away with it, I'm sure, but now is not the time to be sarcastic. This is serious!

'And typically,' I continue, 'after a first kiss there is ... a *second* kiss.'

'Your counting is getting really good!' Star jokes. 'Do you know what comes after second? I'll give you a clue ...' She makes a 'th' sound, but it makes my blood run cold.

'I just ...' I start, and Star knows her gag hasn't landed with me – she didn't realise this was no time for jokes. She quickly rearranges her features into something less mocking and more concerned, all raised eyebrows and crinkly eyes. 'I've been first-kiss obsessed. But now I don't know how to go about a second kiss! And I mean with Duncan. I deffo want it to happen with him. He's a nice kisser.'

Lucy shakes her head good-naturedly. 'Oh, babe,' she says kindly. 'Sometimes I think you don't have enough real problems, and so you make them up.'

'This is a real problem!' I say.

'You're going to be *fine*,' Star insists, putting a hand on my arm. 'Lucy is being cynical, but what she's really trying to say is you'll be OK. If you like Duncan and Duncan likes you, a second kiss will happen before you know it. Just try not to worry, all right?'

'All right,' I say, and Lucy and Star accept what I'm saying at face value, like absolute goons, and we crack on with our Harry Styles and Tom Holland fanfiction, laughing about a plot line we've been writing about them teaching a theatre class at Crickleton as substitute teachers. Meanwhile my head is swimming with different scenarios involving Duncan: What if he's changed his mind? What if I've put him off kissing for life? What if he thought the kiss was OK but wants to try it out with a bunch of other girls too? Because it was his first kiss as well! He might want to sow his wild oats now! Or it could all go the other way. What if he gets way too serious way too fast and I end up married at fifteen after lying about my age and eloping to Gretna Green? How does everybody else figure this stuff out?! Lucy and Star never seemed to be this confused about their relationship. WHY DOES THIS ALL FEEL SO DAUNTING?!

Fancying people is exhausting.

2

Later that evening, Star's dad, Bo, drops me off at Grandma and Grandad's bungalow. We were all going to have a sleepover at Star's, but then she remembered she has to get up at 5.30 a.m. (!!) to drive three hours to a fencing tournament and I love the girl, but not enough to get up at that time *on a weekend*. I've not stayed over with Grandma and Grandad for ages though, so it will be nice. Grandma always sneaks into the tiny spare room and puts the bedside lamp on before bed so it's cosy when I go in, and leaves a chocolate on my pillow, like at a posh hotel. She's so cute. They both are. And they let me have Pop-Tarts, which Mum is *not* allowed to know about. She'd go bonkers! *Growing bodies need more than just sugar for breakfast*, she says. Grandma says what's the point in being a grandma if you can't treat your grandchild to something ridiculous though, and who am I to argue. I like the strawberry ones with the icing on best. They're a real treat.

'Isn't that the French teachers from your school?' Bo asks as we round the corner to G&G's street. I look to where he's pointing, only to see Madame Jones (aka Carrie, as we found out when we hosted the French exchange last month) and Monsieur Brown (Joel, which is funny because he looks more like a Ted or a Dave) HOLDING HANDS! And laughing! And kicking at the autumn leaves on the pavement at their feet! Gosh, their relationship has evolved quickly since the Frenchies went home, when they almost snogged in front of all of us. You don't think of teachers as having their own love lives, do you. Not until they flop into each other's arms as Monsieur Brown's love rival pulls away with a bus full of kids to go back to France, and he stakes his claim. I must make an involuntary noise, because Bo laughs and says, 'I know. Imagine, teachers *dating*.'

'It's weird,' I say, observing them through the car window. They seem so happy. 'I feel like I'm supposed to be grossed out – Monsieur Jones is famous for his coffee breath – but I think they got together over the French exchange and we all saw it happen and it was … nice?' I say. 'Like, Monsieur Brown got all jealous when Madame Jones was flirting with the teacher from France, and I once walked in on Monsieur Brown and Madame Jones kissing. I probably shouldn't tell you that because it was during school hours, but they tried to pretend it didn't happen. I think it's polite if I pretend it didn't happen too. But yeah, it's kind of … heart-warming?' I say.

'I've heard falling in love can be all right, yeah,' Bo says teasingly. I give him a cheeky eyebrow raise and he chuckles. It makes me laugh, too, though. I like Bo. He's a cool dad. 'And perhaps his lady friend there *likes* coffee breath,' Bo reasons. 'Better than having gingivitis and smelling like a sewer rat.'

'That's true. Small mercies. Just goes to show that there's hopefully somebody for everyone.'

'Oh, I'd say so.' Bo nods. 'Everybody has their person. Trick is to enjoy the journey to finding them too.'

Hmmmm. That's quite a poetic thought, actually! *Enjoy the journey …*

We keep driving, and I start to wonder if *my* breath is OK. The list of things to worry about keeps growing! I don't even remember Duncan's breath. It didn't smell of anything, did it? I surreptitiously cover my mouth and blow, trying to smell if I'm repulsive or OK. I can't tell. I take that as a good sign. If my breath was as bad as Monsieur Brown's I'd be able to smell it, surely.

We slow down in front of the house. Bo asks, 'It's this one, isn't it?'

'Yup!' I reply, noticing Grandad stood outside at the bottom of the drive with a hosepipe and a look of fixed concentration as he sprays water at the ground. 'Thanks so much, Bo. And sorry again for all the noise we made.'

'Good job I like you lot,' Bo says. 'Otherwise there'd be trouble.' He winks so I know he doesn't mean it. See? Cool dad. 'Now come on, I'll get out and say hello. I like your grandparents. Bloody bonkers, they are. But nice.'

That's about as accurate a statement as I've ever heard about my grandparents.

Grandma comes out of the front door just as Bo and I see that Grandad isn't hosing the ground, he's hosing *into* the ground. He's taken the cover off the drain on the drive and is power-hosing inside, into the drains, and there's an almighty stink of ... poop.

'Taylor! Bo!' Grandma says, right as Grandad says, 'Don't come too close! There's splashback happening here – you don't want to get poo on your trousers!'

I look at Grandma, horrified, and then at Bo, who is staring wide-eyed at the scene in front of him: Grandad in his wellies, the hose in one hand and a massive stick in the other that he's using to fish out discoloured face wipes from the poopy pipes.

'It's these things!' he says, tutting. 'I've told Rachel they're no good, but the thing is, once you've used moist toilet paper there's no going back!'

Ah, so they're not technically face wipes. They're those toilet wipes you can get that are like face wipes, but for your butt.

'And what are we to do,' Grandad continues. 'Wipe our bums with them and then put the tissue in the bin? I don't think so! That's damned unhygienic! I don't care what they used to do in Ancient Rome or wherever!'

'Ancient Rome?' Bo says, as confused as I am.

Grandad stabs at more wet wipes. 'Gotcha!' he says, impervious to our quite disgusted curiosity.

'Sorry about this, Bo,' Grandma says apologetically. 'As you can see, we've a bit of a situation happening. And there's no good time for plumbing issues …'

'No,' says Bo, unable to take his eyes off what Grandad is doing. 'Can I help at all, or … ?'

'No, no,' Grandma says. 'We appreciate you dropping Taylor home. You get off – we don't want to put you off your tea!'

'No,' says Bo again, still staring.

'I did a massive poo, you see,' Grandad explains, even though nobody asked. 'And it must have blocked the drain because the toilet wouldn't flush properly. And so I came out here to check the drain, and no wonder! Do you use them, Bo, the moist wipes?'

'Can't say I do, David, no. Should I invest?'

'Absolutely not!' Grandad says. 'It says on the packet they're flushable but the evidence before me suggests that they got that bit wrong. I think the advert used to say that if you tried them, you'd be surprised. And do you know what, we were, weren't we, Rachel! We still use normal toilet paper, but then we polish off with a moist wipe, because it really *is* surprising what they can do. That's what we call it, *a polish*. A good secondary wipe, just to make sure you're all clean and good to go. But then there's this to contend with, you see …'

Grandma's phone rings then, and it's Mum. I want to tell Bo to go, to leave now and to never mention all this to anyone again – in fact, I'd love for him to erase it from his memory. I'd love to erase it from *my* memory! I've just seen a series of tiny turds down there!

'Hi, Mum,' I say as Grandma hands me the phone, and I have the urge to wash my hands, like they're dirty simply from looking at a poo. 'How's the writing retreat?'

'Good, thank you, bug. Getting loads done. You all right there?'

I move to stand in the hallway so I can hear better, and look out to Grandad fishing a bunch of wipes out the drain and piling them up for Star's dad to see. He's shaking his head and Bo is nodding like he understands something terrible.

'Give the loo a flush, Taylor!' Grandad yells, so I go to the downstairs toilet where the lid is up and Grandad's massive turd is floating around the basin, which is filled with water. If this doesn't flush, it's going to flood the bathroom …

'Yeah, Mum,' I say. 'Everything's … Well, Grandad is

unblocking a drain and telling Star's dad about his massive poos, so it's all the usual goings-on around here.'

I flush. I cross my fingers. The toilet makes a terrible noise, and for a split second I see the water rising like it really is going to overspill. But then it all gets sucked away, and I hear Grandad and Bo cheer from outside.

'Oh god,' Mum says through the phone, laughing. 'My father and his massive poos. It's mortifying! I remember when I was about ten or eleven he did one so big he actually called me and Mum into the bathroom to look at it. I still remember it to this day – and to be fair, it was enormous. But telling Bo about it? That man has no shame!'

'Tell me about it,' I say. 'In fact, can we call you back? I love you a million, but I'm just …' I don't want to get into the ins and outs of clogged drains any more than we already have. I settle on: '… helping with the job.'

I can practically hear Mum smile, even down the phone. 'I suppose you're earning your keep,' she says, as Grandad shouts, 'Give her another flush, Taylor!'

'Oh,' I say, over the noise of doing as I'm told. 'I am. I can promise you that!'

I ring off and go back outside just in time to hear Grandad say, 'Take that, you mighty turd! Get gone!' He turns to the rest of us. 'Good work, team. Those drains will live to fight another day.'

Nobody knows quite what to say. Congratulations? There's an awkward pause.

'Right then,' Bo says eventually. 'I'll be off. Nice to see you both. Taylor, enjoy your sleepover.'

'Thanks, Bo,' I say, and I swear he looks a little ashen, a bit like he might be sick, as he stumbles up the drive and into his car with a weak smile of goodbye.

'Poor bloke,' Grandma says, waving him off with a smile. 'I'll bet he's lost his appetite after all that.'

'Nonsense,' Grandad insists, bending down to put the drain cover back on. 'It's made *me* absolutely starving. It was hard work, sorting all that!'

'Well, you just make sure you leave those wellies outside and wash your hands *twice*,' Grandma says, ushering us inside. 'It's lasagne tonight, Taylor, hope that's all right.'

'With garlic bread?' I ask, because I looooove garlic bread.

'You betcha!' She smiles. 'I know what my favourite girl likes!'

I help her set the table and organise a jug of orange cordial and sit back with my phone for a minute to relax. Star has texted the Members Only group chat, and I know before I look it will be because her dad has reported back on the ridiculous scenes he's just witnessed.

I'm right.

She's sent a single poop emoji.

I send back a face covering its eyes with its hands. I can't even get into it. I don't want to eat my tea recalling what I've just seen.

Hey, Lucy sends then. *Did you guys hear about Veronica Sellers? She's in hospital!*

Hospital? What the heck! I wonder if she's broken her arm or something, maybe a leg. God, that will be a pain, if she's got to hobble about on crutches for six weeks. How annoying for her! Not that I know her that well – she's not in my form, but she is in my set for maths, sitting somewhere at the back, I think. But I'd feel sorry even for a stranger if they were on crutches. I once saw a woman on the high street trying to get up two steps into the pet shop, and it looked like she was in danger of breaking her *other* leg it was that difficult.

'Dinner is served!' Grandma trills from the kitchen, and Grandad and I take our seats ready to eat, waiting for her to bring it through. I look at Grandad and he gives me a gigantic smile as he pours us a cordial from the jug. As I watch him I think, maybe Grandad might have some advice about second kisses? Dare I ask him? He can actually be quite good at love life stuff, even if he is ridiculous. Although, on the other hand, do I really want to take life advice from a man as passionate about moist toilet paper as he is? Hmmmm.

Anyway, as we tuck into the best lasagne ever, I forget all about Veronica Sellers. I'm sure she is fine, really.

3

At school a few days later, our whole year group is called to an emergency assembly because Veronica Sellers is *not* fine. Rumours about what has happened have buzzed about like flies, the whole of our year whispering theories to one another about what could have happened, from an alien abduction to her stomach exploding. Nobody seems to really know. It doesn't seem very kind to guess, although if she *was* abducted by aliens and lived to tell the tale, I'd be very invested in finding out more. I've always wondered if aliens really do exist, and it'd be a great article for *The Instruction Manual*, my brand-new website with Duncan – coming soon to a screen near you! Aliens? What fun that would be to write! Also, hmmmm: I guess at least doing *The Instruction Manual* with Duncan means we'll always be in touch, even if we don't become boyfriend and girlfriend. That could get weird though, couldn't it? Or worse, we could become a couple and then get torn apart by working together! Oh gosh. The worries are endless!

'Hey, Taylor.'

I look up into the handsome face of Year 10 Tommy Tsao. My heart flutters, which I immediately feel guilty about because of Duncan. But I suppose I'm only human, and it's still a thrill that a Year 10 talks directly to me. I can honestly say I don't fancy him any more. I mean, he's fit, obviously, but he's no Duncan Higginbottom, who just seems to get handsomer and handsomer the more I get to know him. I think it's because Tommy Tsao doesn't really have much charisma. Good to look at, but less fun to talk to. Duncan's charisma grows and grows the more you know him, and that makes him the best-looking guy in the world if you ask me.

Mmmmm. Duncan.

And that kiss.

It was *sooooo* nice. I must make it happen again soon, somehow. I MUST! Otherwise too much time will pass and he'll think I don't want to and might give up on me. And that would be *awful*. I think of Madame Jones and Monsieur Brown, frolicking in the late-afternoon sun, hand in hand. I want that for me and Duncan too. I want to walk and talk and hold his hand and …

'Got double maths now,' Tommy says, gesturing to the textbook in his hands. I realise I haven't acknowledged him out loud. My daydreaming is getting worse, because now I've *really* got something to daydream about: kissing Duncan Higginbottom! I snap myself back into the moment and try to look interested in what Tommy is saying. Of course, thinking about Duncan again is one thing – but I can't lose my head over it. One must strive to be a *bit* cool, after all. I don't want to come across as obsessed. That's what *How to Be Parisian When You're Not from Paris* says, on page 43.

Love and Romance

The French girl lives for the va-va-voom of love in her life, and has every right to throw herself into it like the lead character in her own story. She is impassioned and fervent in her devotion. But a warning: whilst 'treat him mean, keep him keen' is a bit old-fashioned, it is still prudent not to become too obsessed. Be aloof occasionally.

It truly is an outstanding guide for life, that book.

Anyway. Tommy Tsao.

'Double maths?' I say. 'Gross.' I don't really mean that but it feels appropriate. Tommy's saying it like he couldn't think of anything worse, but personally I wouldn't mind double maths.

You just have to get on with it, don't you? Maths, conversations with boys you used to fancy but who once threw up on you at a party ... you grin and bear it and then move on.

Jason Clementine turns around in front of us to see who Tommy is talking to. Nosy, nosy. I stare back at him, daring him to get mouthy. When he sees it's me he turns back around again and nudges the guy next to him. They giggle like idiots, but I won't let it bother me. Jason Clementine is basically a three-year-old in a fourteen-year-old's body.

'What are all you lot doing?' Tommy asks, gesturing with his head to the collection of Year 9s.

'Last-minute assembly,' I say. 'Somebody in our year is in hospital and they want to talk to us about it apparently. Veronica Sellers? I don't know if you know her?'

Tommy shrugs. 'Never heard of her,' he says.

'THOMAS TSAO, LESS TALKING AND MORE WALKING, PLEASE!'

It's Mrs Bates, the narky maths teacher.

'Yes, miss,' Tommy replies, whilst rolling his eyes so only I can see. I stifle a giggle – Mrs Bates is *not* somebody I wanna get on the wrong side of.

'You can practise flirting on your own time!' she bellows, and that makes ten other people turn around because FLIRTING?! WHO?! WHAT GOSSIP IS UNFOLDING?! I feel myself turning purple. Urgh, teachers can be meaner than the other students sometimes. It's not right. What if Duncan heard and got the wrong impression? Mrs Bates could ruin my whole love life at this rate.

'We weren't flirting!' I squeak. 'I was just being nice!'

'I beg your pardon?' Mrs Bates says, coming closer. 'Did you say something, Ms Blake?'

I shake my head. You know they're in a bad mood when they *Ms Blake* you.

'No, miss,' I whisper, because I can tell this won't end well. Best to just back down, even though I'd much prefer to give her a piece of my mind. She pauses, deciding whether to drop it or not, before ultimately tutting and carrying on walking.

'She's so rude,' Tommy whispers to me, which makes me smile gratefully, and then he scarpers before he draws any more attention to us. Mrs Bates turns around and shoots me A Look, and I get busy looking at my shoes. School feels like a David Attenborough documentary sometimes, with us all figuring out who is prey and who will do the preying. In this moment, I refuse to get eaten alive – especially by a teacher.

In the hall, Star and Lucy wave me over to a chair in front of them that's empty. I scuttle over, only realising Duncan is in front of *me* as I sit down and think, *Why does the back of that head look so familiar?* He spins around, like he doesn't even have to see me to know I'm there, like he *senses* me, and if I thought a Year 10 talking to me was a thrill it's nothing compared to Duncan giving me a shy smile and looking pleased as punch to be anywhere near me. I don't think I understood what the word *swoon* means before, but that's what I do. I swoon. It's like a full-body gust of adoration that leaves me grinning like a goonie.

'Hi,' he stage-whispers, beaming.

'Hi,' I stage-whisper back. My stomach does eight flips in a row and my heart beats like a bassline. I want to throw myself at him.

'God,' says Lucy, very much *not* in a stage whisper. 'You two are so goddamn cute. When are we all going to double date?'

OHMYGOD! Lucy! I could kill her! At least Star hits her thigh, as shocked as I am that she'd just come out and say that.

'What?' Lucy says, knowing full well she's winding me up, and enjoying it. But before I can tell her to put her big wooden spoon away and stop stirring, Duncan says, 'Yeah, that would be awesome! We should so do that!'

He looks at me and somehow his smile gets even wider.

'OK,' I gulp, and I can feel the satisfaction of playing cupid radiate off Lucy. She's so annoying when she's right. But Duncan and me hanging out again? Yes please! 'Yeah, let's double date. Cool,' I say, trying to sound aloof, as per *How to Be Parisian*.

'Cool,' Duncan says, teasing me with a wink. I narrow my

eyes and open my mouth to say something witty and charming (I mean, I assume it would have been witty and charming, I haven't actually decided what to say yet) but before I speak the head teacher, Mr Logan, strides down the side of the hall, his mere presence enough to make a hush fall over everyone. Duncan turns back around and we all stand up, the mark of respect we have been programmed with since Year 7. As he passes Ms K, my favourite English teacher, I notice her rub a hand over her stomach, and I don't mean to sound offensive but it looks ... bigger? But then her hand drops and she looks normal again. *Interestinggggggggg!!* We accidentally make eye contact and I can tell by the look on her face that she knows I noticed. She looks sheepish, and I give a tiny smile before looking away. I feel like I've done something wrong somehow, that I shouldn't have seen what I saw.

'Year 9,' Mr Logan roars as he reaches the front of the room. 'Sit down, thank you.' He holds his hands out in front of him, palms to the ground, and motions downward. It all feels a bit old-fashioned, standing for the head and whatnot. Not that I'll be the one to bring it up,of course. Although I suppose I could run an *anonymous* article on *The Instruction Manual* about it, if I don't want to put my name to it. I'll have to ask Duncan what our stance would be on that. I could write something like, *Is Standing for the Head a Mark of Respect, or Simply Pandering to Their Power Trip?*

(Yeah, I deffo wouldn't put my name to that! Imagine! It'd be detention until Year 13!)

'I'm sure you're aware that Veronica Sellers was hospitalised over the weekend,' Mr Logan intones. 'In the interest of quashing any rumours or gossip, let me lay out the facts clearly. The doctors fortunately acted swiftly and it seems she will be OK, but Veronica will be absent for some time. She had meningitis, which can be incredibly serious if not treated immediately. As such, please remember that should you have a headache, a rash that does not fade when a glass is rolled over it and/or a stiff neck, under no circumstances ignore it. Tell an adult and get medical attention right away. Any questions you can further direct to the school nurse, or your form teacher. Thank you.' Mr Logan looks across the room and says: 'Madame Jones? You wanted to add something?'

'*Merci*, Monsieur Logan,' she says, and I suddenly remember again how happy she looked walking with Monsieur Brown the other day. How strange she can be so relaxed and normal-seeming outside of school, but then in school she's so formal and *serious*. She takes to the stage in her cardigan and bulky shoes, her face pinched and frowny. What's that story where the doctor has two different personalities? Jekyll and Hyde! She's like Jekyll and Hyde! Monsieur Jones gets the nice version, and we get *this*. She doesn't even smile for us.

'As Veronica's form teacher, I'm putting together a care package to keep her spirits up, to let her know that we miss her,' she begins. 'Because of the nature of the illness, we are all just so thankful it was caught and dealt with speedily. I'd like to get as many people involved as possible, as a real show of Crickleton High encouragement. So, if you could all prepare something for Veronica, that would be super: letters, poems, drawings, photos of her best and more fun times, a small gift if you'd like – whatever you think she'd love to flick through to get her excited about getting back into school as soon as she can, with her friends. As I'm sure you can imagine, it's been a very unnerving time for her and her family.'

Hmmmm, I think. Something to cheer her up? I don't know much about her, to be honest. Awful that she's been so sick though. I don't know much about meningitis either, except the thing about the glass – I remember Mum doing it to me when I was in primary school, but the rash went away when she did it, and it turned out to be a reaction to a new bubble bath. She slept in my bed with me that night though, and kept waking me up to check my temperature. I quite liked that bit, actually. I liked being looked after and cuddled. It makes me feel really loved and safe. A bit like Duncan does.

Oh, Duncan!

* * *

'Mate, it's proper serious,' Lucy says at lunch. 'Veronica could have died.'

'Sorry,' says Star, tipping her head quizzically. 'Obviously the Veronica thing is mega-serious, but I'm stuck on the fact you just called Taylor *mate*.'

Lucy giggles. 'Yeah,' she concedes. 'I don't know where that came from. The point still stands though. I don't really know her very well, but poor Veronica!'

Star nods. 'I was thinking that too. I feel really bad for her, and obviously want her to get well soon. But besides writing that in a card, I don't know what else I can contribute to Madame Jones's care package. She got pooped on by that pigeon recently, I remember that …'

'Which was good for me,' I say. 'Because it made everyone forget about me having a poo in the woods!'

'You had a poo in the woods?'

I look up. Duncan just heard me! He's stood there with his lunch tray and his friend Paul. He's always ribbing me, is Duncan. But not in a mean way. In a way where we're both in on the joke.

'Huh?' I say quickly, trying my best to keep a straight face. 'What? I have no idea what you're on about.' Duncan nods slowly, playing along, his face a picture of *sure, I believe you, thousands wouldn't though*. I look pointedly away. 'Sit down and eat your food, anyway,' I press. 'Before it gets cold.'

'It's a ham sandwich,' Duncan says. 'So please, by all means, continue with your story. I've got all the time in the world! Where were you? Oh yes, pooing in the woods. I seem to remember a bucket and spade back when we took the French exchange students on the Duke of Edinburgh taster day? Right?'

OK, touché, Duncan. He so refuses to let me be anyone but my full self in front of him. Other boys would let me off the hook and pretend they hadn't heard, I'm sure. But then, that's why I like Duncan – he's as much of a pal as Lucy or Star.

I throw a chip at him, and he laughs, taking it as the right moment to sit down.

'You all know Paul, don't you?' he asks, gesturing to the blond-haired, blue-eyed skinny boy carrying a tray of chicken nuggets and garden peas.

'I think we have science together?' Star says with an inviting smile. She's so good at making people welcome.

'Yeah,' says Paul, his voice barely a squeak. 'Hi.'

'Hi,' echoes Lucy.

'Hi,' I say. He looks away shyly, stuffing a chicken nugget into his mouth, and I get the strong sense that Paul isn't used to saying hello to people he doesn't really know. For ages I thought shy people didn't have as many thoughts and feelings as more confident people, but Star said I have to be careful about assuming that. Everyone has the same amount of thoughts or feelings, it's just some of us have bigger gobs for expressing them. That put me in my place, I can tell you. Just because I *can* use my voice, it doesn't mean I always should. Sometimes the kind thing is to invite other people to use theirs.

'We were just taking about Veronica Sellers,' I tell them both, making an effort to look Paul in the eye so he feels included. That's harder than it sounds when the person you're trying to include won't look up from their lunch tray. 'Sounds like she's been really unwell …'

'I'm sure my mum had a friend at school who *died* from meningitis,' Duncan says. 'Veronica's been lucky.'

'Oh wow. That's terrifying! So what are you going to contribute to the care package?' asks Star.

'Probably a poem.' Duncan shrugs. 'I don't know her *at all*. I think she won cross-country in Year 7?'

Lucy nods. 'And Year 8. But that's all I know too.'

'What about you, Paul? Have you had any ideas?' Paul actually looks up when Star addresses him, and I see his Adam's apple bob up and down as he swallows, like he's searching for the courage to reply.

'Not yet,' he says.

It seems like he might be about to add something, but he doesn't, so we all just stare at him until we're certain he's not going to contribute anything else, and then Star says, 'Yeah, it's tricky, isn't it?'

We fall silent, thinking. In *How to Be Parisian When You're Not from Paris* there's a section on gifts. It says:

On Gifting

The true Parisian woman knows that when it comes to gifting, the price tag is irrelevant. In fact, throwing money at a gift to impress the recipient is crass and very un-chic. Gifts should be thoughtful – it is far better to deliver a posy of favoured blooms wrapped in brown paper than an elaborate and impersonal bouquet of overpriced roses, for example. It is the epitome of elegance to gift a stack of favoured chocolate bars wrapped up in coloured twine, a second- (or third-, or fourth-) hand dog-eared book from a stall by the river, a framed poem or sketch scribbled on the back of an envelope … life is made up of moments, and a gift should reflect the tiny thoughtful ways we know a person, if it is to mean anything at all …

Trust Duncan to suggest a poem, then. He knows exactly how to play it!

'Who are her best friends?' I ask, trying to think of something that could be a bit more personal than just a *get well soon* card. 'What does she *like*?' I add, and everyone shrugs, even Paul.

'I think she used to eat her lunch in the library …' says Lucy. 'People like her, but I don't ever remember her having a birthday party or anything like that, you know? Something with all her friends? Not even at primary school.'

Star pulls a sad face. 'You're talking about her in the past tense!' she says. 'She's not dead!' Paul gives a snort of a laugh, even though what Star said isn't that funny. Star notices and smiles. Paul looks over the moon. I look to Duncan and Lucy to see if they've noticed, but I don't think they have. I must just be reading into things that aren't there.

Lucy says, 'Gosh. If I got sick, it's a bit upsetting to think that nobody might know how to cheer to me up.'

'I was just thinking about that,' I agree. 'I suddenly feel really lucky to have you guys.'

'Because we'd know to write stupid stories about Harry Styles and Tom Holland, and send you chilli-flavoured crisps in a beret?' asks Lucy.

'And a blank notebook for every thought you have in recovery, so you can write insightful and provocative articles about the nature of healing and what it means to be alive!' adds Duncan.

'Yes!' laughs Star, reaching over to Duncan for a high five. He gives one with a bemused look on his face, like he understands it is a gesture of acceptance but can't quite figure out why. He'll catch on soon enough, that in Members Only we always do too much.

'You're taking the mick,' I say, eyebrows raised and lips pursed, 'but it's actually very nice to be so understood. So there.' I stick my tongue out, and Paul smiles at me. It makes me feel proud, like I'm winning him over a bit. I suddenly understand Duncan a bit more, if he wants to impress *my* friends. AND! If he does want to impress my friends, that must mean he likes me, right? That he wants to kiss me again? He did say he wants a double date! I got so sidetracked by assembly I forgot that bit. Yay! A double date with Duncan and my best friends! That will be so cool. It's wicked they all seem to like each other – be awful if they didn't. Awwww, we're a new awesome foursome! Maybe we could try setting Paul up with somebody and become a Magic Six? A sexy six? A ... ditzy six-y? OK, let's just stick with awesome foursome for now, ha. I need time to come up with a better name for a six.

At home, Mum's had an email about Veronica, and wants a big Deep and Meaningful about it all. But, to be honest, I'm a bit over talking about it. It's all anyone has talked about all day! We're all just repeating ourselves now – plus it's freaked me out that a) somebody in our year has been so sick, like, that could have been me, or Star or Lucy???? And b) I just keep thinking about how nobody knows how to cheer her up, that she's a bit of a school ghost. I don't mean everyone has to be Ms Popular or anything, but for *nobody* to know much about her or what she likes? Not to be all self-centred or make it about me, but it makes me wonder if I'm doing enough with my life. That's sooooo dramatic, but if I died tomorrow, what would people say about me when I was gone? *She hosted a really good party once.* Is that it? I want to make more of a mark on the world than that! That's why I want to be the best journalist in the country, eventually – so I can write meaningful things that help people connect. That's what *The Instruction Manual* is for – we want it be a website that is doing something concrete and useful. Gosh, it makes me want to launch the thing even sooner, thinking of it like that. *The Instruction Manual* will be my legacy!!

'Taylor? Darling? Are you listening to me?'

I look up from the last bits of Mum's chilli con carne, her concerned eyes blinking madly.

'Urm, to be honest, Mum …' I start. She laughs.

'That's a no, then,' she says.

'Sorry.'

'Just clear the table, you,' she sighs, shaking her head. 'And I'll sit here and give thanks to the lord that you're OK, and that this girl is, too.'

I pick up the plates and scrape the last bits into the bin, and then load the dishwasher. I'm just reaching under the sink for a tablet to stick in the detergent drawer when my phone trills with the sound of a FaceTime.

'*C'est Axel!*' Mum sing-songs, handing it to me. I take it, seeing my French exchange partner's face on the screen, and swipe to accept the call.

'*Bonjour!*' I say, immediately realising I probably should say *bonsoir*, since it's past 6 p.m. That's the thing about languages, I find: I'm much better with them in hindsight than in the moment.

'Hello!' says Axel, his dimples deepening as he waves. '*Ça va?*'

'*Oui,*' I say, because this is a bit of French I feel really confident with. I can do hellos and how-are-yous and sound really authentic! I'm working on the bits after that. '*Ça va bien, merci. Et toi?*'

'*Oui, bien,*' Axel replies, before switching to English. 'I have some news,' he says. 'That is very exciting!'

'OK ...' I say hesitantly. I have no clue what he could be about to say. He's met a wonderful new boy, perhaps? Mum is craning to listen, so I ask, 'Can you tell me with

Mum here? She's desperate to say hi.'

Mum immediately leaps up and comes to the phone, leaning into shot and waving frantically.

'Axel!' she says. 'We miss you so much!'

Axel smiles. 'I miss you too, Erica! How are David and Rachel?'

'They're good,' Mum says. 'They talk about you all the time.'

'Well,' Axel says, and he looks off-screen then and says to somebody we can't see, '*Oui, viens ici.*' An older version of Axel appears then, like a filter to age Axel by about thirty years. He's a bit taller, and a bit wider, but has Axel's shaggy black hair and dimples you could sink a ship in. The only differences are that he's also got loads of dark stubble all over his face, and his eyes are blue, not brown.

'Oh!' says Mum. 'Hello.'

'My father,' Axel says, and the man waves and says, in perfect English, 'Axel enjoyed his time with you very much. I can't wait to meet you all one day.'

'We'd love to meet you too,' Mum says, in an odd voice I've never heard her use before. It's like a whisper and a laugh, both at the same time. She sweeps hair off her face and starts touching her neck.

'We are coming to London,' Axel says. 'So perhaps we could meet there?'

'What!' I squeal. 'You're coming back to England so soon?! Is that the good news?'

Axel nods. 'For my father's work. In two weeks. Are you free? To meet?'

I look at Mum, who throws up her arms in a gesture I take to mean, *Of course!*

OMG! How chic! We're going to London to meet up with my French friend! This is soooo cool. Axel says he'll text me some details and Mum does her whisper/laugh thing again and then as soon as we've rung off I immediately text Members Only.

Members Only

Me: *OMG! Girls! Axel is coming to London in two weeks!*

Star: *What! How come?!*

Me: *With his dad, I think his dad has a meeting there or something.*

Lucy: *Wah!!! Can we come?! I love London!*

Me: *I'll ask Mum! I'll bet you can!*

An alert buzzes on my phone then for an email. It's from Duncan, on our special *Instruction Manual* email address. It says: *We need a planning meeting for TIM content. How about tomorrow? Can you do after school?*

'Mum,' I say, looking up to where she's wiping down the countertops for the night. She doesn't hear me. 'Mum!' I repeat, and she comes to.

'Yes?' she says, a dreamy smile on her face. I crinkle up my face. 'Why do you look like that?'

'Like what?' she asks, and I narrow my eyes at her like, *Honestly? You're going to act like this is normal for you?* But I don't say anything, because then I remember I'm asking her for a favour.

'Nothing,' I back-pedal. 'I just wondered if Duncan could come over tomorrow? We need to have an editorial meeting for the website.'

I deliberately say *editorial meeting* to make sure she says yes, because doesn't that sound so professional?! Like I'll be wearing a pencil skirt in a New York skyscraper, probably carrying a big portfolio folder in shiny black leather and my initials embossed in gold.

'Of course,' she says. 'As long as you work downstairs at the table, that's fine. I'm a go-with-the-flow mum, but I'm not ready for you to have a boyfriend in your *room*.'

'He's not my boyfriend!' I squeal. 'Mum!'

'Your *special friend*, then,' she says, coming over to flick me with the dish towel.

'Oh my god!' I squeal. 'You're so embarrassing!'

'Joy of the job,' she retorts.

I ignore her and email Duncan back that tomorrow is great, and he says he'll bring the Monster Munch. I update the girls on Members Only.

Members Only

Me: *Aaaaaaand Duncan is coming over tomorrow!!*

Star: *As a date?*

Me: *For the website*
We need to plan what we're going to write for it and when we're going to launch
All that kinda stuff

Lucy: *In between snog sessions?!*

Me: *No!*
Well
Maybe! But Mum says we have to stay downstairs so I don't fancy kissing in front of her!

Star: *No, ewwwww*

Lucy: *Nice to hang out with him again though! A sort of non-date date!*

Me: *EXACTLY.*

Hope I get a snog at some point, though!!

I go to bed with the biggest smile on my face. My friends are awesome, I get to see Axel super soon, *and* Duncan is coming to my house tomorrow. Life is *très bon*!! I'm a lucky, lucky girl! Yay!

4

'You all right?'

I look up to see Duncan with his backpack, giving me his lovely Duncan smile.

'Hiya,' I say back, and we stand, and I am *very* aware that we are alone – or as alone as it is possible to be as a thousand kids from school flood out of the building behind us to head home for the day. It's just him and me, for the first time since THE KISS. Should I hug him? Peck his cheek? Fist pump? Engage *somehow* in physical contact? He's holding on to the straps of his bag for dear life, so it's not like I can accidentally brush his stray hand with mine, like they do in films. That would be nice. Imagine a slow, meandering walk as it gets dark by the river, twinkly lights everywhere, conversation falling into a light whisper as we stumble upon a single violinist playing something romantic and sweet, where we dance, and as we sway together we get closer …

Shame it's 3.30 p.m. in Crickleton and not midnight in Paris.

'Shall we?' Duncan says, gesturing with a nod to the way home. 'We've got loads to get through.'

'OK, Mr Straight-To-Business,' I say, giving him a captain's salute. 'Let's go!'

He rolls his eyes playfully as we start walking. 'Well, one of us has to keep us on track,' he says. 'And if you're going to be the beauty, I'll have to be the brains.'

'Urm, I have plenty of brains,' I say. 'So don't worry about shouldering that burden all on your own. Although you don't have the beauty, so … yeah … sucks to be you, I guess.'

'Outrageous!' Duncan laughs, knocking his shoulder into mine.

CONTACT ESTABLISHED!

Only a shoulder knock, but still! It's a start!!

'I think you'd know not to be outraged by me by now,' I bat back. 'Makes me think you're so blinded by my beauty *and* brains that it's slowing your thinking down.'

'My my!' Duncan laughs. 'We're feeling *very* confident today, aren't we?!'

'Just happy,' I say, with a shrug I hope comes off as detached and mysterious.

'Interesting,' Duncan says, and I sneak a look at him from the corner of my eye as we pass the Co-op. His cheeks are flushed and his expression bashful. He must feel me looking, because he turns to me and says in a knowing voice, 'Any particular reason for that happiness …?'

Oh my GOD. Our kiss is like this massive elephant walking with us that we both have to sidestep around and not mention but it is so, *so* obvious we both know it is there. He soooooo wants me to bring it up! I can tell.

'None at all,' I say, in a way that suggests I know what he is thinking but will not be baited. I can't help but grin. We hold our gaze, and it feels so electric, like a million volts sparking through my body, that I have to look away in the end because I feel like I could burst into actual flames! Just from a *look*!

'Yeah,' Duncan says, 'I can't figure out why I feel so happy these past few days either …'

I don't think anybody has ever said anything so romantic to me. Gah! Duncan is happy too! That's good! That's GREAT!

Duncan!!!

!!!!!

Mum is in her study at home, but comes out when she hears my key in the door and immediately she and Duncan are reunited like long-lost friends.

'Erica!' Duncan says. 'Thank you so much for lending us your dining-room table.'

'Oh, my pleasure,' coos Mum, thrilled he's called her by her first name and isn't being all coy and loitering by the door. She hates that. Her favourite friends of mine are always the ones 'who have something to say for themselves, Taylor! Life is too short to be shy!'.

Lucy says the apple doesn't fall from the tree, aka I get my mouthy ways from my mother.

To be fair ... I see her point.

Mum guides us through to the kitchen, where she's set out some after-school snacks like we're seven. I would say something narky, but it's my favourite orange-and-ginger smoothie so instead I just grab one and hand one to Duncan too, who has started to empty his bag of fifty different folders and files and notebooks on to the table.

'God, this is delicious,' he says, pausing to take a big gulp.

'It's Taylor's favourite,' Mum says. 'As are these,' she adds, bringing through the bowls of chilli crisps and a couple of Nutella biscuit bars.

'A feast!' says Duncan.

'And you both understand the rule about staying downstairs whilst you're here, correct?' Mum clarifies, to which Duncan nods, cheeks turning purple.

'Mum!' I say, hiding my face in my hands. 'Oh my god!'

'What?' Mum asks. 'There's no shame here. Better to speak openly and clearly when there are boyfriends involved.'

Now it's my turn to blush. She can't go around using words like *boyfriend*! Not before Duncan and I have had The Talk!!

'No funny business here,' Duncan says, trying not to sound mortified but giving the game away with the tips of his ears: they're still pink. Mum nods at him, approving at his ability to be direct. 'Taylor thinks it's *hilarious* that I've got us on a strict to-do list, but we really do have loads to get through.'

Mum pulls a face, very *yes, she can be quite the taskmaster*!!

'I just need to get my stuff from upstairs. Can Duncan help me do that, Mum?'

'Sure,' she says. 'Go for it.'

I head up, Duncan behind me, past the bathroom where he saw me crying at my party – where I saw him differently for the first time. Was that really only a few weeks ago? So much has happened since then …

'Cool room,' Duncan says, lingering at the door as I hand him my laptop and notes. 'Thanks,' I say. 'It's cosy, you know?'

'Feels like your safe space?'

I nod. 'Exactly.'

God, Duncan just *gets me*.

There's a couple of magazines I want to grab too, for inspo, and a book about writing interesting articles. As I hunt out what else I need, Duncan does exactly what Axel did when he came to stay as my guest: takes in my Harry Styles and Tom Holland posters, my collection of The Body Shop moisturisers.

He runs a finger over my bookshelf, taking in the titles.

'I don't have a lot of books because Mum makes me go to the library,' I explain, grasping my pencil case. 'She says I get through so many books, she'd have no money left over to feed and water me if she bought all of them in a bookshop.'

Duncan chuckles. 'My stepdad has the same rule,' he says. 'Once I started reading two a week, he cut me off.'

'Just a couple of word junkies then, aren't we?' I say.

'Ceeks, actually,' he reminds me, our code for *cool geeks*. I smile again, and he smiles back. Everything he says is just the right thing! 'What's this one?' he asks, picking up my copy of *How to Be Parisian When You're Not from Paris* with his free hand.

OHMYGOD. OK. So. I don't want to panic or anything, but the Bible is like my diary! And I feel so embarrassed that Duncan knows I read this …

'Urm …' I say, trying to sound like I have no idea, like I'm really trying to wrack my brain to place it. Duncan turns it over to scan the blurb, and then opens to the first page. '*How to Be Parisian When You're Not from Paris*,' he reads aloud. '*Darling, you do not have to be of Paris to be Parisian, for being Parisian is an attitude. It is a state of mind. It is a way of being…*'

'Mum got that for me,' I say, cutting him off before he can read more. 'I'm a bit of a Francophile…'

'I figured that out already,' Duncan says, gesturing at the sticker of the Eiffel Tower on my computer. 'You kind of dress French too, if that makes sense. I noticed that when the *Frenchies* were here.'

He smirks as he uses my word, *Frenchies*.

'Or maybe the French dress like me,' I counter, and he laughs.

'That's probably it.' He nods. 'My bad.'

We look at each other again, and Duncan's smile is half serious, half huge, like he can't make up his mind which way to be. I coach myself through not looking away: if that second kiss is going to happen, I have to make sure I'm encouraging it. Duncan takes a step forward, closing the gap between us, and his eyes roam my face like he's trying to commit me to memory.

'You're so pretty,' he says. 'Like, really, *really* pretty.'

He reaches out and smooths some hair behind my ear. I feel like I could turn to liquid at his touch.

'I like that you think so,' I say, and my voice is soft and quiet, coming out that way because if I talk too loudly I'm worried I'll break the spell, the magic of whatever this moment is: him, me, inches apart. My breathing has gone shallow, barely coming out of my throat so it makes tiny little rasps.

'And super clever too,' he says, his words as low as mine. I swear he's got a cheeky glimmer in his eye too. 'Although that goes without saying.'

'Never,' I whisper. 'You can always say that bit.'

'Noted.'

His face comes towards mine, and I wish we weren't both holding all my stuff so that I could lace my fingers between his like I've been wanting to all afternoon. Instead my arms are wrapped close to my chest, cradling everything, but I can't let that get in the way of what's about to happen. I part my lips and take a breath and tell myself to just *enjoy this*. Kiss number two, incoming, and then it won't be long before I can ask him to be my boyfriend and we can live happily ever after. I lean in, and I swear I've forgotten how to breathe. My heart has paused too. Everything is just waiting for what comes next, me and him, kissing again ...

'Taylor!' Mum's voice floats up the stairs. 'I'm going to order Indian for tea! What do you want? Duncan, are you staying?'

Duncan coughs and steps away from me. Dammit!

'Coming!' I shout back, not looking away from Duncan, who pulls a funny face at me so that as we scramble back downstairs to look at the menu, we're laughing uncontrollably.

As we get settled, I quickly text Members Only:

Members Only

Me: *We almost kissed!*
I was soooo good making sure he knew I wanted it!
But then my mum happened
So
I just need to keep my nerve
And find another opportunity!
Although it's not like we can kiss whilst she's in the next room.
What if she walks in?!

'You ready?' Duncan says, after arranging all his pens in colour order. What a *ceek*.

I put my phone down.

'Absolutely,' I say, grabbing a fresh sheet of paper and writing *The Instruction Manual* in the middle of it, in a cloud. I even do my best writing. I know good handwriting has never knowingly seduced a boy, but you can never be too careful.

'Right,' Duncan says. 'So. The whole point of this website is to run stories too long for the school paper.'

'And the stuff they *won't* publish,' I point out. Duncan nods.

'I'm sure you've got a big list of pitches that fit that bill,' he says, smiling.

'You know me so well.'

'So we keep it small for now? You and me and maybe we put up a page soliciting pitches, but we say we might not be able to get back to everyone? We don't want to create acres of work for ourselves, do we? Answering emails isn't as fun as actually writing and editing the thing.'

'Perfect,' I say. 'Yes. Good thinking.'

Duncan paws at a handful of crisps as I write all this down, and then immediately starts coughing like a maniac. Crisps spray everywhere, and he's the colour of uncooked steak.

'Oh my god!' I say, worried he's going to choke to death. 'I'll get you some water.' As I scuttle off to the kitchen I yell over my shoulder, 'Please don't die!'

I fill a glass with water that's not entirely cold, but I figure time is of the essence. Duncan drinks it down greedily, steadying his breathing. I tap on his back, but I'm not sure it's especially helpful. His eyes are streaming, tears flowing down the sides of his face.

'Are you OK?!' I say, and he nods. 'You scared me!'

Mum appears at the door from her office. 'Duncan! Are you all right?!'

'Went down the wrong way,' he says, pointing to his mouth. 'The crisp.' He blinks quickly, in rapid succession. 'Urgh,' he coughs. I can tell he's really trying to gather himself. He keeps coughing and drinking water and we keep staring at him coughing and drinking water. Personally, I'm worried he might suddenly explode again. After a while he steadies himself enough to say, totally deadpan, 'Well, that wasn't humiliating at all.'

I pull a face of sympathy.

'I'll get you a tissue,' I say, patting his shoulder like an elderly aunt.

'I'll stop staring at you and get back to work,' Mum agrees, disappearing. Over her shoulder she shouts: 'Glad you're OK! Be awful if you kicked the bucket on my watch!'

I hand him a Kleenex. 'So you can wipe your tears,' I say.

Duncan takes it. 'It's unfair to pick on a guy who almost just died,' he counters.

I assess him and decide: 'I'm afraid you're going to be just fine. Are you sure that wasn't just a performance to get out of all this planning?'

'Did it work?' he asks.

'Almost,' I admit, smiling.

I grab his empty glass and go to refill it, letting the water run longer this time so it's actually chilled. I even add ice. I get the box of tissues off the windowsill in case he needs more, and decide at the last moment to add in some cordial to his glass. I want him to know I'm thoughtful. That I go the extra mile.

When I turn back around to the dining table, my phone is lit up, and I can tell right away Duncan's eyes are on it. His gaze flickers up to me, and he knows he's been caught.

'I didn't mean to read that,' he says, and I do actually believe him. He's not holding my phone or anything – it's literally lighting up right in front of his face. I grab it, and it's a message in Members Only.

Members Only

Star: *Don't wait for an opportunity to kiss*
   CREATE ONE!!

I gasp involuntarily, and my hand goes to my throat, clutching imaginary pearls. Duncan bursts out laughing, really loudly.

'Your face!' he chuckles. 'Taylor!'

I put my phone down – screen down this time – and smack his arm. He's seen it. He's seen the message, and isn't even trying to deny it.

'Ow!' he says.

'You deserved that!' I say back.

'Be nice to me!'

'Fine,' I say, handing him his cordial.

He takes a big sip and looks at me over the rim. He doesn't even need to say a word. His face is a picture of delight.

'Shut up!' I say, laughing.

'I didn't say anything!'

'You didn't have to. Now. Let's talk about a possible launch event. Maybe a big party?'

Duncan looks at me like the cat that got the cream, he's so happy. He leans across the table, looking to the door, and I don't realise until after he's delivered a peck to my cheek that it was to double-check the coast is clear. I feel his lips tingling on my skin long after he's pulled away. I might never wash my face again!

It's really hard to focus after that.

We work on article ideas until we're interrupted by the takeaway arriving.

'I come bearing gifts,' Mum says, holding up the paper bag she's just retrieved from the delivery driver. 'Duncan, you hungry?'

'Always,' he says. 'Thanks, Erica.'

We decide we're done with our *editorial meeting* and clear the way for plates and poppadoms. We've got a fair amount done, but post-cheek-kiss there was a lot of throwing glances at each other and holding hands under the table, which made the meeting a little less productive (but a lot more fun!).

'Any more news on that poor girl in hospital?' Mum asks as we tuck in.

I shake my head and swallow my mango chutney. 'No,' I say. 'Not really. I mean, none of us actually really know her, so …'

'Oh,' says Mum. 'You mean she's got no friends?'

'Not in an unpopular way,' supplies Duncan. 'Just … she's a bit like me, I suppose. Keeps herself to herself.'

'The boy who never speaks,' I tease, because that's what I used to think about him. Duncan rolls his eyes and gets back to mopping up his curry with a bit of coconut naan.

In the silence, I find myself adding: 'It kind of freaks me out. Like, if I got sick, what would people send in Madame Jones's care package? I want people to remember me, you know?'

'People would have plenty to say about you,' Duncan says. 'I wouldn't worry about that.'

'But I do!' I cry. 'It's my worst nightmare!'

Mum says, 'It all really does remind you that life is

precious, that we should appreciate what we have when we have it. Live life to the full.'

'Exactly,' I say.

'Seize the day!' cries Duncan, waving his hand melodramatically.

'Seize the day!' I echo, and then it hits me: 'That would actually make a really great column. Don't you think? "Taylor Blake Seizes the Day"?'

Duncan nods, digesting this. I can tell he approves by the look on his face. 'OK, OK …' he says. 'I see where you're going with this …'

'I could write all about how life is short, and so hey, everyone! Go get on with the adventure of your life!'

Duncan nods even more, so much so that his head could fall off. He puts on a low, dramatic voice like a newsreader and says: '*"Taylor Blake Seizes the Day" is a brand-new column from* The Instruction Manual's *Taylor Blake, on loudly and proudly living, loving and learning … coming soon!*'

Whoa. I look at him, amazed. Then I look at Mum, who looks genuinely impressed, with her raised eyebrows and big smile. Duncan is a genius! And we all know it!

'Yes!' I say, going in for a three-way high five. 'That's it! I can write a whole bunch, like a series, and that can be part of the launch! God, we're a good team. This has been *very* productive!'

Duncan beams at me. 'Hell yeah we're a good team,' he says, and the way he looks at me gives me butterflies. I could snog his face off right now in celebration! Heck, I could snog his face off in any mood. I just need a way to be alone with him, not at school, not in my house with Mum hanging around … and I need it to be SOON. This waiting game is *killing me.*

5

I am motivated, I am excited, I am *early*.

School doesn't start for another forty-five minutes, but I woke up *bursting* with ideas for 'Taylor Blake Seizes the Day'. I mean, I also have a bit of a tummy ache, but I'm not going to let that stop me. This column could win me awards! Fame! Recognition! So it's double purpose: I'll seize the day *and* make a name for myself by doing whatever activities I come up with, but by writing about it and (hopefully!!) inspiring other people to do the same, I'll *also* become known. Win-win!

I feel like Ms K won't mind if I sit quietly with one of the school iPads in her room. She's always made her classroom a bit of a calm and safe place for us to go if we need it. I mean, whose idea was it to put a thousand or so teenagers in the same building every day and expect us to find peace? It's a madhouse! What was it Axel once said? *School is a palaver.* Ms K's quiet place is really needed sometimes. Often, in fact.

'Miss?' I say, knocking on her partially opened door. At first I don't see her, because she's slumped over her desk, head on her hands, cardigan pulled up over her head.

'It's *Ms*,' Ms K mumbles from somewhere between the desk and her elbow. 'Defining grown women by their marital status with miss or missus when we don't do the same for men is prehistoric and … and …' She pauses and sighs into her arms like she gives up. 'Stupid.'

I've never seen Ms K like this, all moody. Maybe she has her period or something?

'Sorry, Ms K,' I say. 'I can go somewhere else.'

At the sound of my voice she lifts her head, and not to brag, but she seems to soften when she realises it's me. I'm not saying I'm her favourite or anything … but I'm also not *not* saying that, if you catch my drift.

'Taylor,' she says, her smile weak. 'Sorry. I'm not feeling very well. How can I help?'

I hold up the iPad I checked out of the library and say, 'Just wanted to do some research for some articles. I wondered if I could do it in here? But if it's a bad time …'

She shakes her head and motions me in. 'That sounds great,' she says. 'Make yourself at home.' She lifts her head a bit more, and I can literally see the colour drain from her face as she does. 'Oh,' she says in a squeak. 'Urm. Urgh. I think I'm going to be sick.'

Ms K makes a break for it before I can even ask if there's anything I can do to help, scrambling out of the room faster than Star going in for the kill when she's fencing. *En garde!*

Well, this is awkward. Should I go? Or stay and take her up on the offer to come in? I look at the clock on the wall. I've only got twenty-five minutes as it is. I decide to stay. I think I should be here when she gets back so I can check on her, anyway. If I sit near the door at least I'm out of the way, and I can slink off if she gets mad I stayed because she needs some space. Not that Ms K ever gets *mad*, but you know what I mean. She's not herself today.

I settle in and start googling, fresh notebook open beside me like this is my office at *Teen Vogue*. I start with a simple *How to seize the day* and scroll through what I find. I don't know what I'm looking for; I'm more just trying to get a sense of what *seize the day* means to people.

There's loads of stuff about taking chances and how *carpe diem* is the old Latin way of saying it. It's incredible how many people have tattoos of that, actually, as I learn when I click on 'images'. I don't know what possesses me to read an article called 'No One Will Remember Your Name'. Except ... well, I do, I suppose, because that's the huge fear that's come out of the Veronica Sellers thing. It's like it was written just for me! I read:

No One Will Remember Your Name

People won't remember your name. Nothing you do will affect the future. There's not much you can do to affect next week, to be honest. You are nothing. You are totally inconsequential in the grand scheme of the universe because there's only one Cleopatra or Beyoncé or Hemingway in a lifetime, and that's probably not you, my love.

Nobody will remember you.

You'll do your best, day in and day out, for sixty or eighty or a hundred years, and then you'll be gone and your life will never have mattered at all.

Nobody will remember you.

But.

Within the confines of school every day, and work every day after that, you'll taste the dizzying heights of being alive. Your words – spoken, written, whispered – will make somebody else feel less alone, if only for the moment they see or hear them. You'll taste oceans in his kiss, stars on her mouth. Rain happens, and so do rainbows. The storm passes, but it's about who is in your boat because the storm will always come. Holding hands, wiping away tears, chocolate cake. Sad days, duvet days, blue days, red-letter days.

Nobody will remember you.

Life will be hard and it will be mostly pointless. But it's because we're utterly without point that we're endlessly precious.

So steal the kiss, say the difficult thing, take the chance.

Nobody will remember you.

So what have you got to lose?

The words hit me so hard. It wasn't that long ago that Lucy accused me of inventing problems because I don't have any real ones, and even though she was half joking, she was half right as well. Sometimes I think my brain just needs something to do, so it overthinks. But what if I didn't overthink?

What if I did more jumping in with two feet? Just going for it? Take Duncan and our impending second kiss. I'm so *hungry* for it, and I'm sure he wants it too! I just need to go for it! What have I got to lose, indeed. Nothing really matters, so we may as well seize the day. I don't want to be some polite girl waiting to be chosen, I want to *do* the choosing. And I choose Duncan, and I choose writing great articles, and I choose being loud and silly and totally myself because life is too short not to!

Before I know it I'm scribbling down loads of different ways to seize the day. I can take a chance and make my second kiss happen, but I can also do something for others, get some fresh air, treat myself, get political, be fancy, make a fun playlist, make the most of the day, get educated and learn something new, *go* somewhere new too. *Why then the world's mine oyster / Which I with sword will open!* Ha, I forgot I knew that quote. We learned it with Mrs Hawthorn last year. It's where 'the world is my oyster' comes from, and I suddenly understand it more than ever. The world is my oyster, but only if I go for it. And go for it I will.

'You feeling any better?' I say, just before it's time to pack up and head to form time. Ms K is back at her desk, sipping on some water. I didn't even hear her come back into class, I've been so focused on all these ideas fizzing around my brain. 'Was it something you ate, or … ?'

I leave the 'or' hanging there, because she's rubbing her tummy again, like she did in assembly yesterday. And I don't want to add two and two together and get five but isn't throwing up one of the signs of pregnancy?

Ms K gives me a kind of sad-seeming half-smile, like I've asked a silly question. It makes me feel a bit stupid, but before I say anything else she sighs and says, 'It must have been, Taylor. Yes.'

I sling my bag over my shoulder and go to her desk.

'I can go and tell the office if you like. So they can get a substitute teacher? You should probably go home.'

Ms K looks like she might cry. 'I should, you're right,' she says, voice wobbling. 'I'll sort it though. You're a good girl, Taylor. Your mother must be very proud.'

It doesn't feel like a question, so I don't try to answer. I just say, 'Thank you. Feel better, Ms K,' and head off. It's really unnerving when the adults in your life act odd. They're supposed to be the ones who know what is going on! And now, because I'm not used to seeing Ms K so discombobulated, I feel all weird inside too.

I try to explain everything that's swimming around in my head re the column, to the girls during geography, where we're supposed to be working on a group project on low-income developing countries, locating them on a map using compass directions, co-ordinates, oceans, hemisphere and tropics. I MEAN!! Luckily Lucy does most of the work as Star and I talk, because quite frankly my growing tummy ache means that the gross domestic product of Timbuktu is the last thing on my mind. I wish I was at home on the sofa with a nice hot-water bottle. My back kind of hurts as well. It's like I'm falling apart! I wondered if Ms K's period was coming before, without me realising mine is probably due soon too, which isn't fair: I feel like I've only just gotten over the last one.

'So it's like a checklist?' Star asks. 'You'll go through each thing and write about it afterwards?'

'Exactly. And I'm so gonna need help. Like, *go somewhere new?* I'm thinking New York or something! Let's shoot for the stars!'

Lucy looks up from where she's shading something on our poster and says: 'I've never been to London. So my something new could be that. You know – when you go to meet Axel?'

'Yes!' I say, thrilled that she was both following the conversation and also wants to get involved. 'You should both come.'

'That would be so cool,' agrees Star, grabbing a ruler and a fine-liner and deciding to get involved in Lucy's handiwork. 'Has Axel been before? Because we can take him on an open-top bus ride …'

'And to Madame Tussauds to see all the celebrity waxworks,' I add. I have, after all, been giving this some thought ever since he said he's coming. London is so cool. Not as cool as Paris, but still awesome. God, next year in Year 10 we get to be hosted by the Frenchies and I just can't wait. It will be *amazing*. 'Then obviously Buckingham Palace, and Downing Street, and I was thinking about a proper afternoon tea? Somewhere really really nice, where they serve all the cakes and sandwiches on those tall towers. You don't get that in Crickleton.'

I love the idea of travel. *How to Be Parisian When You're Not from Paris* says it is imperative for a well-rounded and elegant individual. It says:

> *Travel makes us kinder, more empathetic, and more interesting. Whether it be a short trip somewhere on the train, or further afield via boat or plane, experiencing a place for the first time, with all the culture that brings, adds magic and charm to our lives in a way that cannot be found any other way ... embrace it, but more than that: seek it out.*

'Have you asked your mum if we can come?' Star asks, and immediately I think, *D'oh! I knew there was something I was supposed to talk to her about!*

'She basically founded the "more the merrier" club,' I say. 'I haven't asked her yet, but let's *positively visualise* it happening. Visualise having the best ever time, that's what they say. What you think, you can make happen!'

'I wonder if I can positively visualise about Tom Holland asking me to the Oscars so I can finally experience the fairy tale in person,' quips Lucy, because out of all of us, 'positive visualisation' isn't really something she gets on board with. That is, until something *she* wants is involved, like when she made us all visualise her passing maths so she wouldn't have to go to summer sessions, AND SHE DID. But I do think that was more about her having me as a study partner than *willing* it to happen.

Anyway. Girls' trip to London? Woo!

(Tummy ache? Boo!)

6

The next day, I have to leave English early because I've got a dentist appointment and 2.30 in the afternoon was the only time they had left. When I turned fourteen, Mum said it was time for me to start booking my own appointments so that I'm not afraid of taking charge of my own life. I think she read that in *Raising Empowered Teens*. She's always giving me responsibilities and nudging me towards sorting stuff out on my own. Anyway, part of making my own appointments is also figuring out how to get there if she's working. Enter: Grandma, my saviour!

'I've had the worst drive here,' Grandma sighs as I climb into her little car. 'Honestly, I think they give away driving licences now. There's so many fools on the road I can't believe they've passed an actual test.'

I lean over and give her a kiss and then close my door.

'You've not been giving people the finger again, have you?' I tease. It's well-known in our family that Grandma is the nicest woman in the whole wide world ... until she's driving. Then all bets are off. It's the only time I hear her swear.

'Only the ones who deserved it,' she replies, a naughty glimmer in her eye. I strap in, and she pulls away from the kerb. 'Right then, boss,' she says. 'The dentist, I believe?'

'Just for a check-up,' I say. 'We shouldn't be long.'

'I hope we are long, actually,' Grandma says. 'Because I love spending time with you.'

See? Nicest. Grandma. Ever.

My tummy ache is getting really bad, but I try not to think about it as we enter Heather's office. She's so nice: she's been my dentist my whole life, and she's always sooooo complimentary about my teeth. Mum has about twenty fillings, so she's always been on at me about good dental hygiene. Heather says it shows.

'Oh my gosh!' Heather says as Grandma and I walk in. 'Taylor! You've blossomed! You're so beautiful!'

I hand Grandma my bag and coat and she sits down in the corner. She gives me a wink, I think because she can tell Heather is embarrassing me.

'Thanks, Heather,' I say shyly, hopping up into the chair.

'The hair, the clothes, the luminous skin, all of it,' Heather presses. 'It's giving young, it's giving healthy, it's giving French – I'm *obsessed*. You done your French exchange yet?'

'Yup!' I tell her. 'It was amazing. My partner was a boy! And so lovely, he got on with everyone, didn't he, Grandma?'

'Lovely lad.' Grandma nods and then says, 'Me and your grandad are going to come with you to see him in London, actually, if you don't mind.'

'Nope,' I say. 'I'm gonna ask Mum if the girls can come too.'

Heather claps her hands together. 'I swear, your family! I've never met a group of people who are related to each other and actually like each other as much as you lot. It warms my cold, old heart, it really does.'

I lean back and Heather pokes and prods, in the way that dentists do, asking me if anywhere is tender. I tell her no, and within five minutes she says she's done, to keep up the good work – just make sure I don't miss that back right at the bottom – and announces that I am free to go.

Right as I stand up, Grandma shrieks: 'Oh! Look! A squirrel!'

We all turn to look where she's pointing, expecting to see – well, I don't know what. Why do we care if there's a squirrel outside unless it's juggling pine cones or doing an impression of the local weatherman? I turn around just in time to see Grandma running a tissue over the dentist's chair, bright red with blood. It makes my heart skip a beat: Why is there blood on the tissue? What's happened? By the time Heather has decided whatever squirrel Grandma has seen has evidently disappeared, Grandma is stuffing the dirty tissues into the bin, wrapping my coat around my waist, and standing behind me to usher me out of the building with a cheery, 'We'll call about booking the next appointment! Thank you so much, everyone!'

It all happens so fast and so bizarrely that it's not until Grandma says, 'Just stay there, darling,' that I realise my trousers feel weird at the back. I touch around to my bum and see the faint smudge of red across my fingertips.

'OHMYGOD,' I say out loud as Grandma puts a plastic shopping bag on the front seat. 'Have I bled through my trousers?!'

Grandma looks at me sympathetically. 'Happens to the best of us, Taylor. Don't you worry. Did you forget to change your pad or moon cup or whatever it is you use?'

I look at her, distraught. 'I didn't know it had come!' I say. 'Urgh! Being a girl is THE WORST!'

I go to bury my face in my hands but then remember the blood and pull them away just in time.

'Do you think Heather noticed?' I ask sadly. I really like Heather. Mum has always said periods are nothing to be embarrassed about, but there's no two ways about it: bleeding on your dentist's chair is the definition of embarrassing.

Grandma shakes her head. 'No, love. It was the tiniest little bit on the chair, and I wiped it all up. Don't give it a second thought. I'll pop into Morrisons to get you some clean knickers and pads, and we'll get you back to ours and cleaned up. I'll let you use my fancy David Bowie hot-water bottle if you like. And we can have beans beside toast for tea.'

I feel so grateful for her that I could cry – or maybe that's just my period too.

'Thanks, Grandma,' I say, pouting to demonstrate how sorry I feel for myself.

'I used to get heavy periods as well,' she says. 'And on an irregular cycle, like you. I know it's always a tough time, whenever it comes.'

I started my periods when I was ten, in primary school. There was only me and one other girl who had it, and we had to use the special teachers' toilet once a month because that was the only loo with sanitary disposal. Mum got me some period knickers last year, that absorb everything, and they've been a game changer. They last all day! Alas, I don't have any on me right now, so clean pants and a pad is going to have to do. And a healthy dose of self-pity, of course. Can't forget that.

* * *

Grandma looks after me like I'm a tiny little baby, not letting me set the table or help get drinks or *anything*. Grandad is out, so it's just me and her, and she sets me up on the sofa with a blanket and her Bowie hot-water bottle, as promised, and gives me two paracetamol that help my tummy ache almost immediately.

'Being a woman, eh?' she says, once I'm settled and she's issued a kiss to my forehead. 'It's full of bloody troubles, isn't it!' She catches herself then, and her use of 'bloody'. 'No pun intended,' she adds, and I roll my eyes good-naturedly. Periods puns, who knew *they* existed?

As she potters about, the French rap Axel introduced her to poetically spilling from the speakers and a little cinnamon candle lit on the coffee table, I flip through my notebook and reread everything I've been jotting down for my new column so I can distract myself. Duncan texts, asking where I was after school, and suddenly I'm in dreamland, thinking once again about how I need to get us alone together, in a way that means Second Kiss City can be reached. I scribble 'The Second Kiss' on a fresh page in my notebook and start to write:

I thought about my first kiss obsessively, for so long. It felt like everyone in the world was getting kissed but me! And I had a few false starts on who it might be with too: an older guy in the year above, my French exchange partner ... or suddenly, out of nowhere, a new friend, a boy I'd never paid much attention to until one day it just felt so obvious that BAM! I wanted to kiss **him**.

It took ages to get there. It felt like we liked each other, and we even went on a date, but it didn't happen! I'd put so much pressure on myself for it to be perfect, without thinking that maybe he was putting the same pressure on it too.

And then, whoa. It happened, and it made me so happy. He's a really good kisser! I hope I am too.

But what about the second kiss? The first kiss, it was sweet and lovely and gentle and, because I'd given up by the time it happened, unplanned (which is the best way for kisses to be, I'm told). Now though, I want more. A first kiss feels like it could be fun, but a second kiss with the same person feels serious, like you might actually want to be girlfriend and boyfriend ...

Doing it feels like saying OK, I liked it the first time, let's keep doing it!

And it's all I can think about ...

'You've got a dreamy look in your eye,' Grandma says as she passes through the living room to take out the recycling. 'If I didn't know any better, I'd think that Duncan boy might be on your mind ...'

I give her a very dramatic, unimpressed look, which makes her laugh. 'Tell an old woman to mind her business if you must!' she chuckles. 'But I know young love when I see it!'

I catch my own eye in the reflection of one of the many mirrors in this house. I look tired and pale, but undoubtedly excited about something.

Duncan, **I text him back.** *Why are you so obsessed with me?!*

Taylor, **he texts back.** *What sane human wouldn't be?*

Cheese!

But also.

SWOOOOOOOOON!!!!!!!!

I decide my notebook scribblings could actually be the basis for an article for my 'Seize the Day' column. After all, it's like Ms K says: the very personal can actually be incredibly *universal*. We did a whole half-term on writing like this, in Year 8. It's not about telling your secrets just to tell them, but writing truthfully. Ms K taught us that if you write your truth, the people reading it don't need to have experienced the exact same thing for them to get closer to *their* truth. Something like that, anyway, if I'm remembering properly. And it's like Mum always says, being honest is never wrong. If I'm obsessed about getting my next kiss with a boy I like, other people must get this way too. Right?? I hope Duncan doesn't mind, but this deffo has to go on the website. It's my truth!

7

I once read that period cramps can be so intense that they're not unlike the contractions somebody has before giving birth. If that's the case? I'm good on ever being pregnant, because HOLY MOLY am I in *agony*.

It's 5 a.m. when I get up to change my period pants, because I've got a funny feeling that with a tummy ache so bad I must be bleeding quite heavily. I don't mean to wake Mum up, but she yells from her bedroom, 'You OK, bug?'

I pad through to her room and she motions for me to climb in with her. I pull the duvet over us and she cuddles me from behind in the exact same way she's done all my life. It's my happy place, right here, just me and Mum, two peas in a pod. Except I don't feel very happy right now.

'It hurts,' I say, and it surprises me how much I feel like I want to cry. It *does* hurt, a low but constant tugging from the inside like little people are in there and are chipping away at my insides with very sharp picks. Nothing seems to help it. It's deeply uncomfortable. No wonder I want to sob! I challenge anyone to feel this way and not shed a tear.

'Oh, love,' Mum whispers. 'Did you manage to get any sleep?'

'Not really,' I admit, a giant yawn adding emphasis. 'I had weird dreams.'

Before I woke up I thought I was floating through the school hall, above the heads of everyone I know. They were all pointing and trying to tell me something, but I couldn't hear them. It was like I had them all on mute.

Mum puts a hand on my back and rubs, the pressure of it helping me feel better, because misery likes company, doesn't it? Being sad alone is no fun, but somebody letting you know that they're there … well, everyone needs their mum sometimes. Some people think they're going to grow up and not need their parent any more, but Mum says she's never needed Grandma as much as she needs her now. For her, the older she gets the more she appreciates her parents. I think that's nice.

'Stay off school today,' Mum whispers. 'You'll be no good to anybody if you've not slept, and you can hardly sit there with a hot-water bottle strapped to you.'

'Will you do me a hot-water bottle now?' I ask in a small voice, like a little kid.

'Course I will,' she says, slipping out the covers like a ninja so she doesn't let the cold air in.

After two paracetamol I drift back off to sleep, waking up at half past eleven feeling much, much better.

'Hello, you!' Mum says, creeping into her room with a hot Ribena and two massive slabs of hot buttered toast. 'I'm working from home today, lucky you.' She pops two more painkillers out of the packet for me, and hands me a glass of water from the nightstand. 'I heard the toilet flush, so I knew you were up. How you feeling? Any better?'

She brushes hair off my forehead gently, and then cups my cheek.

'Yeah,' I say, taking a bite of the toast. I'm suddenly ravenous. She watches me eat, polishing off my first slice in four big bites, and seems satisfied I'm telling the truth. I gulp down the Ribena and ask her to open the curtains a bit. She cracks a window, too, and it's a lovely feeling, being all cosy and fed in bed, with a little bit of a fresh breeze cutting through the room.

'I rang school,' Mum says, 'and said you won't be in today.'

'Did you tell them why?' I ask, suddenly horrified at the thought of Mr Logan getting a TAYLOR BLAKE HAS HER PERIOD note across his desk. To reiterate: periods aren't anything to be embarrassed about – I wasn't raised to be ashamed of ever needing a wee, so why would I be ashamed of another perfectly natural thing my body does? But also, you know, Mr Logan knowing my monthly cycle is a bit weird.

'I can't lie,' Mum confesses. 'In the end, I did. Yes. But don't go mad at me! It's because the woman at the office was a bit funny about it.'

I narrow my eyes. You don't get raised by Erica Blake without coming to learn that whilst she is fun, and understanding, and a lot cooler than most parents, she also does not like to be challenged, and just like Grandad she has a bit of a thing about unnecessary rules and authority figures.

(I know, I know – NO WONDER I AM LIKE I AM! It's a joke Star and Lucy have both made before, thankyouverymuch, let's move on!!).

'I rang and said you were unwell,' Mum explains. 'But she pressed me for more details, which I thought was odd. So I said, *She's got tummy ache*. And the way she replied, repeating *she's got tummy ache*, like she didn't believe me, was really annoying, so I said, *Yes, from her period. She's got cramps and hasn't slept because of her period*. And then she said OK, and hung up. So. It worked, I suppose. But she didn't need to give me the third degree *and* a bad attitude.'

I pop the last of my second slice into my mouth and as I chew I shake my head and say, 'You'll get me into trouble if you're not nicer.'

'I am nice!' Mum says. 'It just really bothers me that

they'd give us the Spanish Inquisition about why you're poorly. It's so *ableist*. Do you know that word? Like, some people have disabilities or chronic conditions and that means they often might not go to school. I'm not talking about *school refusal*, I mean legitimate medical reasons: doctor's appointments or pain management issues. So when school are all, ONE HUNDRED PER CENT ATTENDANCE IS A KEY MARKER OF SUCCESS, it makes some kids feel less-than, because they're never going to be able to attend school one hundred per cent of the time. Does that make sense?'

'It does.' I nod. 'Like if someone has ME? Like Grace Weissman in the year below?'

'Exactly. Obviously you don't have a disability or a chronic condition, and you're not registered as having any issues, but my point still stands: you're ill, and that should be enough. And also, if your body is giving you the cue that it needs rest, or to go more gently, what does it teach you if I say NO! YOU HAVE TO GO IN! NO MATTER WHAT! We've got twenty- and thirty-somethings going into work with chest infections and ending up in hospital because they were never taught how to rest. Well. Not my daughter!'

She shakes a fist at an imaginary judge and jury in the sky, and then smiles and makes a face to appreciate she's being dramatic.

'Thanks for ringing, Mum,' I say, giving her a look I can

only describe as Teenager. I know I can get 'on one', but gosh, do I drone on as much as Mum does when *she's* 'on one'?!

'I've also ordered some heat patches on Amazon groceries, along with hot chocolate, sponge pudding, more baked beans and a nice big pie for tea. You know the things I mean? They're oval-shaped and warm up to act like a hot-water bottle, to help with the pain. Aunt Kate swears by them.'

'I love you, Mum,' I say, because OK, she drones on a bit, but she looks after me soooooo well. I know I'm lucky. Not everyone has a mum who is so thoughtful. Some people don't have a mum at all.

'Wanna have a bath and then come down to watch cartoons on the sofa?' she asks. 'I'll run one for you. Go pick a bubble bath from your collection.'

See? She's the best.

Axel texts that afternoon, saying next weekend he'll be in London from the Friday night until the Sunday morning.

'Do you know what?' Mum says when I tell her. 'Let's book an Airbnb and make a night of it. I can't go on the Friday because I've got a late lecture at work, but we can go first thing Saturday morning and come back Sunday afternoon, if you want.'

'Of course I want!' I say with a little clap. 'And the girls?'

Mum nods. 'And Grandma and Grandad. We'll make quite the motley crew.'

'You're amazing!' I say, leaping up to throw my arms around her.

'Somebody is feeling sprightlier!' she says, laughing as I refuse to let go of her neck.

I ruffle her hair and flop back down on the sofa. 'I am,' I say. 'It still aches, but not as much.'

'See? A little bit of rest and you're good as new.' Mum is pleased, having proved her point. 'No point pushing through at fifty per cent when a day off can put you at a hundred.'

'Yes, yes,' I laugh. 'You're right, oh wise one!'

At 4 p.m. Lucy and Star knock on the door, bearing blue raspberry bonbons and the homework I'll need to catch up on from today.

'We hate when you're not there,' Star declares, squeezing me in a massive hug.

'Taylor sandwich!' Lucy squeals, coming around the other side of me so that I'm between them both.

'All right, all right,' I giggle from where I'm smushed up against Star's shoulder. 'I missed you guys too.'

'Did you though?' Lucy asks sarcastically. 'Or have you been so absorbed in your duvet day that you haven't even spared us a thought?'

I take too long to answer that, because Star bursts out laughing and says, 'Busted!' and then I'm laughing too, and urgh! I feel a million per cent better than I did this morning. Mum is right – rest is never wasted.

'Hello, girls!' Mum says, coming to the door. 'Are you coming in? I was just about to do a round of hot chocolates …'

The girls de-robe themselves of school bags and coats and shoes, and wash their hands before finding spots to get comfy in the living room. Mum busies herself making drinks, and I ask what I've missed out on today.

'Apart from Star getting a red rose taped to her locker this morning? Zero,' Lucy says, straight-faced. 'Less than zero. It's just been another boring day at Crickleton High.'

I look to Star. 'You got a red rose? From who?'

Lucy answers for her: 'Nobody knows! But obviously I am furious. How dare they try to woo my partner!'

Star raises her eyebrows and puts her mouth into a straight line, unimpressed. 'I'm pretty sure whoever it was got the wrong locker,' she says. 'It's a non-story. Just like everything in the new issue of the *Register* is a boring non-story too,' she continues. 'Because you're not even writing for them any more.'

I haven't even thought about the *Register* in a while. That's crazy! It's all I used to think about, but now we've got *The Instruction Manual*, I think about that instead.

'I might still write for the school paper,' I say. 'I just need to focus on my and Duncan's stuff for now.'

Mum delivers our drinks with some biscuits. 'Stay as

long as you want,' she insists to a beaming Star and Lucy. She excuses herself to do a bit of work in her office.

When she's gone, Lucy says, 'Oh!' because she suddenly remembers something. 'We spoke to Duncan at lunch!'

THAT gets my attention.

'Go on …' I say slowly, looking between them. 'This is it, isn't it? The bit where I find out he's totally changed his mind about me?'

'No!' Star interjects, 'It's nothing bad! Something good, in fact!'

'The double date!' Lucy says, waving her hands excitedly. 'How about this weekend? We were thinking bowling? And then Pizza Express for some dough balls?'

My tummy does a flip, and it's not because of my period. This is a nervous/excited flip. An 'OH-MY-GOD-A-DOUBLE-DATE?!' flip. That's so grown up!!

'A double date?' I repeat, letting it digest. 'I mean, yeah, awesome. But also, you're not going to be annoying and say hints about us kissing again or whatever, are you? You'll be cool?'

Lucy drops her jaw like she's insulted by the mere suggestion. 'How very dare you!' she says. 'I would never!'

'Yes you would,' giggles Star, who then turns to me and says: 'The answer is no. We won't be irritating. We'll just have fun!'

'And you know how I feel about fun …' I smile.

'Wicked,' Lucy says. 'I'll book a lane. Remember when we tried to go for my birthday last year and I cried because Mum hadn't reserved a lane and so we couldn't get in?'

Star pats her knee sympathetically. 'Adventure Golf was a cool alternative ...' she soothes, but she doesn't say it very convincingly. Adventure Golf was pretty rubbish, too hot and difficult and boring all at once. We all knew it at the time, and we all still know it now. But the lie must persist, because we don't want Lucy remembering her birthday badly. It's what Grandma would call a necessary untruth.

'Hmmm,' Lucy grumbles.

'And Mum is excited for you both to come to London,' I say. 'She says we can stay over on the Saturday night!'

'Oh!' says Star sadly. 'Really?'

'Isn't that a good thing?' I ask.

She pulls a face. 'I've got a fencing competition Sunday,' she says, sticking out her bottom lip. 'So I don't think I'll be able to go if you're staying over.'

'Oh,' I say, looking to Lucy for moral support. She pulls a *what can you do* face. I mean, we could *not* stay over, I suppose. But a night in London? It's too good to resist! And it's not like Lucy is suggesting we come home on the Saturday night, is she. I think she wants a sleepover as much as I do.

'It's OK,' says Star. 'I'm really loving fencing right now, so ...'

'It's amazing you have a sport you're so good at and invest so much in,' I say, trying to find the good in it. 'I don't do anything sporty.'

'You're good at netball, though,' Lucy reminds me. 'In PE Ms Perkins is always asking you to try out for the team.'

'I think she's just being nice,' I say.

'Well, she doesn't say it to me,' Lucy presses.

'Nor me,' Star says.

I consider it. 'But the netball girls are all so ...'

'Yeah.' Star nods. We don't need to fill in the blanks. Everyone knows netball girls are cliquey without saying it. 'They are. But still, you're good at it!'

'You could try out for the team for your column!' Lucy exclaims. 'I'd totally read that, a column about taking a chance on, like, getting picked or going from good to great.'

'That's not a bad shout, actually,' I say, letting the idea marinate. And yeah, the girls are snooty, but I do really enjoy netball. Maybe I could even get them onside with my daring wit and charming banter!

'I do have some good ideas!' Lucy laughs. 'I'm not totally stupid!'

'I didn't say that!' I squeak.

'Hmmmm,' Lucy grumbles, giving me a look. 'Anyway. You'd love the netball team, if you could crack them.'

I think of that article I read: *Nobody will remember you ... so what have you got to lose?*

'All right then,' I decide. 'I'll do it.'

Well, you don't see anyone all day and then it's like Piccadilly Circus with guests! Right as Star and Lucy are putting their shoes on to leave, Grandma and Grandad knock at the door – which, to be honest, is a formality, since they never wait to be invited in. The knock is more of an announcement of their intention to enter, regardless of what you're up to. You could be butt naked and doing a samba through the living room and they'd only walk straight on past you to put the kettle on.

'Oh! Sorry, love!' Grandad says, bashing the door into Star's butt. She tumbles forward with a yelp, reaching out for the first thing in front of her to steady her fall, which just so happens to be ... my pyjama bottoms.

'Arghhhhhh!' she wails, landing on the ground with a thud. My pyjama bottoms have served as zero help, because instead of supporting her, they've gone down with her: she's pulled them all the way down to my ankles.

'Star!' I exclaim, right as Grandma shoves Grandad. 'Go on in, then, David, you're letting in the cold,' she admonishes as she pushes Grandad over the threshold and then follows him, only to be confronted with me in nothing but my sleep T-shirt and period pants.

'Oh, is it trouser-less day?' Grandma says, clocking me. 'I didn't know.' Mum comes around the corner to see what all the fuss is about, but it's too late: Lucy is leaning against a wall, laughing, and Star is curled up in a ball on the floor in stitches. As for me, I scramble to get decent again, tears of hysterics streaming down my face because oh, for god's sake! Life feels like one embarrassing thing after another! As if G&G have just walked in on me with my trousers pulled down!

'Well,' I say, wheezing in between breaths. 'If that had to happen in front of anyone, I'm glad it's you lot!' Star grabs my arm, shaking with the giggles, and we stand there, holding on to each other – Lucy too – absolutely howling.

It takes about ten minutes for us young ones to stop laughing, to the point where the grown-ups seem genuinely bemused.

'OK, OK, that's all the teenage laughter I can take,' Mum announces, ushering the girls out the door. 'I love you all, but it's time to go.'

'Sorry, Erica!' they chorus, and I can only imagine the running jokes we're going to have about this in Members Only. They'd better not mention it to Duncan tomorrow on our double date.

'I love to see such good friends having fun together,' Grandad says when I join them in the living room. 'We used to get up to all sorts when I was a lad. You'd leave the house at breakfast, and only come home when it either got dark or you were ready for your tea.'

'What did you do all day then?' I ask, climbing back under my duvet on the armchair. I could get used to this cosy living! I check my phone as I ask to see that Duncan has messaged to see if I'm all right. The little cutie.

'Oooooh, all sorts,' says Grandad. 'We used to tuck our trousers into our socks and then put my friend Baz's hamster down and see who could stand it the longest.'

'Oh, David,' tuts Grandma. 'That poor creature.'

'Poor me, more like!' Grandad says. 'Have you ever had pants full of hamster droppings? My mother gave me a right telling off!'

'Were you really naughty, then?' I ask. I love finding out about what my grandparents were like at my age. I often wonder if I would have been friends with them, if we were all fourteen at the same time. I like to think we would have been, but then I also think Mum might have forbidden me from hanging out with such reprobates!

'YES!' answers Grandma for him. 'So don't follow his example!'

I raise my eyebrows at the room. 'All hamsters are safe around me,' I say. 'Rest easy.'

We sit and chat, Grandma saying they're at a Northern

Soul night this weekend, Grandad saying it's time for his annual underwear-buying spree. They ask about *The Instruction Manual*, and are positively giddy when I say we're thinking of having a launch party for it. It's one of the things Duncan and I came up with at our editorial meeting the other night. Before or after he read my text about kissing him, I can't remember. Oh gosh! I get embarrassed all over again at the thought of it.

'Taylor – we can ask at the social club! Have it there!' Grandad says enthusiastically. 'They've got a lovely set-up, haven't they, Rachel?'

Grandma nods. 'He's not wrong. They've got a projector too, so could even put up your website on the screen for everyone to see! For the big reveal!'

'Ooooooh,' I coo. 'Do you think they'd let us have it for free?'

'Leave it to us.' Grandad winks. 'We'll see what we can do.'

I spend the rest of the evening on my laptop, starting a Pinterest mood board for the launch to get ideas for fairy lights strung up and little cakes with our logo on.

Obviously we *need* a logo first.

I see a really gorgeous outfit, too – a long red strapless dress with really high heels with a bow.

Fancy, I think. *In fact, I should have a Be Fancy Pinterest board, since that's a way to seize the day!* It kind of goes against what *How to Be Parisian When You're Not from Paris* says, because French girls err on the side of simplicity. Nevertheless, I add pins of dresses and poufy skirts, neck scarfs and shoes, and the more I pin, the more I keep getting ideas for ways to 'be fancy' in my everyday life. Gosh, this day started out so crappy, and one big sleep and a bunch of visitors later I am feeling back to my old, full-of-life self. I wonder how Veronica is doing, if she's any better. I go on to her Instagram and her last post – from three weeks ago, before she got sick – is flooded with comments wishing her a speedy recovery and 'get well soon!'. With a pang of guilt I remember I still haven't given any thought to Madame Jones's care package for her. Maybe I could just contribute chocolates? Is that a cop-out? I add a row of pink hearts to everybody else's and put my phone away to charge. I should get some sleep – I want to be back fighting fit and ready to *carpe diem* tomorrow! *La vie est belle!* And I wanna be ready for it.

8

*I*t's amazing what a day of rest can do for a girl. I've been up since 6 a.m., ready for DOUBLE DATE DAY (!!) and full of *joie de vivre*. I can see why 'getting up early' was on so many *how to seize the day* lists when I did my research – I feel like I'm beating the rest of the world to something by being up, *and* it's giving me time to really put together a fancy outfit, as per my *be fancy* goal.

I remind myself of all the things I pinned last night, and pull a few things out of my wardrobe to consider as I curl my hair. The thing is, I've always strived for the chic, simple French look, and *How to Be Parisian When You're Not from Paris* is very much team 'don't look too polished':

> *To be chic, one must save the complications. A white T-shirt and well-fitting jeans need only to be*

accessorised with a charming neck scarf or good-quality pair of earrings. A summer dress requires good sunglasses and a straw bag only. Over-accessorising signals a lack of self-esteem: the Parisian woman is confident in her sartorial choices.

On the French exchange the most alluring and well-dressed girls had mussed-up hair and minimal make-up – but the thing is, everything on my mood board is a bit more crazy than that, a bit more … is ostentatious the word? Must google. 'Out there' is another way of saying it. But if Taylor Swift can reinvent her image with every album, perhaps I can be as chameleon-like as Taylor *Blake*. Dressing well is an act of creativity, after all! I think I read that in the changing room of H&M.

I watch a YouTube video on how to curl hair with straighteners, pinning up the top half of my hair and then twisting the flat iron around and around to make a curl. It works! Except on the baby hair at the front I think I leave it sizzling my hair too long, because there's a faint smell of burning hair and then a bit comes off in my hand.

BUT! THAT ASIDE! I don't do too badly!!

The video recommends using hairspray to give it hold, and then brushing out the curls with a wide brush to soften them, which seems like a good way to undo all the hard work I've just done, so I don't. I'm vaguely aware of the 'choose eyes or lips' make-up rule, where you can be bold with one or the other but not both, so choose lips. Then I think, well, lipstick rubs off throughout the day when you talk and eat, not to mention when you kiss, which hopefully will be happening today.

Wait, let me positively visualise.

... It will absolutely happen today!!

Anywoohoo, I try to scrub the lipstick off with a tissue and do my eyes instead. I'm quite good at liquid eyeliner now, and have a cobalt blue one in a set Auntie Kate sent for my birthday, so use that with a bit of mascara. It's a retro look, kind of party-party. I'm into it. It deffo fits the bill of 'be fancy'. It's nice to make the effort. I'm feeling ready for anything!

At the bottom of my wardrobe I find a tutu from last year, which if worn with a leotard would obviously be outrageous, especially for school ... but with a white shirt tucked into it, black tights for modesty (and warmth, it's starting to get chilly out there) and then big chunky boots, it's totally a day date vibe. I still have my period, so it feels nice and secure too, like I can wear my period pants and be held in by my tights and there's no danger of leaking anywhere AGAIN. That *cannot* happen today, or ever again for that matter. Bleurgh.

At the last minute I add in a nod to my love of French style with a neck scarf, too, partially because it's cool, but mostly because I am actually a bit chilly. And of course Duncan told me I dress a bit French, didn't he? Can't let him down! I feel like I look like the lead character from an old show Mum sometimes watches, where the woman walks down a busy New York street and a bus passes by with an advert from her column on the side. Imagine! That would be the height of *ooh-la-la!* New York meets Paris meets … Crickleton, ha.

I look so good that Mum almost chokes on her coffee when I get downstairs. It's taken a full two hours to get glam, after all, so despite me being the first up, she's beaten me to breakfast – it's already past 8 a.m. She looks at me over the rim of her cup, her eyes practically bulging from their sockets in a love-heart shape, like a cartoon. I give a little twirl to show off.

'Am I cool, or am I cool?' I ask, arms open ready to receive her compliments. 'It's giving *girl in a big city with a fancy media career and fantastic taste*, no?'

Mum takes a big gulp and lowers her cup.

'What's …' she starts slowly. She's so impressed by me she can barely speak! I'd call that success! I cock an eyebrow, waiting for her to finish her sentence. It's like she can't decide what to say.

'What's ... ?' I repeat, and she settles on: 'What's the occasion, bug?'

'Life,' I reply. 'I'm seizing the day!'

She nods, absorbing the magnificence of what is before her, i.e. me.

'I know,' I say. 'It's a lot, but I feel *amazing*. Trouble is, if I look this good today, how will I keep it up for the rest of the week?! For the rest of my life?! I'm setting the bar high, I know.'

Mum's eyes trace over me, taking in every last detail of the look.

'I look nice, don't I?' I prompt, because even though I can tell she thinks so, I'd still like to hear it. Call me a greedy ego monster, but who doesn't like words of affirmation! Especially before a date.

'Yes, bug,' she says. 'You look very ... creative.'

She doesn't sound like she means it, but obviously she does because she's got eyes, and the truth is plain to see. Hmmmm. Hopefully the girls will be more effusive with their words, and even Duncan too! He's so nice with his compliments!

At 11 a.m. I meet Lucy and Star at the bus stop at the marketplace. Duncan does drama on Saturday mornings, so he's going to meet us in town after. My first double date! I'm ticking off so many firsts lately, there's just no stopping me. Talk about seizing the day. This is the best thing I've ever done, pledging to live life to the max. It's exhilarating.

'Hey, besties,' I say, approaching them. They're both eating croissants from the bakery, buttery, flaky pastry falling to the ground as they lean over paper bags and try not to get it on themselves.

'Oh!' Star says, mouth full and eyes wide. Her eyebrows shoot up to the moon and she doesn't take her eyes off me as she chews, exaggerating the movement of her jaw and bobbing her head from side to side as if to say, 'Gosh! Eating things is so wild!'

Lucy doesn't say anything aside from hi, but it seems like Star has something to say so we both watch her chew and chew and chew, swallowing in a massive gulp and then wiping at the corners of her mouth with her finger.

'Tasty?' I say.

'Very,' she replies. 'We texted to see if you wanted one but you didn't reply.'

I fish my phone out from my bag and sure enough, there the text is.

'My phone was in my bag,' I explain, somewhat needlessly. She's just seen me get it out, after all.

There's a strange atmosphere, with nobody really saying anything, or … I don't know, it's like Star and Lucy both want to speak but are waiting to see who will go first. Eventually I can't stand it any longer, and I blurt: 'What? Come on.'

'Your outfit,' Lucy says finally. 'I've never seen you look so …'

To begin with I think she is about to compliment me, but when her face falls as she fails to find the right word for ages, I have second thoughts and realise I don't think she is. My heart sinks. Have I got this wrong?

'I think what she means to ask,' Star offers, 'is … what was the … *objective* here?' She holds out a hand and wafts it in my direction like I'm a bad smell.

'The objective?' I repeat, confused. I'm like a parrot today, just copying what everyone else says but sounding confused as I do it.

A dad with a pushchair navigates the pavement beside us, the kid strapped up inside pointing at me and gleefully proclaiming, 'Halloween, Daddy! Halloween!'

Lucy bites down on her bottom lip. Star looks past me, eyes glazing over. I get the sense they're trying not to laugh.

'Oh my god,' I say, the penny dropping. That kid thinks I'm in a Halloween costume?! I know kids don't get *style* but being pointed at and laughed at is a whole other ball game! 'Is my outfit bad?' I ask, panicking. Oh crap. 'I was trying something new! Something fancy! I can't go on a date dressed for *Halloween*!'

Star lunges forward and puts a hand on my shoulder. 'It's just a lot, that's all,' she says, in her kind, soothing way. 'We can fix it, can't we, Lucy? I think it's just …'

'Busy,' Lucy concludes. 'Cute, but busy.'

'I don't have time to go home and get changed!' I moan. 'But what choice do I have?'

Lucy points at the charity shop across the way. 'How about going in there?' she asks. 'You just need to, like …' She appraises me, putting her fingers to her chin and narrowing her eyes. She nods decisively and concludes: 'Swap the shirt for maybe a cardi? Put your hair up?'

'Come on!' says Star, grabbing my wrist. 'It's not a big deal! It's only clothes! Let's see what we can find!'

I try to avoid my own reflection in the shop windows as we head on over. I really thought I'd nailed this.

'I'm such a try-hard!' I wail as the girls stuff me into the curtained nook that passes as a changing room. 'Why can't I have more chill! I should have just gone jeans and trainers, like you!'

'Your lack of chill is part of your charm,' Star tells me, unbuttoning my shirt for me and taking off my neck scarf. She ties it to the strap of my bag in a surprisingly chic way, and Lucy announces from the other side of the curtain that the fashion gods have smiled, and there's the perfect cardi for only one pound fifty. She passes it to me and I am

AMAZED. I look better already, I can see it! Less busy, more refined, more considered. Thank GOD for my friends.

'Hair up, too,' Lucy says through the curtain, since three of us won't fit this side of it. 'In a low bun.'

Star helps me put my hair in what the French would call a *chignon*, and I step out to reveal myself.

'Oh my!' the shop assistant says. 'Now that's impressive, love, repurposing a fancy-dress costume into something everyday. See! We don't have to spend a fortune to look fantastic, do we, ladies?!'

This has been a terrifyingly close call. What a 'mare.

'I'm surprised Erica let her go out like she was dressed,' I hear Lucy say to Star as I go to pay for my new second-hand cardigan. 'You'd think she'd have said something.'

'Maybe she was rendered speechless,' Star reasons.

'I can hear you!' I say, stuffing my change into my pocket. Jeez!!

In the bowling alley I start to feel nervous.

'Breathe, Taylor,' Star reminds me. 'He's just a boy.'

'A boy I LIKE,' I remind her. 'A boy I'm probably going to kiss again!'

'That sounds exciting,' says Duncan, who has, improbably, chosen that exact moment to appear behind me.

'Duncan!' says Lucy, throwing her arms open wide for an

uncharacteristically enthusiastic hug. I think she's trying to defuse the moment – suits me! I am going to pretend that didn't just happen. He's going to start thinking I'm obsessed or something soon, for the number of times he's overheard me talking about snogging. I'm not putting *that* into my 'Second Kiss' article. The authors of *How to Be Parisian When You're Not from Paris* would disown me! Desperado dot com!

'Oh!' Duncan says as Star moves to hug him too. 'This is quite the welcome. I wish everyone was this happy to see me.'

When Star is done I realise it would be weird if I was the only one who didn't hug him, so I take my turn.

'Hey,' he says, voice low and breathy in my ear.

'Hey,' I say back, flushed.

I smile.

He smiles.

He is so, so cute!! I feel the blood in my body rush to my cheeks, making me hot all over. I wonder if he can tell. I wonder if this happens to him too.

'Right then, let's do this!' declares Lucy, dragging up to our lane. 'Prepare to lose so badly you'll want to *cry*,' she teases Duncan, who follows obligingly.

'Who have you been talking to?' he says, straight-faced. 'That only happened ONE TIME,' he jokes. 'I can't believe you know about it!'

'Lol,' says Star.

'I didn't know people still said LOL in real life,' Duncan quips. 'Not under the age of forty, anyway.'

'LOL!' repeats Star, for effect. 'LOL, LOL, LOL!'

I *love* that Star and Lucy are seeing the Duncan I've come to know, the silly and funny one. We all invent stupid ways to throw the ball – between our legs or crazy walk-ups – and between us we hit about three pins total because the ball keeps going into the gutter, but it is *hilarious*. Whenever Duncan comes back from his go he loiters near me, like we've got magnets in our wrists that draw us together. I'm super aware of the nearness of him, for the whole two hours we play. Every time he brushes his arm against mine (does he mean to? Or is it a happy accident? Either way, I don't care!) or waits his turn by sitting a bit close on the wooden bench. I wish I could just grab his hand, or had the guts to ask him if I can, like he did for me on our first date. But I can't, I just can't do it! I'm a big old scaredy-cat. When Star and Lucy share a kiss in front of us, we look at each other shyly, then burst out laughing. It feels like being part of a team. An awesome foursome, but also a cosy two. I like it. I like it a lot. And when Duncan finally takes hold of my hand as we walk to go get pizza, I decide I don't like it. I love it. This is the best feeling ever.

* * *

'This shouldn't taste as good as it does,' Duncan says, coating half a dough ball in garlic butter.

'I can't believe you've never had dough balls before,' Lucy says, shaking her head. 'Who comes to Pizza Express and doesn't have dough balls?!'

'Mum never lets us!' Duncan laughs. 'She said if we wanted dough balls we should have gone to Dough Ball Express!'

'Classic mum humour,' Star snorts, pushing his hand out of the way so she can get to the garlic butter too. Duncan waits patiently, and then resumes pigging out on it. It makes me less self-conscious about chowing down too. I really love food!

'I've had *dough* before, as a pizza base,' he says, popping his wares into his mouth. As he chews he covers his mouth with a hand and continues, 'And I've had butter before. But together? It's heaven-sent! I'm so addicted now.'

There's one dough ball left, which is technically mine, but I see Duncan eyeing it and then looking self-conscious when he realises I've noticed.

'Go on, Dough Ball King,' I say, pushing it towards him. 'It's all yours.'

'You're my favourite person EVER,' he says, blowing me a kiss across the table. I pretend to catch it and press it to my own cheek.

'Get a room, you two,' Lucy chortles, so just to annoy her I blow him a kiss back. Duncan looks absolutely pleased as punch – I'm still getting used to the fact that I always thought boys were unimpressed and too cool to be openly emotional. But not Duncan. He wears his heart on his sleeve and his emotions on his face, and it makes me feel really safe with him, like I'm gonna be OK because every smile and blush and air kiss reassures me he really does like me.

(He does like me, right?)

(I'm pretty sure he does.)

(I'd like to hear him say it twenty to thirty times though, just to be safe.)

(Too much???)

(Probably.)

Duncan makes me relax, and it's easy to be myself around him. He is the best possible addition to the Members Only gang (not that he'll ever be allowed in that text chain!), except instead of him just being one of the girls, I also want to kiss him. Gosh, this must be what it's like for Star and Lucy all the time! I think of Paul, how I meant to invite him along and get him set up with somebody, but it totally slipped my mind.

'I've been thinking about *The Instruction Manual*,' Lucy announces as our starters are cleared and mains delivered. I've got the four-cheese pizza – the more cheese the better for me!

'Oh?' I say. Lucy doesn't tend to pay *that much* attention to my writing – that's what's been so nice about spending time with Duncan. We're *ceeks*.

'Yeah,' she says. 'I'd like to help. I think I could be useful.'

'That would be great,' says Duncan with a smile, but I'm confused. Does she want to write articles? Because that's kind of *my* thing …

'Taylor mentioned having a party to launch the website, to make a splash,' she says. 'And I'd like to be the organiser.'

'Oooooh,' says Star, nodding crazily. 'THAT is a good job for you. You'd make it so good!'

I feel relieved she doesn't want to write, to be honest. I know that's a bit territorial, but it just feels like that is *mine*. Lucy has her own stuff! But to be fair, organising stuff is right up her street. It's a good idea.

'Yeah,' I agree with a smile. 'If anyone can help organise a good launch, it's you.' I look at Duncan.

'Absolutely,' he agrees. 'Nice. I think we're going to do it at the social club? They have projectors, apparently, so we can put the website up on the wall. Taylor's grandparents have sorted it.'

Lucy nods. 'Amazing,' she says. 'And, Star, I haven't mentioned this yet but I think you should do the marketing?

Getting people aware of what's coming, that there's going to be this badass new website for Crickleton High and beyond?'

'For sure!' Star agrees, not missing a beat. 'Yes! I don't want to be the odd one out. Sign me up!'

'Well, I didn't realise I was coming out for a *business* lunch,' Duncan says, sitting up straighter and lacing his fingers together like we're in a boardroom. 'How productive!'

We decide on a date three weeks from now, so we've got something to work towards, and then we get the bill and the girls go to the loo. Look at me on my date, talking about my website, wearing eyeliner. I'm practically thirty years old today!

'This has been really nice,' Duncan says across the table when the girls are gone. He gestures to the space they've left. 'They're so funny.'

I pull a face, one that means *oh yeah!* 'They're wild,' I say. 'But they let me be wild too, so it works out.'

'Yeah,' Duncan says. 'It's been really nice, this.' He smiles, and I mirror him. Then he opens his mouth but then closes it again. I get the sense he wants to ask me something else, so I wait for him to keep speaking. If I try to fill the empty air between us I will just babble, and I don't want to talk so much that he can't get a word in edgeways. And silence, a meaningful look, that's all a gateway to a kiss, isn't it? I look at him and try to keep calm, try to keep breathing and not look too nervous. His eyes soften as he takes me in, and I stand up so we can close the distance between us. He follows my lead so we're facing each other. I dare to lightly take his hand in mine.

'Do you want to walk me home?' I ask, hoping he understands what I'm getting at. I think we both feel a bit too shy to snog right here in the middle of the restaurant. Anyone could see! It would be nice for it to at least be a little bit private.

'Absolutely,' Duncan replies. 'I *really* want to walk you home.'

He grins. It's safe to say he's caught my drift.

We all get the bus back to Crickleton and get off at the marketplace, so Lucy can walk Star home and Duncan can walk me home.

'Hey,' he says when we're at the corner of my street. We've walked mostly in silence, but it wasn't awkward or anything. It was sort of comforting, like we don't have to be constantly jabbering on. What is it they say? It's not about having somebody to do stuff with but about having somebody to do nothing with. He gives me a little tug. I stop walking and face him. I can't keep the excitement from my face. I'm grinning from ear to ear.

'Hey,' I say.

I know how good this is going to be so I don't feel afraid, not any more – I feel like *finally. Finally! Kiss numero dos!* And not even at the top of my drive like last time, where Mum could see. Clever boy, Duncan, having us stop here instead.

I lean in – probably a bit too eagerly, to be honest, but I cannot wait a second longer – and our lips meet through our smiles, and then it's happening. As gentle and soft as the first, only this time Duncan puts his hand up to my face so that he's cradling the side of my head, like he doesn't ever want to let me go.

I don't know how long we stay that way for.

But I do know that by the time I get home, my jaw aches.

9

I'm in the kitchen, working on a column about my failure to be fancy the other day. So far I've got:

Taylor Blake Seizes the Day ... by Being Fancy!

Well, dear reader, what is it they say? If at first you don't succeed ... give up?

Just kidding.

If at first you don't succeed, try and try again!

Unfortunately, that is what I'm going to have to do. I had all the best intentions for embracing a fancy life, but I got so excited that I overdid it. We're talking eyeliner, we're talking lipstick, we're talking tutus and curled hair ... all at once! It's a good job I've got friends good enough to let me know when I've missed the fashion mark, especially considering this was on my way to my very first double date. Lucky for me the object of my affections is a lovely boy who I don't think would be afraid, but it was better to take no chances ... and for those of you keeping track, that second kiss did happen. Yes, I am dying from happiness!

'Oh my god!'

I look up from my laptop. 'What's happened?' I ask Mum, who is stood at the kitchen counter flicking through her post.

'Those miserable, sneaky ... *buttheads!*' she exclaims, staring at the piece of paper in her hands like she's trying to turn it into flames with the power of her mind.

I close my laptop. Mum doesn't lose her cool very often. This is ... interesting.

'Mum?' I repeat, and she turns to me.

'I've been fined for keeping you off school the other day,' she says, in a voice obviously straining to be measured – so it's quite scary, really. Sometimes the less scary thing is somebody just going ballistic and losing their cool. It's when gritted teeth and bulging eyes happen that you have to panic. 'I've had a letter,' she continues, 'that basically says half the population get periods, and it's no excuse to miss school. So instead of school taking my phone call as authorising your absence the other day, they've logged it as an *unauthorised* absence. And that means the council sending me a fine, because the school told them to. A hundred and twenty quid, reduced to sixty if I pay it in the next fourteen days. This is the stupidest thing I've ever heard!'

She tosses the letter on to the counter, frustrated.

'So this is what we get for telling the truth, is it?' she says, less so to me and more to … the world. Like she's complaining to God or something, looking out of the window and up to the sky. 'It's so patronising. And it *reeks* of misogyny. It's so anti-women. Anti-*people*. People get periods! That cause cramps! Painful ones! Where you can't concentrate! It would have been *inhumane* to send you in last week, especially when you'd not slept. If this happened to the majority of the patriarchy there'd be paid-for leave and care packages sent every month, but because it's seen as *a girl thing* we're just expected to get on with it.'

She's on one now. I open my mouth to agree with her, to tell her I think she's right, but Mum just keeps on talking.

'It's a man's world, and we're just living in it …' she says.

'Your head teacher is a man, yes? He's the one who will have passed this on to the council …'

Her eyes are huge like saucers. I feel this isn't about the letter about periods. I know she lost out on a promotion for department head at work last month at the uni, and she's been cross about it since. Called it an 'old boys' network' and said she'd never stood a chance.

'Do you know,' she tells me, 'that most offices are five degrees too cold for women because the formula to figure out their temperature was based on a 1960s, 70 kilo man – women's metabolisms are slower, so we don't run as warm. But nobody cares! I have to keep a blanket under my desk at work, because I am *freezing*!'

Ah. So this *is* about work. I wonder if she'd notice if I slipped off to the loo? I'm bursting for a wee, but I deffo think she'd take it badly if I trot off mid-rant. This is a performance that requires an audience.

'*And* we're fifty per cent more likely to be misdiagnosed following a heart attack, because heart failure trials typically use men. AND cars are designed around the body of 'Reference Man', so even though more men crash cars in the first place, they're generally kept safer because cars are designed *for them*. Women are *fifty per cent* more likely to be seriously hurt. Fifty per cent!'

She finally takes a breath.

'Sorry you have to pay, Mum,' I say, when it feels safe. 'I have seventeen pounds upstairs – I can pay that towards it? If you like?'

Mum's face softens. 'Oh bug, no, no, no,' she says. 'It's not about the money. It's … I just think it sets a terrible example to young people that essentially, something like this says your lived experience doesn't matter. I don't want you to grow up having your body and your pain minimised! School should be empowering you to own your female experience, not lead the way in diminishing it! Spain literally just passed legislation allowing paid time off for periods, for crying out loud! Now THAT is empowerment.'

'Whoa,' I say. 'Really? I always thought we just had to … well, like you say, crack on. That's really awesome that they did that.'

'It is,' Mum says, flopping down beside me in the breakfast nook and slinging an arm over my shoulder to pull me close. She kisses the top of my head.

'I shouldn't have ranted. Sorry. Well, not *sorry*, because I shouldn't have to apologise for caring about stuff, but …'

I put a hand on her knee. 'Mum,' I say. 'It's OK. It's a stupid letter, and a stupid fine.'

She grimaces, and then sticks out her bottom lip, pouting.

'Let's change the world,' she says, and I know she's joking, but …

'Well, yeah,' I say. 'Let's!' It suddenly occurs to me that if we don't try to change things, loads of other people could end up suffering needlessly. Mum is right – periods happen, and sometimes they hurt! I missed a day, but quickly caught up. I don't think I'd be able to criticise Mr Logan and the school in the actual school newspaper, but when *The Instruction Manual* is launched, I could do something there. Or …

'What if we go to the local paper?' I ask. 'I think if we made enough noise, loads of other people would agree with us, and school would *have* to change the rules! The matter just needs a bit of attention on it …'

Mum looks at me in that way she does: impressed but also like she might cry. She opens and closes her mouth a few times, undecided on what to say and inadvertently looking like a fish.

'I actually don't care what you think,' I decide, before she can stop me. 'I'm going to do this. I've had painful periods since I was eleven years old, and every month – or whenever it is they decide to come – it takes me by surprise how horrible they can be. I couldn't bear the thought of anybody going in when they feel how I did last week. It's not like I skip school for a holiday, or even every month. And what did you call it? Ableist? Well. I agree! I'll take it from here!'

Mum does the floppy-mouthed fish thing again, and

then sits up straighter, as if she's resolved within herself to accept I will not change my mind.

'Go for it then, my darling,' she says, nodding with purpose. 'Go give them hell.'

My mind *races* all the way to school. I don't even remember the walk in, I'm so busy thinking about how to go about this. But my feet automatically take me to Ms K's office, and it's not until I'm knocking on her door that I realise I'm even there. It makes sense: she's a cool teacher, the coolest teacher at Crickleton High, and I feel like she gets it, you know? She doesn't ever talk down to us or make us feel like we're idiots because we're teenagers and she's ... well, I don't know how old she is, maybe, like, thirty or something? Twenty-five? Forty? I have no idea how to tell adult ages apart unless they have wrinkles. To me, age is basically: tiny and can't talk, less tiny and *can* talk, primary school, high school, young-looking but adult, parents, grandparents. Those are the categories.

'Oh,' I say, reaching the threshold of Ms K's classroom and seeing her at her desk again. I don't mean for it to come out – I'm self-aware enough to know that it looks like she doesn't want to be bothered.

... And yet, there I am, making noises and letting myself be known.

I wonder what it's like to be somebody whose intentions and actions match? I feel like my head says one thing and my mouth always ends up saying another!

Ms K moves her head the tiniest bit, just enough to see it's me.

'Taylor. Can you pass me my snacks?' she mumbles. 'From my bag?'

I look around, thinking her bag must be at the opposite end of the room from her. It's not. It's at her feet. As in, she could reach it if she just moved her hand.

'Urm,' I say. 'OK?'

I lift up her bag and there's a see-through carry case on top, jammed with granola bars.

'One of these?' I ask, gesturing. She grunts as reply, a grunt I take to mean *yes*. She takes it, her head still on the desk, and opens it without looking. I'm not really sure what to do. Do I stay? Do I go? As it happens I sort of can't take my eyes off her – my English teacher, not acting very teacher-like. It's unnerving, and I feel like I'm seeing something I shouldn't. I vaguely wonder if this is related to her running off the other day to be sick. Instinct tells me not to ask, so I stand there, watching her eat.

After three bites Ms K sighs contently, like a craving has been satisfied. She has come back to life.

'The joys of pregnancy,' she says, pulling a face.

Aha! The belly rubbing! The throwing up! The snacks! I knew it!!

'I didn't know you were pregnant, Ms K,' I say.

She gestures to her stomach. 'I thought it was obvious.'

She doesn't sound happy about it, but I say congratulations anyway. It comes out a bit half-hearted, like that's not the right thing to say. But … babies are a good thing, aren't they? If you're an adult, anyway. If it was somebody my age it might be a different story. But it happens! When I was in Year 7 there was a girl taking her GCSEs who had a baby the day after results day. She's in her final year now, and I heard a rumour she has a place to study at Cambridge. She didn't let it stop her, but there was hell to play about it happening. At one point they weren't even going to let her sit her exams, because her pregnancy would be a distraction to the other pupils! There's the patriarchy again.

Anyway, I digress.

'Yes,' Ms K says, and I regret coming here at all. I'm intruding, I'm sure of it. Who says 'yes' to *congratulations?!* I'm in over my head here …

'You're not intruding, you know,' Ms K says, like she can read my mind. Maybe that's what makes her such a good teacher. SHE KNOWS WHAT WE ARE ALL THINKING. 'I was just having some nausea. It's a good job you came – I couldn't even get my own bag off the floor. I'm feeling much perkier now though.' She gives a wan smile. 'Urgh!' she mutters, shaking her head. 'It's a roller coaster!' She studies my somewhat bemused face. 'How can I help, Taylor? I owe you one now ...'

'Urm,' I falter. 'Well, the thing is, it's about my period. Or everyone's periods, actually.'

'What a way to start a conversation,' she chuckles. 'You certainly have my attention.'

I explain everything, all about the letter Mum got and how it's unfair and how I want to change policy. And she listens, nodding along like she's absolutely with me, like I'm making a lot of sense, which is encouraging. I'm not crazy for caring about this, then!

She waits for me to finish and then asks: 'And so how can I help, exactly?'

'I just thought you might know how to contact the local paper,' I say.

She nods, understanding what I'm saying. 'Bold move,' she notes.

'I'm a bold girl,' I reply. It makes her laugh.

'That you are, Taylor. That you are.'

Ms K googles the number for the *Crickleton Chronicle*'s news desk, writes it down, and hands it to me.

'Thank you,' I say. 'I suppose I could have googled that myself, it just didn't occur to me it would be that easy.'

'My pleasure,' she replies.

I start to pick up my bag, and can tell Ms K has more things to say, so stand up straight and look directly at her, waiting. She gives me another weak smile, as if she isn't sure she can say what it is she wants to. I cock my head quizzically, and say, 'Yes, miss?'

She takes a breath.

'Taylor,' she says. 'I don't mean to pry, and this is very unprofessional of me, but am I right that it's just you and your mum?'

'No *just* about it, Ms K,' I say.

'No.' She smiles, and somehow I can tell it was the right thing to say. 'It's always been OK, then?' she presses. 'You've never felt like you … missed out?'

'With no dad?' I ask. She gives a wee shrug, like it pains her to ask. 'No,' I say, and I mean it. 'Mum has always been so honest about how much she wanted me, and very clear that a sperm donor isn't my "dad", just somebody who helped her when she needed help. She said if I got a maths tutor and scored an A on a test, does that mean I got the A, or the tutor?' Ms K's features soften, like this is exactly the thing she wanted to hear. 'I think it's her way of saying the person who helps us doesn't get the credit,' I add.

Ms K digests what I've said, and the bell goes – meaning

I'll be late for form time if I don't get a jog on. I've probably already said too much. Ms K didn't ask for my life story!

I turn to leave, because this is all a bit intense for eight thirty in the morning, but then have a huge twinge of guilt that I've not been helpful *enough*. It's hard to know where the line is, what with her being a teacher and all.

'Are you like my mum, then?' I say, lingering by the door. 'You'll be a solo parent too?'

'It seems that way, yes,' Ms K says. 'But, Taylor, I thought I was sad about that, and then you've just made me so hopeful and excited. I just … well. If I do half as good a job as your mother has obviously done with you, I think I'll be very proud of myself. Thank you for your kindness.'

'No worries,' I say. 'It's like my mum says, we're all just trying to get through a day, aren't we?'

Ms K lets out a bark of a laugh.

'Get gone, you,' she chuckles. 'You're showing me up with how wise you are now. And remember!' she adds: 'Don't sound hysterical and worked up when you speak to the journalist, just lay out the facts. They speak for themselves, OK?'

'OK,' I say.

It's soooo nerve-wracking calling the paper. We're not supposed to get our phones out at school, but me and the girls find a quiet place behind the industrial bins and I do my best impression of somebody who knows what they're talking about as I'm connected to Pria Kaur on the news desk.

I half expect her to tell me to call back when I'm older, to refuse to take me seriously because I'm 'just' a teenager. But she listens properly, and asks really good questions, and to be honest I even impress myself as I give my answers. I sound quite confident and knowledgeable! It must work because ... Pria Kaur is coming to interview me after school!

'What's all this about getting interviewed?' Duncan asks after English, as we head to lunch. Lucy has maths clinic and Star has fencing practice, so it's just him and me.

'How do you know?!' I say. 'Are you psychic now?'

'I've always been psychic,' Duncan bats back. 'And also Calum Maggiore told me in PE this morning.'

I shake my head, although I shouldn't be surprised. This school is rife with gossip – everyone is always talking about somebody else.

'It's not about *The Instruction Manual*, by any chance, is it?'

I shake my head. 'No,' I say. 'It's about ...'

I stumble over my words. Am I really going to say the word *periods* to Duncan?

'About ... ?' Duncan repeats, corners of his mouth curling upwards, amused. I know he thinks I'm super confident and vocal, so on the odd occasion I stumble over my words he *loves* it. Not in a nasty way. He goads me with a sort of fondness, because he knows I like the verbal sparring of it all.

'Periods,' I declare, doing my best not to lower my voice. I may as well own it, may as well at least act like it doesn't make me cringe to talk about it to a boy I like. And yet, isn't that just the thing? THERE IS NOTHING TO BE EMBARRASSED ABOUT.

Some things are easier in theory than in reality, though.

'I'm going to need more information,' says Duncan, creasing up his face, confused. 'How did that happen?!'

As we drop our bags at our lockers and head to the cafeteria, I explain. Duncan – to his credit – barely bats an eyelid.

'My mum has been teaching me about periods since I was four,' he says as we join the queue for some lasagne. 'For all the exact same reasons as you say: it's normal, it happens, everyone needs to understand it more. And for what it's worth,' he adds, 'Mum also went through early menopause, so I also have more knowledge than I probably should about what happens when periods stop, too.'

'Duncan Higginbottom, the Period Expert?' I say.

'DUNCAN GETS A PERIOD!' Bobby Hasstlehoff shouts out to the dining hall. I hadn't realised he was behind us.

'DUNCAN IS ON THE BLOB!' he presses, reaching out a hand to ruffle Duncan's hair.

'Grow up, mate,' Duncan says, and Bobby mimics, in a high-pitched voice, *'Grow up, mate.'*

Paul joins us then, instantly understanding that something has come to pass. He says hi, Duncan and I say hi back, and then the three of us just look at Bobby, straight-faced, blinking, saying nothing. It takes the wind out of his sails, because Bobby looks between us like he doesn't understand why we've stopped reacting, and the longer he frowns the funnier it becomes, until Duncan and I burst out laughing and Bobby storms off, saying something about going to the toilet 'to get away from these weirdos'.

'Bullies, man,' Paul says, letting me get my food before him. 'They just can't take a joke.'

It's really nice to eat lunch with Paul as well as Duncan, because he's a bit more chatty in a smaller group. He asks loads of questions about *The Instruction Manual* and how I found the French exchange.

'I prefer German,' he explains, 'so I didn't do the exchange. I don't even think I'll do the German exchange though.'

'It's a lot of pressure, isn't it?' I say, trying to be empathetic. Inside I'm thinking, *Why wouldn't you want to try everything life has on offer?!* Seems rude to say that, though.

'Did your friends do the exchange as well?' he asks. 'Lucy, and … what's the other one's name?'

'Star,' I say. 'Which is fitting, because she lights up my life.'

Paul smiles at that.

'You're very …' he says.

'Yeah,' Duncan agrees. 'She is.' He winks at me, letting me know the blank space is a good thing.

'So, Star,' Paul repeats. 'Cool. I'll remember that.'

'You coming with us to this interview?' Duncan asks, looking at his watch. 'Taylor, we'll have to go in a sec.'

I glance at the wall clock and see it's almost time.

'Yikes,' I say. 'Let's make like a tree!'

'And leave?' Duncan asks. 'God, that's a dad joke.'

'Oh!' Paul says, only just getting it. 'Leaf. *Leaves*. Leave! Ha!'

Oh god.

Paul declines accompanying us, which is good because I feel like I'll talk more freely with just Duncan there. I appreciate his moral support, because even though I did myself proud on the phone, my palms got sweaty and my heartbeat was going really, really fast. I feel the same now. Am I really going to do this? Put the school's policy out on blast?

'You're gonna be great,' Duncan whispers, knowing I'm nervous without me even having to say it. 'Just be yourself.'

'Taylor?' says a tall woman with cropped black hair and

massive eyes as I approach the bench near the school gates, where she said she'd wait.

'Yes,' I say. 'Hello.'

She's really nice, actually, inviting me to sit down beside her and offering me a cup of tea from the flask she's brought with her. Duncan puts his bag on the ground and sits on that.

'I really do think you've got a fantastic point,' Pria tells me, 'and I'd love to support you drawing attention to the cause. I actually had endometriosis myself, I don't know if you've heard of that? It can cause really painful periods because of a problem with the lining of the womb. I used to be in agony with my periods, and it felt like I was just supposed to get on with it – not even the doctors took my pain seriously until a few years ago. I spent half my life in agony! So let's make sure people know what school have said, shall we? It's the modern world, after all. We shouldn't have to grin and bear it or hide our pain any more. And I have a feeling our readers will be outraged on your behalf. More of us struggle than you'd think.'

'Exactly,' I say, with a firm nod of my head. 'I really appreciate your support, Pria.' It feels good to be validated by somebody so professional. If there's a tiny voice in the back of my head telling me I could get in trouble for having an opinion about all this, she quietens it down.

Pria asks me some of the same questions she did on the phone, and a few more, and Duncan nods along as I answer, letting me know I'm doing well. And then Pria says, 'As a journalist, I'm supposed to be impartial, but I'm just wondering if you've thought of any kind of protest, something the school body can get involved in?'

The way she says it is part curious question, part instruction. She holds my eye, and I can tell she's imploring me to say, *Yes! That's exactly what we're going to do!* but for some reason the words won't come out of my mouth. A protest? How would I ever go about organising one of those? And what would it achieve?

It's Duncan who says, 'We are, actually! Next Tuesday, at nine a.m.! Tell everyone in the article to bring their placards and their spirit!'

Pria smiles, satisfied. 'I think that's great of you,' she says. 'Causes like this need a call to action. I'd doubt just an article will do much to change things, but an article followed by a peaceful protest certainly could. Sometimes change needs a bit of noise.'

She clicks her pen, our interview over, and tells me she'll be in touch.

'Sorry for jumping in there,' Duncan says once she's gone. 'I just got excited.'

I feel a bit shell-shocked, like the adrenaline is coursing

through me but also there's so much of it I don't even know where to begin: I've forgotten how to speak, how to function.

'You all right?' Duncan asks.

'Yes?' I say.

'This is good, Taylor. You're doing a good thing.'

I look at him, thankful that he's here. 'Yes,' I say. Then: 'Do you think I'll get in trouble?'

Duncan shrugs, and then smiles. 'Yeah,' he decides. 'Probably. But I think it will be worth it.'

I hope he's right!!

'Also,' he says, looking at his wristwatch. He's like my official timekeeper today. 'You're late for netball try-outs.'

'Gah!' I squeal, grabbing my stuff. I'd totally forgotten about netball try-outs! Thank goodness for Duncan. 'OK, gotta go. Thank you for staying for the interview! And for saying about the protest!' I'm already backing away, heading off to see if I really am any good at team sports. 'I appreciate you!'

Duncan laughs, pulls a face. 'I appreciate you too, Taylor Blake,' and then he blows me a kiss.

'Cheese!' I shout in return, but secretly I am over the moon. I catch it and hold it to my heart, happy as happy can be.

10

Members Only

Me: Urm ... so I only went and got a place on the netball team!

Lucy: Yassss queen!

Star: We knew you would! What position?

Me: Not sure yet, probably wing attack or wing defence, I think

Star: You're gonna be soooooo busy

Don't they train twice a week *and* have at least one match?!

Me: Yeah

Mum said the same

But I think if I just get up earlier I'll have no trouble seizing the day!

Lucy: LOL

Star: In other news, thanks for my chocolate lolly, Taylor! Have fun this weekend!

Me: ???

I didn't give you a chocolate lolly

Star: Oh. Really?

Me: Really.

Lucy: OMG Star! It must have been the same person who left you the flower!!

You've got an admirer!

Star: Weird.

Anyway...

Love you guys! Send pics with Axel!

I'm so excited to have a fun weekend. To recap, the things I have on my plate right now are:

- My 'Taylor Blake Seizes the Day' column research/writing
- *The Instruction Manual* in general
- *The Instruction Manual* launch (Lucy and Star are managing most of this though)
- Impending London trip to see Axel (tomorrow!!)
- New netball team status: 2–3 practices and matches a week (mostly lunchtimes)
- PERIOD PROTEST (official name)

- Ongoing development of things with Duncan. We have kissed twice and had two dates. What now??? I need him to be my boyfriend! Not sure how to raise this with him.

Obviously I also have school, homework, and my friendships. And being a nice daughter. And a good granddaughter! Let's seize! That! Day!! Aye, aye, aye, I am booked and busy.

But.

When I got up early the other day I really did realise it's sooooo good to have all that extra time in the day, so I'll keep doing that, and stop wasting so much time on e.g. reading love stories for hours before bed, or curling my hair even though it makes me feel fancy. Priorities!!

Anyway, gotta get to sleep now, because tomorrow is SEEING AXEL DAY!!! It's been taking me ages to get to sleep at night, bizarrely. I've always been so good at sleeping, but lately all my thoughts whizz around asking for attention and I end up staring at the ceiling and trying not to forget all the things I need to remember.

It's a lot.

Good, but a lot.

Oh my gosh. Well. It's all very well saying a 9 a.m. train isn't that early, but then we had to leave the house at 8 a.m. to make sure we were at the train station on time (we got there at 8.20, so now we're all freezing on the platform) and so I've been up since 6 a.m., like I've promised myself I would. Except I didn't go to bed until really late because I started reading the new Holly Bourne book, even though I said I wouldn't read before bed any more and do work instead. But I love reading so much! And this isn't a romance, it's a call to feminist arms, like all her books are. Maybe there's something else I can cut from my days instead of reading …

OK, I'm coming up with nothing here. I like everything I do. Hmmmm.

'The cold makes me need to pee,' Grandad announces as we cradle hot chocolates Mum has got for us at the café on the platform. 'Hold this, would ya, Taylor?'

He hands me his cup and toddles off down the platform to the loo. Mum yells after him, 'Dad! Be quick! The train will be here in a minute!'

'Your father hasn't peed quickly since he was thirty-five,' Grandma says with a chuckle.

Lucy pulls a face. 'Do people pee slower when they get older then?'

'Do they!' hoots Grandma. 'Cakes have been baked and cooled in the time it takes David Blake to use the bathroom. Whole episodes of television have been watched! And god help us if he needs a number two. I call him worry wipe, you know – he does a poo, comes out of the loo, and then worries he's not wiped properly. I had to start buying those moist toilet paper things to set his mind at ease, but that's a whole other story.'

'Worry wipe?' Lucy repeats, looking green.

'Bet you wished you never asked now, don't you?' I say. Lucy smiles weakly.

'Are they always like this?' she whispers.

'TMI personified?' I say. 'Yes.'

She nods, and then goes back to being quiet. She's been a bit monosyllabic since we picked her up, to be honest, which is just *soooo* not like her. I wonder if she's missing Star, or has decided she feels guilty about coming without her after all. Star seems to be the object of somebody else's affections lately too, what with the rose and the sweets – but surely Lucy isn't worried about a mystery admirer? She and Star are rock solid!

'He'd better not be any longer,' Mum says, checking the tickets on her phone for the millionth time. She's normally a lot more relaxed than this. I wonder what's making her so jumpy. 'Look, the train is coming.'

The train pulls up to the platform and slows to a stop right as Grandad comes out of the toilet.

'Cutting it fine, Dad,' Mum says to him, like *he* is the child, and Grandad shrugs.

'Stop fussing, you. This is supposed to be fun!'

'Hmmmm,' says Mum, checking herself out in the reflection of the closed train doors. She's worn her hair down, something she only ever does for special occasions, all flowy and wavy over her shoulders. *And* she's wearing lipstick.

'You look good, Mum,' I say as the doors sigh and part, and we stand back to let off a man with a pram.

'*On y va*,' Mum instructs, once the coast is clear.

'What does that mean again?' Grandad asks, following me aboard.

'It means get your butt on the train, Dad,' Mum says. 'Come on, this way.'

Excitingly, the train is very quiet, so we get to spread out over two table seats in the middle of the carriage and play Heads Up! together. Grandad holds the phone up to his head as Lucy cries out, 'It lives in a cupboard normally, under the stairs!'

'Dobby!' Grandad cries, thrilled he remembers the little house elf from Harry Potter.

'No, you plug it in!' Lucy squeals.

The timer on the game ticks, letting them know they're running out of time.

'A hairdryer!'

'NO!' shrieks Lucy, so that a few people in other seats further down the carriage crane their necks to see what they're doing. She's too competitive and too involved to notice, or care. I'm getting the sudden feeling it might have been a bad idea to pair up *I'm not bossy I am instructive* Lucy with a man who is so laid-back he's horizontal.

'You clean things with it!' she cries.

'A feather duster?'

'YOU DON'T PLUG IN A FEATHER DUSTER, DAVID!' Lucy yells.

The timer on the app counts down 3 ... 2 ...

'COME ON!' Lucy shouts, but then the timer hits 1 ... and the round ends.

'A VACUUM CLEANER, DAVID! IT WAS A VACUUM CLEANER!'

Grandad nods in understanding. 'Ahhhh,' he says. 'So I wasn't far off with the feather duster then, was I?' he chuckles. 'Right ballpark, wrong game, ha ha ha.' Lucy's face is like thunder: she's furious.

'I thought he'd be loads better than this,' she whispers to me as he ducks down to find some crisps in his bag.

I give her my sympathetic face. 'You thought wrong,' I say, but then I shouldn't get too cocky, I suppose, because I'm paired with Grandma and the last time we played this together, she ended up crying because she got frustrated 'with the stupid blinkin' phone! Games shouldn't be on phones, they should be on the table in front of you!'.

Spoiler: it wasn't the phone that made her lose. She was just bad at it.

We play some more Heads Up!, get off one train to switch to another, the one that goes into St Pancras, and then we play Dobble, which I like because I always win. I don't know what it is, my brain just works fast with pictures, so I can match up the images really quickly and usually get rid of my cards in record time.

'God, I love this part of the journey,' Mum says, noticing that we're almost there. We speed through Kentish Town and Mum points out a pub. 'I met Malcolm Williams in there once,' she says. 'Back in the day.'

'Who?' I ask.

'He was in a boy band when I was a teenager,' she says. 'He was my Harry Styles.'

'There's only one Harry Styles,' Lucy says, and Grandad pipes up: 'I don't know who either of you are on about, so how about that.' Once the train comes to a stop we scurry off to pour out on to the pavement near the Eurostar entrance.

'I wish we were going to Paris,' I sigh, noting that in the queue you can tell who is French and who is not purely from how shaggy and chic their hair is.

'London not good enough for ya?' jokes Lucy, lacing her arm through mine. We exit and make a right so we can cross the road. 'Look at this place! I can't believe this beautiful building is a TRAIN STATION!'

'Well,' Mum says, as we wait for the green man to light up. 'Technically that bit is the St Pancras Hotel, and the train station is behind it. But still. It really is gorgeous, isn't it?'

'Dreamy,' Lucy comments, so lost in taking it all in that I have to pull on her arm so she doesn't get left behind.

Mum has organised with Axel's dad, Lucas, to meet in the lobby of the hotel opposite the train station. It's *very* hipster and cool. It makes me feel super grown up and *chic*. I try to act like I come to places like this all the time, with the dark wood and moody lighting and people in baggy trousers and designer T-shirts. I'm in a more Frenchie outfit today, having learned from my 'be fancy' mistakes, including my Converse and pleather jacket. When I spy a really fashionable woman in Converse too it makes me happy. I chose right!

'I can barely bloomin' see,' Grandad stage-whispers to Grandma. 'Why do they turn the lights down when somewhere is supposed to be impressive? Is it so they don't have to dust as much?'

'Dad,' my mum says to him. 'Get in the spirit, would you? I couldn't bear to invite Lucas to McDonald's. Let's show them the nice bits of London!'

'Taylor!' comes a voice. Axel. He's stood up by three cosy-looking sofas in the corner, beside his taller and yet identical father. They're both smiling widely, and Axel has his arms open, ready for a hug. He looks exactly the same as he did when he was my exchange partner. I know it wasn't long ago, but things can change, can't they? And you can remember things as better than they were, too. Not with Axel, though. His eyes are as dreamy as ever, the dimple on one side of his face deep enough to fall into. He flicks his hair from his eyes, and then quickly hits the *play* button on his phone. 'Non, je ne regrette rien' blasts out, and Grandma and Grandma start clapping.

'That cheeky little love!' Grandma says, because he's playing 'their' song, the song they played for Axel when they had us both over for tea.

I hug Axel really hard and really tight, and then step back so Grandma and Grandad can do the same. He hugs Lucy too, and then turns to look for Mum, who is talking to Lucas in French. He says something and pulls a funny face, and Mum roars with laughter and then leans in and touches his arm. I catch Grandma and Grandad exchange a glance, but before I can think anything of it she's realised we're all staring at her and snaps out of it.

'Axel! Darling!' she says, cutting her conversation with Lucas off short and reaching out for him instead.

We collapse down into the squishiest, most luxurious sofas I've ever sat on: me between Lucy and Axel on one,

Grandma and Grandad on another, and then Lucas and Mum on a third. We order skinny fries and burgers, and Mum and Lucas decide to order a bottle of wine, too.

'It's our little holiday, after all!' Mum declares, pouring some for the four adults. We lose ourselves in eating and napkins and drinks and chatting about everything and nothing.

'And so?' Axel says, licking ketchup off the side of his hands. 'How is Crickleton?' I love how he says it: *Creek-ul-ton*.

'Same as ever,' I say with a shrug. 'School is busy ... I got on the netball team!'

'Netball?' asks Axel.

Lucy leans over and explains: 'It's like basketball, but you can't travel with the ball.'

Axel pulls a face like he doesn't fully understand but knows that isn't hugely important. 'Huh,' he says, before turning his attention back to his burger.

'And your boyfriend?' he asks, in a funny voice. He *loves* that I went on a date with Duncan – when I told him over FaceTime he whooped and applauded.

'He's not my boyfriend!' I say. 'Not yet. But ...'

'She wants him to be!' Lucy supplies. 'They're *very* cute together. A good match!'

Axel grins. 'I saw this, I think, on my visit.'

'And Pierre?' I say. 'How is he?'

Axel's smile gets even wider, and he's literally got stars in his eyes. Oh gosh, to be loved by Axel! It must be quite a thing.

'*Parfait*,' he says. 'It is a bit of a dream, I think. To fall in love is …'

He doesn't finish his sentence, but instead kisses his fingertips like a chef pleased with the meal they've just prepared.

I laugh, but notice that suddenly Lucy has welled up. I stare at her for a beat, making sure I'm not seeing things, and she sees me watching and fixes her face so it looks happy again.

Strange.

'Beautiful!' she says, but I can tell there's something off about her. I try to get her to look at me by staring some more, but she is wilfully ignoring me. Hmmmm.

'Are you OK?' I ask, because if she's upset I can't just ignore that. She waves a hand.

'Yeah, fine,' she insists, not very convincingly.

Axel senses we need a moment alone, and tactfully heads off to the loo. I lean in close to her and say, 'What's up, Luce?'

'I'm fine! Honestly!' she says, a bit too brightly. Her eyes glaze over as she looks across the coffee table, getting misty. But then I see her focus, her brow furrow, and then she smiles, just slightly. I follow her gaze.

It's Mum and Lucas. They're nursing their wine and talking in hushed voices like they're on a date or something. Grandma is busy trying to download the Citymapper app that our waiter has told her and Grandad about, so they can navigate themselves to a Bowie exhibition Grandad wants to see. Grandad is talking the waiter's ear off about it.

'Mad for him, I was. Papered one of my bedroom walls in tinfoil to get that Ziggy Stardust look, and cut my hair two different lengths. I *lived* for his music, I did,' he's saying.

I want to tell him to be quiet, to ask everyone if they're seeing what I'm seeing. Because I think Mum is … *flirting*?!

'Axel!' his dad says suddenly, still laughing at something Mum has said, which I didn't catch because of Grandad listing his favourite Bowie albums to his new BFF. '*Ça va?*'

Mum looks all dreamy and happy and smiles lazily at Axel too.

'*Oui,*' he says. '*Fantastique!*'

'We thought,' Lucas says, 'that you could explore together? If you have the app the waiter suggested, and agree to meet back up in, say, three hours? Four?'

I look to Mum.

'Really?!' I say. 'Us too?'

'You too.' She nods. 'I trust you.'

'Ohmygod!' I squeal. 'That's so cool! On our own in London?! Yes!'

All my worries about Lucy and Mum and Lucas disappear because what-the-what?! I get to roam the streets of London like I live here?! Like I belong?! Without parents?! That is AMAZING.

'What are we waiting for, then?' I say to Axel and Lucy. 'Let's ditch these guys and EXPLORE!'

'Charming!' Grandma says, but with a smile – she's not really offended. She gets it. Grandma always does.

'And, Mum,' *my* mum says to her own. 'You know where you're going, right? If you want to head off, I'll stay and take care of the bill. Let's all meet at Nelson's Column in Trafalgar Square at, say, five p.m.?' She looks to me and Lucy and Axel. '*Everyone* knows where that is, so if you get lost or separated, ask in a café or a shop, or look on one of the big black maps at the street corners. Stay together, and have fun … but also be sensible. But have fun. Sensibly. You know the drill.'

'The drill?' Axel asks.

'It's another way of saying *you know what to do*,' I explain. 'Let's go!'

We say our goodbyes and spill out on to the street, alone.

'Which way?' Lucy asks, looking left and right.

'Urm …' I say, unsure. Axel pulls out his phone.

'Shall we go to Leicester Square?' he asks. 'The famous Leicester Square?'

'Yes!' I say. 'Great idea!'

'On we go!' Axel says, pointing towards the main road. 'We can get the Tube. It's OK?'

Lucy looks at me. 'Just don't lose me!' she says. 'Do NOT let go of my hand, OK?'

I entwine my fingers through hers. 'I promise,' I say, and we head off into the city.

11

We get the Piccadilly Line from St Pancras station to Leicester Square, swiping through the barriers with our debit cards and getting in the way on the escalators. I didn't know you were supposed to only stand on the right, so that people can walk past you on the left! Not until some man barged into me and shouted it at me.

'Right! Stand on the right!' he shrieked. 'Can't you read?!'

I should have been mortified, but he was so purple and mad I burst out laughing, and then we all laughed, and now we keep randomly saying to each other STAND ON THE RIGHT! CAN'T YOU READ! and it's funny all over again.

'Whoa,' Lucy says, when we elbow our way out of the busy station and find our way to the square itself. It feels huge – there's a million people, and even though there's a garden bit in the middle, it's all super overwhelming with the big screens with massive adverts that light everything up, and street performers painted like statues and moving when you give them a pound in their box. A group of boys are breakdancing too, and we stand and watch them for a while. They get all the crowd clapping along, and I don't know how they do it without snapping their necks – one guy literally spins on his head and then falls to the ground! Axel says, 'Cool,' with genuine awe, and it makes me feel proud. Like yeah, England, baby! It IS cool here!

'It's a bit like being in the centre of the universe, isn't it?' Lucy says, when the breakdancers finish their performance for a rest. 'If it's not happening here, it's probably not happening anywhere. Do you know what I mean?'

'I do,' I tell her, linking my arm through hers. 'You know some of the biggest magazines in the country have their offices around the corner?'

'Yeah, but who reads magazines any more?' Lucy asks. 'Millennials?'

I pull a face. She's not wrong. 'Even Mum has said that one reason *The Instruction Manual* is such a good idea is that it's online, to be fair,' I say. 'But still. *Stuff* happens here. Talent spotters and fashion people and … something called fintech? But I'm still not sure what that actually is.'

'Taylor! Lucy!' Axel calls. I look across to where he's stood with his phone up to his face, about to take a photo. Instinctively I kick a leg up and tip my head and make a peace sign. 'Yes!' yells Axel. 'Perfect!'

He's laughing, which only makes Lucy and me bolder with our poses. Before I know it we've commandeered a statue of Mr Bean on a bench, with Lucy flinging an arm around his shoulder like they're old friends, and me sticking my finger up his nose. Axel runs over to a Mary Poppins statue and copies her pose, even going as far as getting a brolly out of his rucksack to hold it up like she does. Lucy squeals and says, 'Wait!', getting her own brolly and switching it. He looks *much* better holding her red polka-dot umbrella than his boring black one. She loops her scarf around his neck and holds it out, telling me: 'Cut me out of the shot, so it looks like the scarf is floating behind him!'

I decide to pay £2.99 for a sandwich from Boots just so that I can sit next to Paddington Bear on a bench and pretend it's marmalade. Lucy climbs up beside a statue gripping on to a lamp-post and dancing, holding her leg up impossibly high until she slips and almost breaks her neck.

'Ow!' she says, pouting. 'That hurt!'

'But look,' Axel says, showing her the photo he took. 'It is a beautiful picture, no?'

To be fair, it is.

'You should send that to Star!' I tell her, and immediately

regret it. I feel like I've done something wrong by bringing her up, because a cloud passes over Lucy's face and instead of enthusiastically jumping on the idea like she normally would, she simply says, 'Yeah,' in a super half-hearted way. Axel looks at me. It feels like a betrayal to return Axel's look, acknowledging between us that she is *definitely* not herself all of a sudden.

'I think it is time for ice cream,' he announces, trying to save the mood. 'Come with me.'

Axel leads us to a huge Baskin-Robbins and says we should all get the biggest sundaes they have, because his dad is paying. We end up with massive scoops of bubblegum and caramel and strawberry shortcake, smothered in syrups and topped with chocolate sprinkles and marshmallows. Axel takes a selfie of us all in the shop to send to his dad as proof of life (and proof of ice cream), and we sit in the window so we can people-watch and gradually feel more and more sick from all the delicious sugar. It's wonderful.

'What is happening there?' Lucy says, after some moments of comfortable silence. She gestures to just beyond the glass, at a few people scattered through the crowds, all doing a dance. Like, a choreographed one – not just dancing that happens by accident.

'Urm …' muses Axel, as confused as we are.

Some other people join in with the dance routine. There

doesn't seem to be any rhyme or reason to who is taking part: they aren't wearing costumes and they all look totally different. There's a woman in a hijab and an old man in an army shirt and two people who must be twins. A man who is a priest or reverend or someone who wears a white dog collar joins in, followed by a handful of other people who come in at the exact moment that everyone's hands go in the air, until almost every single person except two – a man, beaming, and a very perplexed-looking woman – are dancing in perfect unison, twirling and jumping and smiling, smiling, smiling.

'What the … ?' I say in wonderment.

The grinning man then moves into the middle of the people, who shift to make a space for him. He gestures to the woman he was with to come closer, to follow him, and she looks around at all the happy, waving people as confused as we are, her face the perfect arrangement of: *What is happening here?!*

The man gets down on one knee and holds out a velvet box.

'He's proposing!' squeaks Lucy. 'Oh my god!'

The woman holds a hand to her mouth, speechless but happy – then she starts crying and nodding, very obviously saying yes.

The man fits the ring to her finger, stands up, and picks

her up to twirl her around and around. The dancers all cheer and clap and then finish off their routine.

And after, when it is done, they all … just walk off. Like it never happened.

'A flash mob,' Lucy says, her voice full of admiration. 'I thought that only happened in movies.'

'Whoa,' I nod. 'Same.'

I don't think we can quite believe what we've just seen. It was amazing!

'Hey,' Axel says, scraping the very last of the sauce from his cup. He's got a smudge of it on his top lip. It makes him even cuter. 'You know, you are as romantic as this, I think, Taylor.'

He gestures to where the flash mob have just performed.

'OK …' I say. 'I guess …'

'I am thinking, you know. To make Duncan your boyfriend. Why not do this big display for him? If he is your first boyfriend, it is important to be very, very special when you ask him.'

'You think I should organise a flash mob?' I say, because I am a confident girl but I truly cannot imagine myself doing *that*.

'I don't know,' says Axel. 'Perhaps not exactly this, but something special nevertheless.'

'How do you know the word *nevertheless*?' Lucy asks,

smiling. 'How is English your second language and you know *nevertheless*?!'

Axel shrugs. 'I think I am simply very intelligent,' he says, and Lucy throws a napkin at him, laughing.

I tell Axel all about *The Instruction Manual*, and seizing the day, as we walk down to Buckingham Palace. Axel has seen it before, and me too, but Lucy hasn't, so we decide to go and see if King Prince Charles is home. Even now it feels weird to call him *King* Charles – he's King Prince Charles! I don't know. It makes us laugh. We did a massive project on him when I was in primary school, so I know more about him than a lot of people, weirdly.

'So basically,' I'm saying as we sidestep some horse manure on the Mall. 'I feel like this seizing the day thing is working already, because I'm not sure if we'd have arranged the protest on Tuesday without it. It's making me braver!'

'I do not think the world is ready for Taylor Blake to be braver ...' Axel teases, and I shove him with my shoulder.

'Oi,' I say.

He holds up his hands in surrender. 'It is a good thing!' he says. 'You are already so brave! It's good!'

Lucy seems worlds away, not really listening to us. Again.

'Earth to Lucy!' I say when I spot it. 'Are you with us?'

She adjusts her gaze and gives me a half-smile. 'Yes,' she

says. 'It's weird to see black cabs and cars or whatever drive down here, isn't it? You'd think it would be a private road.'

'People still have places to be,' I say. 'Although imagine your drive to work taking you past a palace.'

'I think this about Paris,' Axel says. 'Going past the Tour Eiffel to get to school – can you imagine?'

'No,' I say. 'Although when I live there, obviously that will be my life.'

'Obviously!' Axel laughs.

Lucy's phone pings, and it's a text from Star to Members Only, featuring the newspaper article about the Period Protest.

'Taylor!' Lucy says, shoving her screen under my nose. 'Look! You're famous!' I look at what she's waving around, grabbing her phone and reading over what it says UNDER A GREAT BIG PHOTO OF ME LOOKING CROSS!!! Omg.

Schoolgirl to stage peaceful 'Period Protest' outside Crickleton High against 'sexist, antiquated' health policy

Students of all genders expected to assemble next Tuesday as part of a school-wide demonstration

Student protesters will assemble outside Crickleton High next week, holding signs they say 'communicate the rights of anyone who menstruates' to take a stand against a rule denoting any period-related absence as 'unauthorised'. The entire student body is invited to create signs and peacefully protest to allow menstruation to be considered valid for 'authorised absence', in line with other illnesses.

Crickleton High student Taylor Blake, 14, spearheaded the movement after receiving a fine for unauthorised absence recently.

Blake says, 'It's totally nuts to think half the people who go to Crickleton High will have stomach ache, back ache, headaches or migraines, every single month, and yet are expected to carry on like they're totally fine.'

'Nobody is asking for special treatment here. This isn't about a monthly excuse to miss lessons – it's about the very real pain and upset so many of us endure, that the school should be proud to say they understand.'

'There's no point coming in unwell and not being able to concentrate. Personally, whenever I have to miss school I always catch up, even if that means doing it from the sofa with a hot-water bottle and blanket.'

Fellow student Duncan Higginbottom, 14, agrees. 'This is something that might only affect half of us, but it is important to be an ally in times like this. I can't help but think that sexism is at play, and if the shoe was on the other foot school would allow periods to be justified time off. We're not asking for a revolution, just for some basic human empathy.'

Mr Logan, Crickleton High Head, has not responded to a request for comment.

The protest will happen at 9 a.m., just inside the main school gates, on Tuesday.

'I'm excited for this!' Lucy says as we linger by the gates to Buckingham Palace, where the King's Guard stand either side with their guns and funny hats. She frowns at the sight of them.

Axel is reading the article beside me.

'Do you understand all that?' I say, impressed.

'Mostly, I think,' Axel says. I give him a look. 'Well, I think it means you are ... how do they say? A badass?'

'She *is* a badass!' Lucy squeals with a clap. 'Yes!'

They high-five each other, and I pretend not to get it but I secretly do. I'm really proud we got the newspaper to write about it, and can only hope loads of people show up so it's not just me and my handful of friends on our lonesome. Although, even if it is, who cares? I've made a stand against something I think is wrong. That's seizing the day!

'Bit much, isn't it?' Lucy says, observing the Beefeaters even more closely. 'What's wrong with a regular security guard in a portacabin?'

'Mum says people wouldn't travel from all over the world and contribute millions to the economy if they didn't dress so silly,' I say.

'I like it,' Axel says. 'It feels important, like history is still alive.'

LIKE HISTORY IS STILL ALIVE?! God, this boy is poetic.

'What?' Axel says, when I look at him like he's magic. He wipes at his lip with a finger self-consciously.

'Nothing,' I say, shaking my head. 'I'm just glad we're here, is all.'

He grins. '*Moi aussi*,' he says, and then Lucy walks too close to the guards and one of them barks, 'GET BACK! GET BACK!' and she squeals and leaps back to the pavement and looks like she might cry.

'Hey!' I shout. 'There's no need to be mean!'

A few people around us snigger, and I take Lucy's hand.

'Come on,' I say. 'Let's get to the palace.'

* * *

'As a French person,' Axel says as we walk. I can already see that the flag isn't up, so I take that to mean nobody important is home. 'I have experience with protesting. We do it often.'

'I've never done one before,' Lucy says. 'It feels big. Good. Fun, but fun because we're actually *doing something,* if that makes sense. We're not just complaining and hoping somebody else will do something.'

'Exactly!' I say. 'This is exactly it! And that, to me, is *seizing the day*. Although I am worried we'll get in trouble …'

'You will,' Axel warns. 'But then you'll get results.'

I shake my head and smile again. See? WISE.

We walk up the steps to the fountain opposite the palace and look at the big gold statue.

'Whoa,' Lucy marvels.

'I know,' I say. 'They don't really *do* "understated", do they?'

We walk around the edge until we're directly opposite the palace.

'Ta-da!' I say, with jazz hands. 'Here she is! Although there's no flag flying, so King Prince Charles must be somewhere else today.'

Lucy frowns.

'It's very big,' she says.

Axel and I look at each other.

'Yes …' I say. 'Palaces tend to be, as I understand.'

'Ha, ha,' she replies, rolling her eyes. 'Well done you for not being overly impressed. I, on the other hand, will get on with *enjoying myself*.'

'Fair point,' I say. 'Come on then, let's go up to the gates. Mum was once here on a school trip and the queen happened to be driving up in the back of her car and when Mum saw her she cried! The actual Queen!'

'If that happens to us, we'd better run,' Lucy says. 'The Queen has been dead for years!'

We last about five minutes at the palace before we decide that actually, it was cooler back at Leicester Square and if we're quick we'll have time to do M&M World before we have to meet back up with Mum and Lucas. We're stuffing our faces with overpriced candy by the time we make our way to Trafalgar Square and bump into Grandma and Grandad.

'My babies!' Grandma shrieks across a bevy of people, who all turn and stare at her, horrified.

'Ssssh!' laughs Grandad, and they hold on to one another's arms, chuckling, like they're a pair of teenagers. I've never seen them like this before!

Grandma pulls us all in for a hug, saying, 'You little loves. I love you all! I'm so happy we're all here together!'

Grandad peels her off us and says, 'Rachel, you're scaring the poor things.'

I look between them. They're red-nosed and rosy-cheeked and glassy-eyed.

'Have you had fun?' I say. 'Did you enjoy the exhibition?'

'It was fine,' Grandad says.

'He got bored,' Grandma supplies. 'He lasted half an hour and then wanted to go.'

'Hey!' Grandad says. 'You were bored too, Rachel Blake.'

'Rachel Blake is Seizing the Day!' Grandma says, raising a fist triumphantly. I give her a look.

'That was supposed to be funny,' she says, looking at me. 'Not micky-taking.'

'OK ...' I say. Something is ... *off*. They don't seem quite themselves. Everyone is acting strangely today: Lucy, Mum, and now my grandparents.

'So what did you do after?' I ask, and Lucy stage-whispers, 'Isn't it obvious?'

I don't get it. Why is it obvious?

'We found a tequila bar,' Grandad says. 'By accident. And they were doing a tasting, so ...'

'We tasted it!' Grandma supplies, giggling.

The penny drops then.

'You're drunk!' I say, genuinely shocked. I've never seen

them drunk in my life! I didn't even know old people could *get* drunk!

'Oh hush,' Grandma says. 'We've had fun, is all. We're on holiday!'

'Here, here!'

Mum's here now too, and she looks as flushed and happy as Grandma and Grandad too.

'Have you had a nice time, bug-a-boo?'

She pulls me in close and kisses my forehead, and does the same to Lucy for good measure. Lucas takes care of Axel, kissing his temple, and then we're a group of seven happy tourists in the middle of Trafalgar Square, in varying degrees of loopy.

'Onwards?' Mum asks, pulling up directions to the Airbnb on her phone. She's booked a place near to where Axel and his dad are staying so we're all close, and she charges up ahead, squinting at her screen and following the little blinking dot that will lead us to where we're meant to be. We've all got our backpacks with us, like an army of particularly deft tortoises.

The Airbnb is amazing. We're just behind Covent Garden in a rooftop flat that has a tiny, winding staircase all the way up – it felt like going up to Rapunzel's tower. But then at the summit a big metal door pushed open to reveal a humongous open-plan living room with massive velvet sofas and ginormous windows highlighting the London skyline, twinkling lights and gorgeous sunset included. As soon as I flop down on an overstuffed armchair I feel exhausted. We must have walked ten miles today!

'You know what I think we should do?' says Axel, kicking off his shoes.

'What?' asks Lucy, over the noise of Grandma and Grandad saying, 'Blinkin' heck! This is some gaff, innit!'

'Order pizza,' Axel says. 'For delivery. And watch a movie?'

'Ohmygod, yes!' I say, thrilled he hasn't suggested sneaking out to an all-night rave or similar. A night in after our day of fun sounds *parfait*. 'Let's google the best pizza in London! Only the best!'

Mum seems disappointed when I tell her the plan.

'Oh,' she says. 'You don't want to go out?'

Lucas frowns too. 'A night in? When we are in *London*?' he asks.

'Can't fault 'em,' yawns Grandma. Grandad has already dozed off in the chair opposite me. 'I'm not long for bed, to be honest.'

'Terrible!' Mum admonishes us. 'What party poopers!'

'What it is, *party poopers*?' asks Axel.

His dad laughs and translates into French.

'Oh,' says Axel. 'Well, yes. But sometimes it is nice to be a party pooper.'

I reach out a hand to give him a high five, because he's right! Seizing the day is grand, but so is snuggling down with your besties for a movie marathon.

'Perhaps, if they are having takeout, we can try the tapas place I mentioned?' Lucas says to my mum. 'They can party-poop in peace?'

Mum grins, obviously thrilled with the invitation, but straightens up her face to turn to me and ask, 'Would you mind, Taylor? I suppose you don't want us here cramping your style anyway ...'

'Of course they don't mind,' Grandma answers for me. 'We'll be here if they need anything,' she adds, winking at me to say, 'And to pay for the food.'

I smile back. This sounds like an impeccable plan!

'Don't stay out too late,' I tell her, in the exact same way she tells me. 'And be back at a reasonable hour. I trust you.'

'You're too smart for your own good,' she giggles, pulling on her coat and stumbling out of the door like a teenager about to go out and cause mischief.

Lucy finally tells me what's wrong with her after Grandma and Grandad have gone to bed and Axel has fallen asleep before we've even got to the best bit in *Mamma Mia!*. It's like once I stop asking her what's wrong, she wants to tell me.

'My mum got a new job,' she tells me as Sophie whips her blonde hair around on the beach and sings 'Honey Honey'.

'Oh,' I say, because it's quite hard to speak when the boys on-screen are dancing that way.

'It's head of department,' she presses, and Sophie's fiancé kisses her on the sand. It makes me think of Duncan – I haven't texted him all day because we've been having such a good time! I'll text him before bed. Gosh, how nice to have somebody to think about, how nice to watch a kiss in the movies and think, *Well, I don't have to be jealous because I have that too!* I mean, not on a beach in Greece. But still.

'It's an hour away, Taylor – we're going to have to move!'

That gets my attention. I hit pause on the remote.

'What?!'

'Yeah,' she says. 'I don't want to move!'

'I don't want you to move either!' I say. 'Are you sure?!'

'She got *head of department*,' Lucy sighs miserably. 'It's way more money and exactly what she's been after for ages. Why does everyone's mum want to be head of department all of a sudden? I don't know what to do!' she says, tears welling up her big blue eyes. 'I don't know what to tell Star!'

And then that's it, the water gates open and she sobs and sobs, throwing herself into my arms.

'Oh, Lucy …' I say, wracking my brain for the best thing to say. I'm panicking, to be honest, because I don't want her to move away! But I know this isn't about me. But also, a friend moving away kind of is about me??? I'm going to miss her so much!

'We'll sort something out,' I say, trying to sound soothing and calm. 'Maybe you can live with me and Mum or something?'

'Yeah,' she says with a sniffle. 'Maybe.'

We both know that will never happen, but it is a tiny comfort to make believe.

'You have to let me be the one to tell Star,' Lucy says then, seriously. 'OK? Not being funny, but you're not very good with secrets. But you have to swear down, all right? She's gonna be …'

Before she can finish the sentence she starts sobbing again, and I sense this isn't the moment to defend my honour re being accused of being a bad secret keeper. I can totally keep secrets!

'I get it,' I say. 'You and Star are like … water and cordial. You belong together. It will be hard for her to be apart from you. I understand.'

Lucy looks at me with her big watery eyes. 'Thank you,' she says. 'I've been so worried about her. I know she's strong but she's also, like, you know … she can be strong because she's got us, and without us …' Her voice wavers into sobs again.

'Oh, pal,' I say. 'I'll look after her.'

'OK.'

'OK.'

I take a breath. 'When *are* you going to tell her though?' I ask. 'Just so I know.'

Lucy shrugs. 'I'm not sure. Soon. You know. It's just a lot. I want to make sure I do it right.'

I nod uncertainly, but then Lucy starts crying loudly again and I know I can't push her on it. Star already thinks something is really wrong, and the longer Lucy leaves it the more Star is going to be wondering, which doesn't seem fair. I lie awake for hours after we've gone to bed, worried about it. I don't want Lucy to move – Lucy is my best friend! She's a pain, and a gossip, and very, very, bossy, but she's also loyal and supportive and hilarious. I wrack my brain to remember *How to Be Parisian When You're Not from Paris*, and in the careers and jobs bit I'm pretty sure it says:

> *A Parisian woman is not defined by her work, but by her life – her friends, family, style, culture, the kindness she sprinkles throughout her days. It is, though, inarguable that a woman who spends her days doing something she cares about is a woman who will always have purpose. And a woman with a purpose is the chicest thing of all.*

I don't know if that means we should support Lucy's mum's ambition or not. I look at the clock. Ten past one. It's going to be time to get up in a few hours. I need to get to sleep …

Just as I'm about to finally drift off, there's a noise outside my room and the light comes on: Mum is home. I look at the clock again. It's half past one! My mother has stayed out until half past one! In the morning! Outrageous behaviour. She'd better not be a grumpy grump tomorrow because she's tired. That's what she'd say to me.

I close my eyes again and try to breathe deep. The thing is that now not only am I thinking about Lucy, I'm thinking about Mum and Lucas too. Has she been with Axel's dad this whole time?! Why is everyone acting so unbelievably bonkers in London?!

12

*T*he thing about having fun is that nobody tells you how *exhausting* it is. London this weekend was *amazing* – well, except for finding out about Lucy's mum and her new job. I hate having to keep that a secret from Star, but I understand that Lucy is still processing and doesn't want to worry Star until it's absolutely certain. Not that Lucy is concerned about worrying me! But then, I'm glad she can talk to somebody. A problem shared is a problem halved, that's what Grandma says. But surely it won't really happen. Surely Lucy can't leave Crickleton High. It makes no sense! It wouldn't be fair! Maybe I could talk to her mum for her, try to make her see sense. It could be my one good deed for someone else, a way to seize the day by trying to help.

Anyway, getting up at 6 a.m. today was HARD. Yesterday

was an inset day so I got to sleep in, but I'm still sleepy. I'm outside in my bare feet, because I read that one must literally 'ground' oneself first thing in the morning. The thing is, the ground is kind of wet, and it doesn't feel grounding so much as ... cold. I've got a hot water with a single piece of lemon, and in between sips I'm trying to close my eyes and breathe in the day, setting good intentions for what's in store – namely, THE PROTEST. It's today! I wonder if anyone will actually come ...

'Taylor?'

I look up. Mum is sticking her head out of her bedroom window.

'What are you doing?'

'Grounding!' I shout back, before remembering it's very early and I should probably whisper. 'Grounding,' I hiss. 'To help seize the day!'

'But it's half past six!' Mum hisses back.

'I like getting up early!' I murmur back. But then, right on cue, I give a massive yawn that kind of disproves my point. I blink. Mum frowns. 'Fine,' I say, trudging back inside.

I chuck the half-finished hot lemon water in the sink and make a cordial instead, then fling bread into the toaster. As I'm waiting I look through Pinterest on the iPad, getting some ideas about what to wear today to be 'fancy'. I quite like the idea of a blazer, mostly because I've actually got one, with a big flouncy blouse underneath, which I don't have, but

Mum does have a collection of lacy collars you can tie around your neck to dress up an outfit, so I might do that. Then, so I don't make the same mistake as the other day, I'll pare it back with jeans and boots, so instead of loads of fancy things all at once I've just got one or two fancy things. I think I'm getting the hang of this seizing the day malarky! Look at me go – up with the larks, hearty breakfast, great outfit, and I'll still be early for school! I've got it licked!

OK, so the heel on my boot breaks on my way out of the door, so I have to scramble about finding different shoes to wear and end up being five minutes behind schedule. Room for improvement here, I feel, even though it's not technically my fault.

I'm a bit sweaty as I round the corner to the school gates, and I must be in a world of my own (I can hear Lucy saying, 'Aren't you always, Taylor?!') because I don't realise there's chanting happening until I'm face-to-face with a massive crowd of students holding signs and saying, 'Get with the times! Get with the times! Period pains aren't a crime!' I can see Desiree Sanders, her sister Jessica Sanders, Penelope Richards, Sasha Broadwell, Horrid Anna … Natalie Redcock (still an unfortunate name), Tommy Tsao, Bilious Billy off the bus. The whole bloomin' school is here! I see Calum Maggiore, Trevor McGregor …

Well done on the boys for showing up, as they well should!

'Can you believe this?' Duncan smiles, gesturing to the crowd. 'Look at what you've done!'

He pulls me in for a big hug, but I'm too shocked to hug him back. Instead I stand there like a limpet, my arms soggy cardboard at my sides.

'Even some teachers are here!' Duncan presses, holding me by the shoulders and giving me a slight shake.

'Get with the times! Get with the times! Period pains aren't a crime!'

The chant feels like it's getting louder.

'They're all here because of you, Taylor. Well done,' Duncan says, and I finally make eye contact with him.

'Whoa,' I say.

'I know.' He grins.

Lucy and Star make their way through the crowd and hand me a placard they've made that says, *PERIOD PAINS MIMIC CHILDBIRTH! THAT'S HOW MUCH THEY HURT!*

'This is amazing!' Star says. 'I've seen some teachers out here too! Ms K and Madame Jones and even Mrs Bates from maths!'

The reporter from the paper is here, stood off to one side taking it all in and making notes in her pad. Beside her is another woman, holding a camera and recording it all.

'Bobby Hasstlehoff has a big sign that says *Just get on with it*,' Lucy says, rolling her eyes. 'But everyone else thinks this is such a good cause, Taylor!'

I can't believe I did this. And if even Mrs Bates has got involved, it's obviously not just something I care about … there must be two hundred people here, all chanting, chanting, chanting.

'Get with the times! Get with the times! Period pains aren't a crime!' I recite along with everyone else, and honestly, I don't think I've ever been so proud. This feels like ACTION.

It gets a bit boring saying the same thing over and over again, so me, Duncan, Star and Lucy peel off for five minutes and try to come up with a new chant.

'We bleed for five days without dying, but you're out here doling out … fining?' contributes Lucy, which makes us all laugh because the sentiment is there, but the execution is not.

'Periods are not shameful, but sometimes they are so painful?' says Duncan, which isn't as funny but has got a better rhythm.

'How about, "Mr Logan doesn't get it, we'll catch up, just let us rest up",' says Star.

There's a lull in the chanting, noticeable enough that the four of us all turn around at the same time. It's Mr Logan. He's striding down the path towards us, tie flitting in the wind and hitting his purple, angry face. My whole body flushes hot – Mr Logan is angry? MR LOGAN IS ANGRY?! How dare he! We are angry! I am angry! He doesn't get to be angry! HE is in the WRONG!

I decide to improvise.

'What do we want?' I yell, looking right in Mr Logan's direction. 'Period justice!' I supply. Then I say, 'When do we want it? Now!' The next time I say 'What do we want?' Lucy and Star and Duncan all yell 'Period justice!' until the rallying call catches on like a Mexican wave and everyone is doing it. Mr Logan stands there, eyes narrowed and face furious, obviously unsure about what to do.

'WHAT DO WE WANT? PERIOD JUSTICE! WHEN DO WE WANT IT? NOW!'

'Get inside,' Mr Logan says, quite quietly really. But he's like a whistling kettle, starting out softer and suddenly screaming bloody murder. 'GET. INSIDE!' he yells, but nobody listens. Finally he positively BELLOWS: 'GET! IN! SIDE!'

A hush descends as his seriousness lands, broken only by Tommy Tsao shouting back at him a simple: 'No!'

There's laughter, and Mr Logan locks in on me, knowing that since I organised it, I'm probably the one most likely to get the crowd to listen. But I can't, can I? I can't back down, because that would be like saying he's right and we're wrong, and we're not.

'We're doing this peacefully,' I shout, but my voice isn't very loud.

Mr Logan reiterates that we should come inside now. 'Point made,' he says. 'Very good. Now. You're late for class, which I am willing to overlook if you go quickly and quietly. Thank you.'

Lucy hands me a megaphone. Where has she got that from?! She shows me how to press the button, and I hold it down as I repeat: 'This is a peaceful protest!'

Everyone looks at me, and nobody moves. Nobody does what Mr Logan says.

'My name is Taylor Blake, and I get painful periods!'

The crowd applauds me, which is a peculiar thing to clap about if you think about it, but I think they're letting me know I have their support.

'Every month I get a period, and sometimes it's OK. But sometimes it is not! With my last period, I had cramps so bad that I had to stay off school. But when I was honest about this, I was told that is not a legitimate reason for missing class, and my mother was sent a sixty-pound fine. THAT IS NOT FAIR! If most men got periods, there'd be measures in place to support them, but instead our head teacher is telling those of us who menstruate that we must simply GET ON WITH IT! No matter the pain, no matter the mess, no matter the hormones or trouble. We're not asking for a free pass, for a blanket excuse every month – although if we were, that would be FINE and we would DESERVE IT. As it happens, most of us do not want our lives interrupted every thirty days, we *want* to get on with it all. But sometimes we can't. Sometimes we hurt, badly, and what kind of message does it send to tell us our pain does not matter? What example is that to set for us? All we want is for period leave to be an authorised absence. We don't want to have to lie, or accept an unauthorised absence for telling the truth. What do we want? Period justice! When do we want it? Now!'

The crowd roars into life, joining me in the chant again.

'WHAT DO WE WANT? PERIOD JUSTICE! WHEN DO WE WANT IT? NOW!'

Mr Logan turns on his heel and marches back into school.

'That was amazing,' Duncan yells over the chants. 'Really amazing!'

I grin at him. It feels good to stand for something, to bring everyone together in a common cause. I have no idea what I just said – I've somehow managed to blank it all out – but after another forty-five minutes I decide it must have worked because Mr Logan comes back and says, 'OK, Ms Blake. You win. Be in my office tomorrow morning to discuss this further.'

I feel a bit famous at school. Everywhere I go, people tell me, 'Good job, Blake!' or 'Well done on the protest!' Even

Mrs Bates passes by before lunch and says, 'Wonderful work this morning, Taylor. You should be proud.'

'Whoa,' says Lucy. 'I think that's the first time I've ever heard her say something nice.'

'Same,' I say. 'It feels odd.'

Lucy laughs. 'Come on, it's pizza day. I'm starving,' she says, heading into the cafeteria.

'Can't,' I say, 'I've got netball practice.'

'At lunch?' she says.

I nod. 'Got a sandwich in my bag to eat after,' I say. 'You'll have to enjoy the pizza without me.'

'OK,' she says, doing a pretend pout. 'It won't taste the same with you gone.'

'No,' I giggle. 'It won't. You'll have to find a way to force it down.'

'So long, fair friend,' she says, holding out a hand so her fingertips brush mine. 'Don't forget about me …'

'What's your name again?' I say, holding out my own hand but already walking off, backwards, so that we're no longer touching.

My sandwich is all squashed at the bottom of my bag, and mayonnaise drips on to my netball shorts as I eat. I'm bright red and panting, and don't really feel like eating but I've only got ten minutes of lunch break left because practice ran over.

I've got a mouthful of tuna when Ms Perkins comes into the changing room and says, 'Great effort, today, Taylor. I'm posting team positions for this weekend's match later on. Are you available?'

I nod, because I know it's rude to talk with your mouth full.

'Thadda girl,' Ms Perkins says, tapping the doorframe twice with her palm. 'You're a hell of a wing attack.'

'You really are,' Josie says. I don't know her very well – I don't know any of the netball girls very well. All I know is that she's always centre position. She's slight and fast and doesn't ever seem to run out of energy. Case in point: she's somehow clear-skinned and ready for an afternoon of lessons, not a wheezing breath in sight. Meanwhile I feel sick from stuffing down some lunch and am still postbox red.

'Thanks,' I say, trying to quickly get changed with two bites of my lunch still in my hand. This is an action that only serves to make me more out of breath. How is it nobody else is struggling like me?!

'A group of us do a conditioning session most afternoons after school,' she says. 'You should join us. You know. If you want.'

She gives me a small smile.

'Conditioning?' I say. I feel like this word only applies to haircare, and yet I also suspect this isn't what she means. My top sticks to me as I pull it on, my body still slick with sweat.

No way am I putting that lacy collar on for the afternoon. Or my blazer, come to think of it. I loop them both through the straps of my bag. I'd head out in just my bra if that was allowed. I'm boiling.

'Yeah, like general fitness? Basically we go running,' she explains. 'And then do some star jumps or burpees. It's so that we're speedier and have more stamina on the court.'

'Oh,' I say, and I get the impression she doesn't think I am fit enough, even if she does think I'm good with the ball. 'So you go running every single day? As well as practice and matches?'

She shrugs. 'Yeah,' she says. 'But we keep it fun.'

I nod. If I started running every day after school, when would I write? I'm already behind on articles for my 'Seizes the Day' column, which all need to be uploaded to the website ready for the launch. Right now the whole site is password protected, allowing us to add to it and change things and make it look really, really good before we take the password off and it becomes public.

'I have a meeting after school,' I tell her. 'I'm launching a website.'

'Maybe next time?' Josie asks as we head out of the changing rooms together. I catch sight of myself in the mirror — I've got crumbs around my mouth and my hairline is wet.

'Maybe,' I say, and I can't shake the feeling that I'm going to end up joining their running club whether I want to or not.

'Whoa,' says Lucy when I walk into Ms K's classroom after school, ready to talk about the party for *The Instruction Manual*. 'You're looking a bit ... dishevelled. Are you OK?'

I flop down at the table and put my head down.

'I'm tired,' I say. 'It feels like this day has been going on for twenty years.'

Star rubs my back sympathetically. 'You *are* doing a lot,' she points out. 'I know you're trying to seize the day and whatnot, but ...'

'But what?' I say. 'I'm enjoying everything! I'm just ... sleepy, is all.'

Duncan arrives and settles in, and Star and Lucy take us through everything they're thinking for the launch, from who to invite to food to goodie bags they've found sponsors for.

'Are you serious?' Duncan asks, wide-eyed. 'This is more than I could have ever come up with! You guys are amazing!'

'Compliment accepted,' Lucy says, exchanging a high five with Star.

'I would hire you to organise my birthday party, if I was the sort of guy who had birthday parties,' Duncan notes.

'You don't like birthday parties?' I ask, incredulous. I mean, you think you know a person!!

'Not really,' Duncan says. 'The idea of sending out invitations and being the centre of attention as everyone sings "Happy Birthday" and you blow out candles on a cake? I can just about do that in front of my family. That's it. It's just not me. I'll be celebrating at home, hopefully with chocolate cake. That's my only birthday wish.'

'Wait, when's your birthday?' I ask, realising I do not know this information.

'Next week,' Duncan says. 'But forget I told you that. Thank *you*!'

'No promises,' I say, scrunching up my nose teasingly. 'But it's noted that you prefer no public displays of celebration.'

'Thanking you,' Duncan says, scrunching up his nose too. We realise Star and Lucy are staring at us, watching this back-and-forth with smirks on their faces. I just know they're going to rib me about this later. I think it's a bit *too* obvious how into Duncan I am. I just really like being around him though! Playing it cool takes waaaaay too much energy, and as established, I am all out of energy for the day.

'Tay?' Lucy asks. 'Anything to add?'

I shake my head. I'm so tired I can barely speak. 'No,' I say, forcing a smile. They've done a great job and it's going to be a wonderful party – but right now I just want to get home. I'm starving, and have loads I need to do. I see them all exchange a look, like I'm not being enthusiastic enough. 'Really,' I say, offering up my own hand for a high five. 'You've nailed it.'

They say OK, and thanks, but I get the feeling they wish I was a bit more engaged.

Tomorrow.

I'll make sure they know how much I appreciate them tomorrow …

At home, Mum is in the kitchen making shredded pork tacos, singing along to whatever she's got on the Alexa and smiling to herself. I'm normally at Grandma and Grandad's on a Tuesday, but today they're meeting up with friends they met on holiday and have stayed in touch with, so I'm home.

'Oh hello, darling,' she says, giving me a kiss on the cheek. 'I didn't hear you come in.'

I pad over to the cooker. 'Smells amazing,' I say. 'When will it be ready?'

'About twenty minutes,' Mum answers. She moves around the kitchen with grace, grabbing stuff from the cupboards and washing up as she goes.

'OK,' I say. 'I'll set the table in a minute. I'm just going to try and do some homework first.'

She smiles, her cloud nine floating this way and that.

'No problem, darling,' she says, and it's like she doesn't even really see me. She's in her head, thinking about something else. I watch her for a minute, lost in her own thoughts. There's something different about her, even though she looks exactly the same. It's kind of nice to see, actually. She's all … *chilled*.

'Everything all right, Tay?' she suddenly asks, snapping me out of my staring. She must have sensed my curiosity.

I blink and nod. 'Yeah,' I say, 'totally. Was just thinking.'

I slouch off to the sofa and pull out my history folder to do some work. But the next thing I know, Mum is shaking me awake.

'My love, you fell asleep,' she whispers. 'Do you want to eat, or go to bed?'

'Bed,' I mumble. I feel like I've been pulled out of a dark black cave. 'Bed!'

I head upstairs and get under the covers, fully dressed. What a superb start to the day, and what a whimper of an end. Urgh. I set an alarm for the morning, but I'm so tired I'd be surprised if I even hear it.

I'm out like a light.

13

I wake up at 7 a.m. – an hour later than I wanted to – and immediately feel annoyed that I've overslept. I've got so much to do! I'm going to have to choose between eating breakfast and sorting out a good 'fancy' outfit, and I certainly don't have time to do my grounding in the garden with a hot lemon water. *NOT SEIZING THE DAY* here. In fact, feeling *behind* the day already! This feeling of beginning behind the starting line is made even worse by a text from Josie, giving me details for her conditioning club after school. I'm not sure I technically agreed to join that, but she seems to believe I'm a definite yes. *Hey Taylor!* her message says. *Conditioning Club is right after school today since there's no netball practice. We meet in the PE block and it lasts about an hour. See you there! Xx* I feel like I've got no choice but to text back a thumbs up and *Great!* even though the thought of it makes my whole body want to go back to bed. It feels important to, like, get involved when I'm asked, and I'm worried that if I don't go then the girls will all think I'm stuck up or something. But I thought playing netball would make me fitter after a while anyway. I don't get why I have to do extra to get fit enough to play in the first place? Anyway. Josie has been really nice to me. I can't let her down.

I throw on jeans and a T-shirt with my Converse – a safe and comfy choice. Sometimes I wish we had to wear a uniform for school, if only for the ease ... but then I think about how much of a penguin Morgan across the road looks when she's in uniform for her private school and I think nah, I'm good. Wearing our own clothes is way better. At least we get to be comfy. I can't imagine having to wear a tie every day, especially in a heatwave. And a shirt, tucked in? No.

Anyway, Mum is already at the table with a coffee and a book. I pour some cereal and chomp it down quickly – so quickly that Mum looks up and says, 'Whoa, horsey! What's the rush?'

'Hungry,' I say. 'STARVING, actually.'

Mum nods. 'I suppose you did miss dinner last night. Do you want me to make some pancakes? Fill you up?'

I look at the time on my phone to decide if I've got the fifteen minutes it will take for Mum to cook and me to eat. But I don't even notice the time, because I've got more texts waiting for me. In Members Only, Star, who is quickly becoming our very own media monitor, has linked to another article about the Period Protest. The headline says:

STUDENTS PROTEST OVER RULES ON PERIODS

*Crickleton High students fight for the right
to rest during monthly menstruation*

I don't even read the article though, because Lucy has also texted – and not to Members Only. Oh gosh. I feel like I know what this is going to say before I even read it. My stomach goes heavy. There's only one thing she could be saying if it's on a side chat from Star.

'Taylor? Pancakes, yes or no?'

I tear my eyes away from my screen. 'I'm OK,' I say with a weak smile. 'I'll take a banana with me just in case.'

I open the message and my biggest fear is confirmed: *Mum accepted the job*, it says. *We're officially moving* ☹.

'No!' I squeal. 'Nooooooo!'

Mum looks at me. I said I wouldn't tell Star, but Lucy never said I couldn't tell Mum.

'Lucy's moving,' I say. 'Her mum got a new job.'

Mum tilts her chin, absorbing what I've said.

'I see,' she says with a nod. She folds down the corner of a page and closes her book, setting it in front of her. I don't want to cry but I feel it welling up. Instead I focus on the empty cereal bowl in front of me and think about breathing in, and breathing out. Mum reaches across and holds my hand. My eyes adjust and I can't quite look at her, but I do end up seeing what she's reading.

'Is that French?' I say, voice wobbly but grateful for the shift in topic. I distract myself by picking it up. It is! Gosh, Mum is such a show-off. Imagine being able to read a novel in another language.

'Just greasing the wheels,' she tells me. 'Use your French or lose your French, that's what they say! I realised how rusty I am at the weekend.'

I nod.

… And then I start crying. Little tears, and muffled sobs. Trying to distract myself is NOT working. Lucy is moving?! This can't happen! I don't want to talk about anything else, even if that something else is Axel. I need to do something! I need to ACT, like I did with the period stuff. If something isn't right, you have to try and change it, don't you? I can't just sit by and watch my best friend get carted off halfway down the country.

'Oh, my love,' Mum says, pulling me towards her.

'What will we do without her?!' I cry, and Mum sighs.

'I know,' she says. 'I know.'

Mum's book about raising empowered teens says not to try to provide the answers for your kid, but to be with them as they figure it out themselves. I wish Mum could just tell me how to fix this, but I'm not mad she isn't. I'm so lucky she listens to me. I cry a bit more until I run out of tears, and then lie against her, my mind racing but my breathing calmer. Eventually, it comes to me.

'Do you think it's rude if I go in and talk to Lucy's mum?' I ask. 'Maybe I could change her mind or something?'

'You could never be rude, darling,' Mum says, patting my hand. 'You do what you feel you have to do. I'm sure she'll know it's only because you love your friend that you'd dare.'

That's how I end up bombing it to school on my bike – it's the fastest way to get down the hill and to the gates with time enough to spare to head down to the science block and seek out Saoirse, Lucy's mum. I hate bringing my bike to school. I did it for a month in Year 7 to get extra house points – it was part of a healthy habits campaign – but gave up in the end because coming *to* school down a hill is one thing, but the getting back up that hill home? Horrible, a nightmare, do not recommend. A thumbs down from me.

I see Saoirse in the corridor outside her classroom, carrying a stack of textbooks.

'Hello, you,' she says in her soft Irish lilt. I've always

found her voice very comforting, like she could never be unkind with a voice like that, even if she is a teacher. 'What are you doing in these parts?'

I open up my arms, an offer to take some of her load. She hands half the books over and gives a big sigh, as if to say, *Phew! That was getting heavy!*

'Actually,' I say, 'I wondered if I could talk to you?'

Saoirse nods, and she obviously gets what it will be about. She looks up and down the corridor, puts the textbooks down next to a display about condensation, and opens a classroom door. I follow.

'Lucy told me about your new job,' I tell her, getting rid of my own pile of books on the desk Saoirse leans against. 'Congratulations,' I add, because that seems like the polite thing to open with.

'Thank you.' Saoirse nods, pressing her lips together. 'Although you don't seem very pleased for me really.'

I've never had a very good poker face, that's what Grandad says.

'It's just …' I say, and those tears prick at my eyes again. But I can't cry – I'm so tired this morning that if I cry I worry I might not stop! And if anyone has something to cry about, it's Lucy.

'You don't want us moving,' she supplies, and I nod, miserable.

'Lucy is my best friend,' I say. 'And I know she doesn't want to move. If she did, maybe I wouldn't feel so sad, but I am sad, because I'm sad for her. She was so not like herself in London, Saoirse, so quiet and gloomy. She's settled here, and happy, and that doesn't happen by magic. My mum moved schools when she was in Year 9 and she says it almost ruined her academic career because she just never got settled in her new school. I know it's not any of my business what *you* do, but ... I had to at least tell you how upset Lucy is. She can't move!'

Saoirse sighs.

'It's hard,' she admits. 'There's just no room for upward movement here at Crickleton High, and this new job as head of department ... it's what I've always wanted. Not to mention the money ...'

'I understand,' I say. A rogue tear falls down my cheek. I wipe it away with the back of my hand. Everything just feels so heavy right now. Lucy moving, netball, *The Instruction Manual*, getting up early ... not to mention Duncan. I want to spend *more* time with him, be boyfriend and girlfriend. But if I carry on this way I'm in danger of letting 'us' fall by the wayside because of everything else, even though he's as wonderful as ever. I thought life was supposed to be FUN. But, now I properly think about it, aside from my weekend in London I don't feel like I've been having very much of it. I'm just always so busy, lurching from one thing to the next. It's exhausting.

Hmmmm.

I don't know what else to say. I just sigh, accept the offer of a tissue, and then tell Saoirse I'm grateful she heard me out.

I wish I could go back home to bed.

I wish I had a magic wand to have more hours in a day.

If I did have a magic wand though, I'd use it to keep Lucy here first.

Double history, maths, and then French class – what a morning! I feel run ragged, but now I've got my meeting with Mr Logan just before lunch so have to stay sharp. It's taking everything I've got not to let my mind wander over to Lucy, who I still haven't seen this morning, and so I end up making notes on an article about it, just to get it out of my head. I write it under *Taylor Blake Seizes the Day … by Doing Something for Others (or Trying To)*.

I've only got the beginning, but it has already helped to write about it:

Well dear reader, I thought that doing something for others would be an easy, straightforward thing, an instant way to seize the day. But I was wrong!

Just like embracing fancy, perhaps I overcomplicated the mission by being too ambitious, but then again, ambition is my middle name! My mum has always said women and girls have to reclaim it, because the patriarchy can make us think ambitious girls and women are too greedy, when boys and men are allowed to be as hungry for life as they want. So here I am, shooting for the stars.

Here I am also going off topic a bit, which, again, is quite like me. Ooooops!

Anyway. Doing something for others. I could have held the door open for someone, or given a stranger a compliment. Instead I tried to help my best friend change the trajectory of the rest of her life. Because she has to move house! As in leave our school, our friendship group, our town. And all because her mum has a new job. But I thought, what if I talked to her mum? Could an outsider's perspective help change her mind? Unfortunately not ...

I'm quite pleased with it. I like writing in a chatty, informal way, like the person reading it is my friend and not a stranger on the internet.

'*Taylor?*'

Madame Jones. Eeeek! She's caught me making my notes

instead of working through the exercise she's set. I quickly push the paper under my French work and get back to the task.

'*Je suis desolée*,' I squeak, feeling myself blush. Star turns around from the front, where she sits. Madame Jones has assigned seating in her classes, so you can't sit with your friends and get distracted. She tilts her head, a question. I roll my eyes, an answer. Star creases up her face like she doesn't understand, even a bit like she's concerned about me. I look away and focus on my worksheet. I can hardly explain it all with my eyes, can I? I'd look like I was having a fit.

My stomach growls. I should have taken Mum up on her offer of pancakes this morning. I had my cereal, ate my banana at break, and had half of a protein bar I found at the bottom of my bag and I'm still counting down the minutes to lunch. I'm being excused from French twenty minutes early to talk to Mr Logan about the Period Protest, so hopefully I won't miss it. If the meeting drags on too long I'll get a jacket potato so well cooked it's practically ceramic! And we can't have that. But then, I suppose justice is a more pressing matter than a tuna mayo potato. Just.

Five minutes before I have to go, I raise my hand to remind Madame Jones about leaving early.

'*En français, s'il vous plaît!*' she trills, like I'm an idiot.

'Urm,' I falter. '*Je ...*' OK great, I've got as far as saying 'I'. How on earth do I say *I have to go talk monthly bleeds with our clueless head?!*

'Hmmmm?' presses Madame Jones.

'*Je ... dois ... partir?*' I say, and I can see her have to fight with herself not to tell me to state the sentence, not ask it, but she seems to accept my barely passable French as good enough.

'*Tu peux y aller,*' she says with a wave of the hand. I think that means *scram*.

'*Merci.*'

I grab my stuff and give Star a wave as I leave, Converse squeaking on the floor of the corridor and echoing eerily. I hate walking through school by myself – it feels unnatural. There's the odd noise from each classroom as I pass, and my shoes stop squeaking when I get to the carpeted part of reception and the senior leadership team's office, but I still don't like it. Schools should be loud and noisy and full of people. Being the only one in a long corridor is giving horror movie.

'Taylor Blake,' I announce to the secretary, an older woman called Mrs Mackenzie who looks annoyed at being interrupted. 'I have an appointment.'

She looks over her appointment book, squinting.

'So you do. Take a seat and I'll let him know you're here.'

I wait ages, watching the hand of a big clock above Mrs Mackenzie's head pass one minute, then two, and eventually five. It's amazing the thoughts you can have in five minutes – I've totally convinced myself Mr Logan is pulling some sort of power move, showing me who the real boss is. By the time Mrs Mackenzie says I can go in, I've rehearsed about ten different speeches in my head, ready to give him a piece of my mind!

'Taylor,' Mr Logan says as I enter. He stands up and extends a hand, which I shake suspiciously. So we're handshakers now, are we? Hmmmm. I don't buy it.

'Hello,' I say, taking a seat. I don't know what to expect. Do I launch into my monologue? Or wait for Mr Logan to speak?

'That was quite the spectacle yesterday. I assume you've seen the local news today?'

Star showed me on her phone before French class – there's footage of the protest, and a series of photos of everyone with their (quite frankly spectacular) signs. It is, in a word, AWESOME.

'I have,' I say, not letting my glee show. 'I think the issue resonates with people a lot more than we might have first assumed.'

Listen to me! Talking like the King! I feel like I'm acting in a play!

Why yes, kind sir, the people of yore are quite taken with our plight.

'Interesting,' says Mr Logan. 'And here was me thinking folks simply wanted to miss a few lessons and enjoyed the excuse.'

He looks at me, and it's a freaky sensation, knowing you're being goaded by the head teacher of your school. There are so many wonderful, encouraging teachers here, and yet Mr Logan is, to put it bluntly, a total dummy. It's like he wants me to pop off, to lose my cool. I suppose if I did, I'd prove I'm just a stupid kid who knows nothing, instead of what he probably thinks I am: a threat. I mean, I must be. I got the papers here! Not many 'kids' can say they've done that.

'When we students care about something, we come together and make it known,' I say. 'I think that's very admirable. We need to feel empowered to use our voices, and apparently here at Crickleton High, we do.' God, my heart is beating like a big brass band. *How* my voice isn't quivering like I feel on the inside is beyond me. All I know is, bullies respond to strength, and so I cannot let Mr Logan see that I am afraid. 'The question is,' I add, 'are people going to listen?'

Mr Logan sits back in his chair, raising his eyebrows.

'Indubitably,' he says, picking a word I'll bet he thinks I don't know.

I mean … I don't know that word, but whatever. I'm not going to give him the satisfaction of saying so.

'At the end of the day, sir,' I say, sick of his idiotic smirky face already, but knowing that staying polite and calm is absolutely key, 'the students – and some teachers – have done their best to tell you what they need. As the head of this school, it's up to you if you respond positively to that, or ignore us because you think your judgement is the only right one.'

Mr Logan runs his tongue against his teeth. I *might* have just taken this a bit far. But then, I've not got anything to lose. I'm pretty certain he won't expel me or anything like that – this is essentially a chat to see who will back down. And the fact that I'm in this room at all means it *cannot* be me. I don't want Mum to get fined again if I miss school for something totally out of my control, and I don't want that for other people either.

'Very well,' he says, lacing his fingers through each other and resting them on his desk. 'Missing school for period pains will be downgraded from an unauthorised absence to an authorised one, assuming parental sign-off and that it will not exceed more than two days at a time. All work must be caught up with within one week, and should this privilege be abused, it will be revoked. We will give it a trial period until the end of this academic year, and then review.'

OMG! I've ... won?! Ideally he wouldn't put a time cap on it, because two days isn't always enough for severe period pains, but for now I will TAKE IT. A victory! I have changed a rule at this school, by standing up for myself and others! HUZZAH!

'Thank you, sir,' I say, standing up. I think I should leave ASAP, before I do anything that could be used to change his mind. I hold out a hand, a peace offering, and for one horrid minute I think he might not take it. But he does – it's a hard, angry shake. When my hand is on the doorknob he says, 'Taylor? If I might give you some advice?'

I turn around. 'Yes, sir?'

'Go steady. You're getting a name for yourself as quite the troublemaker.'

I think about this for a moment, because my instinct is that trouble is bad, and this is a warning. But I also know that actually, I've done a good thing today, and I won't let anyone – especially not Mr Logan – take that away from me. What did Axel say? *Expect* trouble, that's how you know you're getting somewhere.

'I think some trouble is good trouble, sir,' I say back.

!!!!!!!!

HOW COOL IS THAT!

I disappear before he can say anything else.

'Did you really say that to him?!' Duncan asks, slack-jawed, when I report back on the meeting to him. I really want to make time to spend with Duncan amidst the current madness of my life. It's like I crave him or something, like he's a bar of Dairy Milk. I made sure I caught up to him and Paul as I was leaving school in the afternoon, Star by my side.

I shrug.

'Yeah,' I reply. 'He deserved it!'

'Incredible scenes,' he says.

'Truly,' agrees Star.

Lucy isn't with us – she left quickly after school. Star asked me what I think the matter is, and I said I didn't know. God, I hope Lucy tells her the truth soon – Star needs to know, so she can start getting used to it!

'Well done, Taylor,' says Paul.

'Thanks,' I say. 'I'm happy!'

We swap stories about our days, but Star doesn't stay long.

'I'd better go,' she says. 'I'm going to try FaceTiming Luce at home, see if she'll open up and tell me what's going on. I really do think there's something.'

Duncan nods thoughtfully.

'Even I think she seems a bit off,' he says. 'And I don't even know her that well yet.'

Star seems to accept this. 'Yeah,' she says. She looks to me like she's going to ask again if I know anything, but I look away to Duncan. He smiles at me, and I'm just so grateful for him. I'm so tired, and I'm cramming eighty million things into every single day, but Duncan? Duncan is still as lovely as ever.

'Bye, then,' Star says, and I give her a hug and we watch her go.

'Bye, Star,' Paul says. 'Nice to see you. In fact, actually, I'm walking that way. I'll come with you?'

Star shrugs. 'OK,' she says.

'Are *you* OK?' Duncan asks, after Star turns around and waves one last time.

'Me?' I ask.

'I feel like you're so busy,' he tells me. 'I want to ask you to hang out again soon, but I'm worried you won't be able to fit me in.'

'Really?'

'Yeah! Of course! You're, like, my favourite person!'

'I am?' I say.

'Oh my god, you're such a plonker,' he says, stepping towards me. 'An adorable plonker who keeps yawning, but I'm trying not to take the yawning part personally.'

He takes my hand lightly, holding me like I could break, and our noses touch … then our lips, even though we're in front of school and everyone can see. Squee!!

I can't believe how many kisses I've been having lately.

We might not have seen each other all weekend, but crikey me, when I do see Duncan it's MARVELLOUS.

'Hey,' he says, when we're done snogging.

'Yeah?'

'You know I said I don't like a fuss from people on my birthday? I was wondering if you wanted to come for cake at my house at least? I wouldn't mind you there.'

'Oh, well,' I say. 'If you wouldn't mind ...' I'm taking the mick, but Duncan gets the joke.

I wonder what to get him as a gift. I really want to get him something thoughtful and considered, like when he bought me a copy of Dr Seuss's *Oh, the Places You'll Go!* after we talked about it. Maybe something to do with our website? I'll ask Paul what he thinks.

My phone pings. It's Josie.

Are you coming? her message says. *We're waiting.*

'Gah!' I screech, because I'd totally forgotten. 'I'm late for running club!'

Duncan looks surprised. 'Running club? You've joined a running club?' he asks.

I'm already walking away from him, my brain focused on the next thing I have to do.

'For netball,' I say, walking backwards up to school. 'They call it conditioning? I don't know. Josie said I should go!'

I'm shouting now, to bridge the distance between us.

'You're doing so much!' Duncan shouts back.

'I'm seizing the day!' I shout back.

OK. I really am exhausted. Josie's conditioning class was *a lot*. We ran around the block, we did burpees and star jumps, seriously, at one point I thought I was going to be sick. I've had to drink five glasses of cordial since getting home, and ate three portions of Mum's mushroom risotto! And she'd added chicken to it! I'm in bed trying to write a column for 'Taylor Blake Seizes the Day … by Getting Political' but I am so, so tired I don't get very far. Maybe my next article should be 'Taylor Blake Seizes the Day … After a Very Big Nap'. Living life to the full is hard work! I'm finishing the day exactly as I started it: absolutely zonked …

14

*O*MG. I've woken up so sore. Josie's conditioning club was so hardcore that my body is determined to remind me of it. I lie in bed moving various body parts – first a leg, then an arm – in a world of pain. Every muscle shouts at me to stop! Even when I go for a morning wee I feel stiff like an old lady just from bending down to sit on the loo. I'm going to have to let Josie know that I'll come when I can, but there's no way I'm going to all of the sessions. I like netball, but never thought there'd be stuff I'd have to do outside of Ms Perkins's practices in order to keep up!

I flop back down on my bed and check my phone. *INTERESTING* ... Duncan has messaged, asking if we can do another double date this weekend ... *in the woods.*

Duncan: I've found this thing called forest bathing. Google it! Could be a really nice way to chillax, man

Me: Chillax?!

Duncan: Go with it...

Duncan: Seriously though. Are Star and Lucy free? I'm thinking picnic, walk in the woods, looking at the clouds... it will be nice! Especially since you've been so busy. You can CHILLAX!!

I mean, what a guy. Aside from questionable and continued use of the word *chillax*, he's so thoughtful. He knows I've been running around like a crazy person and he's found something calming and charming to do. Of course I want to do that! I immediately text the girls:

Members Only

Me: Anyone up for forest bathing this weekend?

Star: Forest bathing?????

Me: It's Duncan's idea! He just asked me, and said we should all do it.

Star: But what is it?

Me: OMG
I AM SO GLAD YOU DON'T KNOW

>BECAUSE I DIDN'T KNOW!
>Tbh it sounds like just going for a walk in the woods
>I'm gonna write about it for my column

Star: OK, googled it
I found a blog that says:
Forest bathing is essentially going for a walk in the woods. Except, instead of walking for exercise, try to focus on the nature around you: how the sun streams through the canopy of trees, or how the birds sound.

Star: I'm in!

>**Me:** Yay! @Lucy?

Lucy doesn't answer the text, and doesn't answer me when I pick up the side chat from earlier, either. I don't want to outright say I tried to talk to her mum, but I assume Saoirse will tell her and then Lucy will let me know she knows. Right? Like, I don't want to show off about trying to be a hero, but also, it would be nice if she knew. Lol.

Anywoohoo, even in English she barely speaks, even though Star and I sit on the same table with her, all in a neat little row. She came in late and is keeping her eyes fixed straight ahead, barely a half-hearted smile to be had.

'Did you see the text about this weekend?' I ask her in a whisper when we're set on task. 'Can you come?'

'Sure,' she replies, like she couldn't think of anything worse. 'I think I can.'

Star leans across her and says, 'Don't bother, Taylor. She's not giving anything away. I've tried a million times to get it out of her, but this is what she's like.'

I reach under the table and squeeze Lucy's hand, surprised when she squeezes back. I decide in that moment not to push her. She'll talk to Star when she's ready – my job as a friend is to be supportive up until then … and then I'll have to be strong and support them both. Maybe Duncan will support me. But then will Duncan need support for me supporting them? Will it just be a big long chain of people supporting each other?

Whoa. Maybe that's what being a person is. Just everyone helping everyone else.

That's quite a nice thought, actually.

'Taylor? Would you mind holding back after class?'

Ms K. She's stroking her belly, but if you didn't know she was pregnant it wouldn't be at all obvious. She's wearing a loose, baggy top, but you can't see a bump or anything yet. She's looking at me all frown-y and strange. Immediately I scan my brain for a history of everything I've ever done wrong. I'm not sure what I'm in trouble for, though.

'OK …' I say. Maybe it's about another writing

competition. If it is, I don't know when I'll be able to write something for it! It's netball practice again at lunch! There's no time!

'You doing OK?' she asks, when everyone else has filed off to chemistry.

'Yes ...' I say. 'Fine, thanks. How are you?'

Ms K nods, but doesn't answer. Instead she presses: 'It's just, you don't seem like yourself, Taylor. You seem distracted and worn out. I hope I'm not overstepping, but you're normally so full of life, you see, and I know not everybody can be firing on all cylinders at all times, but it's just ... well. For you it's seems a bit unusual. I know you've been busy setting up your website, and that the Period Protest went ahead and was really effective. I was there, by the way. Well done. But ... Ms Perkins mentioned in the staffroom that you're in the netball squad now, too. That's a lot for a person to be taking on, is all. So I thought I'd ask. Are you sure you're OK? Because I can help, if you're not.'

'Yeah,' I say, with a shrug. 'I'm fine.'

She looks at me. Blinks. And in the few seconds of silence between us, I ask myself, *Wait, AM I OK?!* I decide that I am. Of course I am! How many times do I have to tell people: I am seizing the day!

'OK, well. Glad to hear it,' Ms K says. 'And if you're ever not OK, my door is always open, all right?'

'All right,' I echo.

'Any chance of some submissions for the *Register* any time soon? Or have I lost you to *The Instruction Manual* now?'

I take a deep breath. 'I'll be back,' I tell her. 'Once the website is launched. Journalists can't write for just one place, after all, can they?'

'No,' Ms K smiles. 'I suppose not. Well. You go steady, all right?'

'Too late for that advice!' I joke. 'I'm busy seizing the day, miss! Getting things done! Carpe diem, et cetera!'

Ms K laughs, but reluctantly. A pit grows in my stomach – she always laughs at my jokes, does Ms K. It feels strange to have one land badly.

'Thanks for your concern,' I add. 'But I'm late for chemistry, so …'

'Chemistry?' she repeats. She looks to the clock. 'Oh, crap! I thought it was lunchtime! My Year 7 drama class will be waiting for me in the hall!'

She stands up and grabs her bag.

'Go, go,' she tells me, batting me out the door with waving arms. 'And any problems about tardiness from your teacher, blame my pregnancy in totality, OK?'

'Mark her, Callie! MARK HER!'

I'm desperately trying to feed the ball through to the goal

attack, having intercepted it from the bibs like an absolute pro. I love that about netball, how you can sail through the air and grab the ball and totally change the direction of play. There's no time to think about anything else when you're playing: it's just you and the other players, all after that little orange ball.

I move left, move right, pivot to throw the ball back down the court and then leg it to the other side so I can get the ball back again. It's not until it's in the hands of the goal attack and then sailing into the net that I realise how quickly I managed to think. Or, rather, not think: I just *acted*. Bam, bam, bam, running the court like a boss!

'Nice work, Pandora!' I shout to the goal attack, going in for a low five. It's only a practice, but I like the team spirit aspect of playing and training, too. Saying good job, being told good job, all the ways we have to work together as a team.

'Back at ya, Tay!' she shouts, and we assume positions to return to play.

I don't even care that I have to scarf down my cheese sandwich in the changing rooms again – something is clicking with netball. And if it wasn't for my column I would never have gone to try-outs! So even though Seizing the Day is tough in some ways, with netball I feel like I've really discovered something I like, and that's *very* cool.

I tell Grandma, Grandad and Mum as much over dinner. Grandma has made chicken pie and mashed potato, and it is soooooo tasty.

'Well, that's really nice to hear,' Mum says as she serves up second portions for us all. 'I used to like that about running – especially in Paris. Pounding pavement, letting my brain switch off and just sort of ... meditate, I suppose.'

'I get the same in the garden,' Grandad agrees. 'When it's me and those begonias, I am truly happy.'

Grandma chuckles. 'I'll be getting jealous if you keep on like that!' she says, issuing a wink at me to let me know she's winding him up.

'Oh, if you're going to be envious of anything, keep your eye on that cheeky minx, the late-flowering wisteria. Just when you think you can't be surprised, out she comes showing off her blooms for the second time this season, making all the other plants jealous.'

'Ooooh,' says Grandma. 'I could never begrudge the wisteria. Not when she brightens the place up like she does.'

I stifle a yawn.

'Banter not up to par?' Grandma asks.

'Sorry,' I say. 'It's not you, it's me.'

'I've heard that before,' Grandad says. 'Brenda Rose, summer of 1973. Broke my heart, that girl. I listened to Diana Ross's "Touch Me in the Morning" on repeat for two whole weeks, until my brother got so sick of me he snapped my cassette tape.'

'Tape?!' I say. 'Whoa.'

'I know,' says Grandad. 'And I'd recorded off the radio, so the first ten seconds was missing and the DJ talked over the end. You don't get that on Spotify!'

'Nope,' Mum says. 'I had to download songs off the internet one by one, illegally! But at least I was able to get the whole thing.'

'We'd lose you on that computer for hours,' Grandma remembers. 'And you used to come home and talk to your friends on that messenger as well. Now there's phones, I suppose – they should call them mobile computers!'

I yawn again.

'OK, you,' Grandma says. 'I'm going to start taking this personally.'

I scrunch up my eyes and give them a rub. I see my phone light up on the arm of the sofa, and Duncan's name above a text, but I don't even have the energy to reach over and read it. I send him mental vibes instead, saying hi.

'I might need my bed soon,' I tell Mum. Then to G&G I say, 'After pudding, of course.'

'Oh, of course,' Grandad says, finishing up. 'Can't send you off without some crumble and custard. People have been imprisoned for less.'

I help load the dishwasher and Grandad sets out pudding bowls and lets the crumble cool out of the oven. It glistens gorgeously with crispy brown sugar on top, all the filling bubbling out at the side.

'Yes, yes, as long as Taylor's happy with it,' Grandma is saying as I go back through to sit down again. 'We *love* having her here. Of course we do!'

'What's this?' I ask.

'This weekend,' Mum says. 'I'm thinking of heading down to London overnight again. I've got some bits I need to do.'

'Oh,' I say. 'Yeah, whatever. If Grandma lets me stay up late again …'

'You,' Grandma says, jabbing a spoon at me, 'need all the sleep you can get! You're going through a growth spurt, that's what I think. You need good food and a boatload of rest. Mark my words!'

'Yes, boss,' I say, giving her a captain's salute. 'Now. Where's the double cream?'

Urgh. The next morning I wake up before my alarm, which seems horribly unfair considering I'm getting up so early anyway! I have a funny feeling in my tummy – not like a tummy ache exactly, and not period pains, but like everything is jangled up and jiggly and unsettled. I squeeze my eyes shut, but can't get back to sleep. The feeling in my chest tightens and gets worse, and in the end I get up, wash my face and brush my teeth (I can't STAND morning breath!) and go downstairs with the laptop to write some articles. I manage to get two done, feeling bleary-eyed as I write about the joys of getting up early …

Taylor Blake Seizes the Day … by Getting Up Early

I love my bed almost as much as I love Harry Styles and Tom Holland. I like being cosy under the duvet, with an extra blanket on top and loads and loads of pillows. I read in bed, have done my homework in bed, spend hours on FaceTime with my best friends from my bed … it's the snuggliest place in the world!

But!

When I embarked on the task of seizing the day, many an article agreed that starting the day as early as possible is the best place to start. After all, you can't seize the day if you're asleep.

So I've been getting up at the crack of dawn, sometimes as early as 6 a.m. Everything I've read would have you believe it's easy to leap out of bed at that time, and that it gets easier as time goes on, but I have to admit that it hasn't been so easy for me. I've felt tired, and groggy, and a bit resentful that it's supposed to be good for you, if I'm honest. My English teacher is pregnant, and everyone tells her to enjoy the sleep whilst she can because once the baby comes she won't be getting any. I even caught her asleep at her desk one day! I know the feeling ... She won't be able to sleep soon because of a new baby, and I haven't been sleeping much because I like to get up early to seize the day! I could fall asleep at my desk too!

I've made 'healthy' drinks like hot water with lemon or mint, and even stood outside on the grass in my bare feet before everyone else is awake. Am I crazy? Maybe. But my research said standing barefoot on the grass is called 'grounding', and that it's really important to feel the ground beneath our feet and the sun on our faces as close to waking up as possible. I suppose it was kind of nice? Calming. I think two extra hours in bed might be more calming though!

The bonkers thing about getting up early to seize the day is that I've been able to fit way more into my days ... but doing more makes me really tired, and so I could do with the extra sleep!

Do I recommend seizing the day by getting up early every day? I don't think I do!

This article probably isn't my best work, but it's an all right start. I can't help but think about how negative I must seem, complaining about getting up early, but I'm only trying to tell the truth. The thing is, so many of my other seize the day experiments seem to be failing too I'm worried this whole column is falling apart. Is my conclusion to all of this going to be don't bother?! It's not worth the effort?! Don't get up early, don't dress fancy?? Although DO protest for stuff that isn't right, and travel to new places. Maybe it's OK if I get a fifty-fifty success/failure ratio.

I quickly eat some toast, swiping away a text from Members Only without reading it because to be honest I just don't have the room in my head to process it. Then I head upstairs to try and figure out yet another *fancy* outfit to wear. Maybe trying to be fancy every day is too much? Perhaps I could do every other day, or twice a week? I yawn again as I rifle though my clothes. How cruel that I couldn't sleep when I am so tired – I could crawl under the covers again right now, and probably sleep for another three hours! But it's time to go. Urgh!

I pick out some flared jeans and my Converse with my (p)leather jacket and a neck scarf that at the last minute I take off from around my neck and tie around my hair. I think about what Ms K said, about not doing too much. But surely seizing the day means doing a lot! That's the point!

I yawn again.

No. It's OK. I'll be fine once I get going. I will!!

15

'Oooooh, David, look there – they've got more of that root vegetable compost you like, the one that always sells out.'

It's Friday night, and I'm at the garden centre with Grandma and Grandad. Rock and roll, baby! It's something I normally love, because garden centres are the most barmy places in the world. There's garden stuff, and plants and flowers and gnomes and benches, but then the one we go to also has two cafés, a bed and bath section, a farmer's shop, toy section *and* a book section (but the books are always ones you've never heard of). Today though? I feel ... antsy. Grandma says it's literally like I've got ants in my pants. I'm *agitated*. I can't keep a thought in my head, and I'm a bit touchy, like I've lost my sense of humour.

'Bring the trolley, Rach,' Grandad says. 'I'll stock up.'

'Oh yeah?' Grandma says. 'Going to put it in the garage that we've got all that room in, are you?'

She winks at me, the joke being that Grandad is the biggest hoarder you've ever come across, and because Grandma makes him keep all of his stuff in the garage it is stuffed to bulging.

'Oh aye,' Grandad says, lifting up a bag of compost with a big huff. 'You all like to make out like I hold on to too much stuff, but the moment you need a bit of wood or string for the garden, or a job doing in the house, it's all, *David, you're a hero! You've always got just what we need! Thank you!*'

I pull a face. 'I don't know if I've ever called you a *hero* …' I say teasingly.

'Well, if you haven't, it's about time you did,' Grandad shoots back, and a passing woman in a beret looks between us with a smile, seemingly enjoying our conversation.

Grandad bends down with a theatrical moan, hoisting up two more bags of compost. When he's done he stands back to catch his breath and suddenly Grandma shrieks, 'David!'

She does it with such urgency that I worry she's dropped something, or is warning Grandad he's about to walk smack-bang into a lamp-post, like he did at the seaside one summer because he was too busy looking down at the ice cream he was eating. He ended up with a humongous red welt on his forehead, and a splattering of 99 with red sauce all down his best summer shirt. The stain never did come out. Grandma said it was a blessing in disguise. She hadn't ever liked that shirt anyway.

Grandad looks up, startled as I am, and we both watch as Grandma does a slow-motion 'run' towards him. She stops inches from him and raises a hand to his cheek, spreading her fingers out so she's cupping the side of his head essentially, and she exhales a big kind of *sexy* sigh and says, 'Thank you for stocking up on the compost. You're my *hero*.'

She leans in and kisses him on the mouth, lingering for a beat too long to be funny – I actually have to look away. Having grandparents in love is nice, but, like, I don't need to *see* it.

'Very good,' Grandad says as they part, but he's blushing, like he actually quite liked the kiss. I wonder if that's possible, that kisses never get old, that you never take them for granted. That's quite a nice thought! I hope kissing Duncan never gets boring for me. In fact, if we could do that again soon, that would be really nice. I feel like I'm so jam-packed with stuff to do at school that all my breaks and lunchtimes and after-school walks home are taken up with writing and netball and catching up on homework I should have done when I chose to outline another article. I need to keep a check on that. We can't just be text pen pals!

Weird. Thinking about Duncan, now it's like I can actually see him in front of me, beside the woman in the beret who just eavesdropped on Grandad's and my conversation.

'Taylor!'

Oh! It IS Duncan!

'Hi!' I say, and immediately feel self-conscious because we're surrounded by grown-ups and you know what they're like. Grandad only has to see me *talk* to a boy to ask if he's my 'fancy man'. Once the penny drops that this is *Duncan* – Duncan! DUNCAN!! – they'll be smiling and saying *awwww* and being excruciatingly awkward.

Duncan holds his arm out for a hug, less self-conscious than me. Obviously I wrap my arms around him, but I keep it quick. Gosh, he smells just like himself though. Woody? Can woody smell *nice*? On Duncan it can.

'Hey,' I say quietly, smiling stupidly.

'Hey,' Duncan says back quietly, smiling stupidly too.

The woman in the beret says, 'Taylor, I have heard *so* much about you. I'm Ronnie, Duncan's stepmum.'

She holds out a hand, and I shake it, and it feels incredibly formal.

'Oh god, what am I doing?' she laughs. 'Can I hug you? I feel like I know you already!'

'Sure,' I say, submitting to the request. She smells good too: apricot-y.

'All right, Duncan,' Grandad says, holding out a hand. Grandad clearly doesn't think it's too formal to shake hands. 'Nice to meet the lad who's been putting a spring in my granddaughter's step.'

'Thank you, sir,' Duncan says, and Grandma says, 'None of that, Duncan. He's David, and I'm Rachel.' She gives him a wave. 'Nice to meet you.'

There's a beat of nobody knowing what to say next, and it feels like Duncan and I are on show, like the adults are waiting to see what we'll do next.

EMBARRASSING! Soooooo embarrassing.

'Well, Taylor, I'd love to invite you over one afternoon. We do a mean board game session in our house,' Ronnie says.

'That would be nice,' I say. 'Yeah, thanks.'

'I'll have Duncan sort out when.' She smiles. 'Maybe for his birthday!' He looks at her, and she winks at him. 'Anyway, I'm just going to see what they've got in the toy section for my niece, if you'll excuse me. David, Rachel, nice to meet you too.'

We watch her go, and I stare at Grandma and Grandad expectantly, waiting for them to need to be somewhere else. They grin back at me. Nobody moves.

'Shall I meet you at the tills?' I prompt, and they leap into life.

'Oh, yes, of course,' Grandma says, right as Grandad says, 'There's no rush.'

'They want to be alone,' Grandma whispers at Grandad, who says, 'What? Stop talking into my bad ear!'

Grandma pulls on his arm.

'David!' she says, not bothering to try and hide it now. 'We're cramping their style!'

Grandad looks at us and says, 'Ohhhhhh!' I love that man so, *so* much, he's funny and kind and patient ... but dear lord my mum is right: he cannot take a hint to save his life.

When they've ambled off, Duncan says, 'They seem super cool. My grandparents aren't like that at all. Mine are quiet and don't know how to talk to me. I only see them at Christmas, really.'

'Oh,' I say, because I can't imagine that. I see Grandma and Grandad all the time! And I *like* that!

'They're a good time,' I tell him. 'I think they're still quite young, though, for grandparents.'

'Cool,' Duncan says.

'Yeah,' I say.

I get a flash of an idea that I could snog him, right here in the garden centre. Should I? Dare I?

'You've got that look,' he says.

'What look?' I ask.

He shakes his head, like he doesn't know what to do with me.

'I'm excited for tomorrow,' I tell him. 'Just going to the forest, no schoolwork or articles or anything. Just …'

'*Being*,' Duncan supplies.

'Yeah,' I say. 'I haven't even told anyone this yet, but yesterday afternoon Mr Singh asked me about running for student council. And all I could think was, no! Nobody ask me to do more things!'

Duncan considers this. 'You don't have to do everything,' he says. 'Did you tell him no?'

I shake my head. 'I said I was flattered, and had never even considered it, but I'd have a think over the weekend.'

'Nicely avoided.'

'I accept the compliment.'

Ronnie reappears then, waving Duncan over from near the toys, and so we say goodbye.

'Tell your mum I say hi,' he says as we hug again. 'My new BFF.'

I roll my eyes. 'She's away this weekend,' I say. 'And I will forget by tomorrow, so … no. Tell your BFF yourself when you next come over.'

'Which will be …' Duncan asks, raising an eyebrow.

'Soon,' I say. 'I hope.'

'Me too. But see you tomorrow? Forest bathing?'

'Tomorrow.' I smile. 'Can't wait.'

* * *

Grandad makes his famous full English for breakfast the next morning – famous only amongst us Blakes, but still. I always look forward to it after sleepovers and on Boxing Day. The thing is, by the time I set off to meet everyone at the forest, I'm so full it's a struggle to get going.

'I think I ate too much,' I say as I bend over and pull on my wellies. As I stand, and as if to prove my point, I accidentally let out a high-pitched squeaky fart.

'Sorry, love, did you say something?' Grandad says, his favourite joke whenever somebody fluffs. I pull a face and look left to right, left to right with a smirk.

'Guilty, your honour,' I admit.

'I wouldn't do that in front of your boyfriend,' Grandad says, right as Grandma comes out of their bedroom with some dirty laundry.

'Don't be ridiculous,' she says. 'Farts are universally funny, and we all do them. Louder the better, I say. Better out than in!'

'Thanks for the romantic advice,' I say, laughing.

'Well,' Duncan says, as him, me, Star and Lucy walk down the path into the heart of the woods. 'You got yourself a fan yesterday. Ronnie says to come over next weekend for board game day. And for birthday cake? But only if you promise not to make a fuss of it being my birthday.'

'Oooooh,' Star says. 'Meeting the family? That's major! And on a special occasion, too.'

Lucy smacks her arm. 'It's normal!' she says. 'Don't make her nervous!' Lucy looks at me. 'Star wouldn't let me meet her dad until, like, last year or something. As if parents are supposed to be kept hidden away or something …'

'Maybe it was you I was trying to hide,' Star quips, but she pulls Lucy in for a kiss on the cheek to let her know she doesn't mean it. Lucy grins, but then looks down at the floor. She still hasn't told Star about moving, then. She's got 'I'm keeping a secret' written all over her face! I think Star has decided to ignore it. I mean, if somebody says everything is fine no matter how many times you ask, I suppose eventually you stop asking.

'I'd love to come over on your birthday to ignore the fact it's your birthday. Yes,' I tell Duncan. 'Thank you.'

'Pleasure.' Duncan grins.

We pass the river where we made Angel Delight when the Frenchies were here, on our Duke of Edinburgh day. 'It's really beautiful here,' I say.

'Yeah,' Duncan says. 'We go for summer walks through here sometimes, but it's nice with the autumn leaves and cooler breeze.'

'And what's our destination, *exactly*?' Lucy asks. 'I am

totally down for whatever, but ... the vibe is *admire the trees*, right? That's the objective?'

Duncan smiles. 'The objective,' he says, 'is to be together and be in nature and eat this food I've packed in my rucksack. And then Taylor can write about it for "Seize the Day".'

'Seizing the day by admiring the trees,' Lucy says with a nod. 'Got it.'

'Do you ever get told you're a bit annoying?' Duncan asks, and Lucy pretends to be shocked and outraged.

'How very dare you!' she gasps. 'I get told that all the time, but how rude to bring it up!'

We all burst out laughing, and keep putting one foot in front of the other until we've walked quite a way. We fall into a companionable silence with each other, not talking, but aware that we're all OK with it – the only sound is the leaves crunching underfoot. The sun does its best to push through the leaves, giving everything a syrupy glow. It's ... really nice. Just the birds and the trees and the sun. The air feels cleaner, and I have the sensation of my shoulders dropping. I hadn't realised I'd been holding them hunched up, tensed. Knots across my shoulders loosen, and I think about nothing, really.

'This is really relaxing,' Star says quietly, like she doesn't want to interrupt the peace.

'Yeah,' Lucy says, nodding, and I can hear the awe in her voice.

We walk even further, and when there's a nice flat clearing with some old giant logs to sit on, Duncan suggests stopping. We set up a picnic: Duncan has a blanket, a flask of hot chocolate and some biscuits, and finger sandwiches he says Ronnie insisted he bring. We sit and eat and don't really talk about anything, really – nothing big or huge or heavy. One of us points out a bird or a squirrel, somebody else says the hot chocolate is good.

'I didn't know how much I needed this,' Lucy says with a sigh.

'Same,' Star says, taking her hand and leaning into her. I shift over on the blanket so that I can lie down, my head on Duncan's leg.

'Is this OK?' I ask.

He smiles. 'It's perfect.'

Duncan takes off his jacket and drapes it over me, and I want to tell him he'll get cold, that it's not necessary, but my mouth doesn't work and my eyelids are so, so heavy. Star starts telling everyone about a stuffed teddy bear holding a love heart that somebody left on her doorstep, and I want to ask so many questions about that but, before I know it, I'm in a sublimely deep sleep. I'm so tired. So, so tired …

* * *

I don't know how long I'm out for, but I know I'm woken up by the most echoing pig snort I've ever heard in my life. It happens, and I hear the shrieks of laughter from Star and Lucy, and it's then my eyes fling open and I see Duncan staring down at me, half horrified and half holding in a laugh of his own.

'What was that?' I say sleepily, and in unison all three of them answer: 'You!'

'What?' I say, sitting bolt upright. I rub my eyes. My mouth feels dry as the desert.

'It was cute!' Duncan says, and the way he's defending me makes me *know* it was me.

'Oh,' I say. 'Sorry. I don't usually snore.'

Lucy laughs. 'Well,' she says. 'You do. But I understand why you don't want to admit that to Duncan.'

I spot an errant biscuit on the rug and grab it to hurl at her. She shrieks, but I miss. I get up to run after her, a rush of energy coursing through me after my nap, but Star protects her and I can't reach her.

'It's going to start getting colder soon,' Duncan says, once we've calmed down. 'We should head back.'

'OK,' I say.

As we begin the trek I slip my hand into his.

'This was a good idea,' I tell him. 'Thank you.'

He grins. 'I could sit in an empty room on the floor and still have fun with you.'

I look at him, my heart swelling eighty million sizes and threatening to burst.

'I feel the same about you,' I say.

'Urgh,' tuts Lucy. 'Why don't you start a mutual admiration society? You could print each other's faces on T-shirts and wear them to school.'

'Not a bad idea, actually,' Duncan says, squeezing my hand with two quick pulses. I play along.

'We could get matching hoodies, too.'

'Oooooh, and gloves! Our faces printed teeny tiny on each finger!'

'We'd have to do commemorative plates as well,' I say. 'Like the royals.'

'And tea towels.'

'You two deserve each other,' Lucy laughs, and this time I squeeze Duncan's hand.

'Good time?' Grandad asks, when I get back to theirs. Mum decided to make her London trip two nights instead of one, which was fine by me. I know she's a single parent and she dates sometimes, and goes to her writing groups and occasionally, when she's in the country, Auntie Kate comes to stay, but I do get that, you know, it must be nice for her to go away sometimes, to a big city, where she's not anyone's daughter or mother or whatever and she can just be ... well, Erica.

'Yeah, actually,' I say. 'I mean, I don't see how forest bathing is any different to just *going to the woods*, but it's always fun with the girls, and Duncan gets on with them really well too.'

'Nice boy,' Grandma says. 'Lovely eyes.'

'Yeah,' I say, but I don't really want to get into it with them. I yawn.

'All that fresh air must have tired you out!' Grandma says. 'You need feeding, get your energy up. What do you fancy?'

Grandma sets about making tea, and I scroll through my phone, passing the time. When Axel FaceTimes, I answer right away.

'That was very fast!' he says, when his beautiful face comes into view.

'My phone was in my hand!' I say. Pierre comes into view.

'Hello, Taylor!' he says with a wave.

'Pierre!' I say. 'Hi!'

Axel comes back on-screen.

'My father has gone away for the weekend, so we are having, how do you say? A slumber party?'

'A sleepover!' I say. 'Awwww! I'm having a sleepover too! At Grandma and Grandad's!'

I spin the phone around so everyone can wave at each other.

'Hello!'
'Hello!'
'Hello!'

Axel shows me around Pierre's house, an apartment with his mother and grandmother in the centre of town. It's sooooo chic, with big high ceilings and wooden floors, and I get a jolt of a reminder that I love France, and simply *must* move there.

'Gorgeous,' I say. 'Just like you two!'

Pierre pecks Axel's cheek, and asks, 'And Duncan? I talked with him and he said you two are …'

'Yeah, yeah,' I say, quickly going through into the other room. I'm not talking about this in front of my grandparents, I'm just NOT. 'We are,' I say.

'*Fantastique*,' Pierre says. 'This makes me so happy.'

We ring off because tea is ready and promise to talk again soon. Seconds later my phone beeps, from the Members Only group chat. Star has sent a photo. It's of me and Duncan, when I was lying in his lap. He's looking down at me, smiling, looking happy, happy, happy. I'm smiling back, and framed by the trees and the dappled sunlight, it could almost be a movie poster or something.

You guys really are the cutest, Star writes, and seeing that? I kinda couldn't agree more. I bet everyone wishes they were young and in love!

16

'I can't believe this week is over already,' I say to Mum as I try to finish my English homework before tea. I'm sat in my netball uniform, having come from an after-school match. We won! Seven to two! And I got player of the match! So yet again, netball is proving to be a superb addition to my days (even if it means still doing my homework at nearly 7 p.m.). The past six days have been a whirl of activity, yet again. I barely know my own name!

'Time flies when you're having fun!' she smiles, stirring a pan of risotto on the stove. She's barefoot, in her apron, hair piled high on her head with a clip I'm pretty sure she's nicked from me, but now isn't the time to go hurling accusations around. There's something different about Mum lately. She's ... I don't know. Smiling more? Even though she's always been happy. Looking younger, somehow? Even though she's never been an 'old' mum, if you know what I mean. Maybe it's that she seems more relaxed? Even though I've never really thought of her as a stress head or anything. I just can't put my finger on it.

'You're in a good mood,' I say. I have an idea of what could be making the difference, but I'm not 100 per cent sure yet.

'Am I?' she says, like butter wouldn't melt. She grates some Parmesan and pours herself a glass of white wine.

Hmmmm.

On Saturday morning, I spend ages getting ready to go to Duncan's house, to have this infamous games night (but in the afternoon) with his family. I've got him a second-hand copy of the Holly Bourne I've just borrowed from the library, because I think he'll like it. And because he doesn't want a fuss for his birthday, I've put it in Christmas wrapping paper for a joke. He can't complain then, can he? Lol.

I don't feel nervous per se, but I deffo want to give a good impression. I leave my hair down, straight, and put on some cargo trousers and a T-shirt so I'm comfy, but also cool. I take a big hoodie in case I get cold. That's the thing about houses you've never been to – you never know what their temperature will be. I know exactly how to dress in my own house (medium-thin layer underneath, medium-thick layer as a jumper, our house is the perfect temperature), how to dress for Grandma and Grandad's (thin T-shirt and nothing else, because their house is hotter than the sun) and roughly what to wear at Star's (vest, T-shirt, hoodie, potentially a coat ... her dad is *very* stingy with the heating). Also, smells. Every house has a different smell, doesn't it? Gosh, there is so much unknown I'm walking into!

Duncan picks me up after his Saturday drama class, Ronnie driving and his dad, Miguel, in the passenger seat.

'So nice to meet you!' Miguel says as Duncan helps me in the car and then shuts the door behind me. Like a true gentleman!

'And you,' I say, smiling. 'Miguel? Is that a Spanish name?'

Miguel nods. 'It is,' he says. 'Not that I've got an ounce of Spanish blood in me. My dad just liked the beer and thought it sounded exotic! Ha!'

'That is, unfortunately, true,' Duncan says with a grimace.

'Am I allowed to find it funny?' I say, and Miguel says, 'Abso-bloody-lutely! My dad was mad as a box of frogs!'

'All strapped in?' asks Ronnie, and I nod. 'Let's do this!'

Well. The thing about Duncan is that I am coming to understand he's got layers, like an onion. And I'm learning more and more about him – that he's not as quiet as I thought, that he's funny, that he's a good kisser. And as we pull up to his house, I learn one more thing about him: he lives in a mansion!!

Well, maybe not a mansion, but his house is absolutely massive, with big black gates that automatically open as Ronnie pulls up on to the drive and then close behind us like magic. It's like something from a movie set. Seriously, the house could come straight out of a horror movie, but in a good way? It's all different levels, with red brick and plants growing all the way up it, and the windows all have shutters. There's a wrap-around porch that goes around the whole of the house, with outdoor furniture on it. Sofas, but for the outside! Like from an American movie! When we get out of the car, Ronnie says, 'It would be nice to take you through the front door, Taylor, but we're a bit muddied up after a morning walk so let's go via the boot room.'

I don't even know what a boot room is! I think it's a room just for shoes, but ... muddy ones? We go in a door at the side of the house, so I get a glimpse of the garden: a rolling meadow of a thing with a trampoline sunken INTO THE GROUND so you don't even have to climb up on to it, and I swear it looks like a tennis court down at the bottom. We take off our shoes, and the floor is warm, like a radiator on a very low setting. I look at Duncan, who shows me through to the kitchen, where I sit and wait whilst he gets changed out of his drama stuff.

'What can I get you, Taylor?' Miguel asks. 'I'm making coffee, but we've got juice, cordial, tea …'

'Cordial, please,' I say.

I just can't get over this house! It's like the size of our house, Grandma and Grandad's, AND Star's, AND Lucy's put together! It's a wonder they don't get lost on the daily.

'Sitting room?' Ronnie asks, and Miguel says yeah, let's get cosy. 'I'll go drag Melvin from his room, then.' She nods.

'Ronnie's son,' Miguel explains. 'He's on a gap year before uni. Just earning some extra money before he goes travelling.'

The sitting room is, predictably, very big for a 'cosy' room, with massive sofas and a big coffee table with games piled high beside it: Scrabble, a million different Top Trumps, Cluedo, Monopoly, BOP IT, loads! Duncan sits beside me and grins. I smile back, then he leans over and gives me a peck on the cheek, in front of everybody, just like that!

'So this is Taylor, is it?'

Duncan looks up. 'Certainly is,' he says. 'Taylor, this is my annoying stepbrother Melvin.'

Melvin reaches out a hand to shake mine, like we're in a business meeting and I've just offered him a great deal.

'Annoyingly charming and funny and family board games champion,' Melvin says. 'Don't let the slightly dusty boxes fool you: We still play all that kids' stuff, don't we, D?

Although he's as much as a loser as ever, aren't you, little stepbrother?' Melvin says this in a funny voice, letting me know he's only teasing.

Duncan sticks out his tongue and Melvin does the same, and then we're off! God, I don't know where the day even goes: his stepmum and dad are as funny and laid-back as my mum, and I didn't even know Duncan had an older stepbrother, let alone one who is as dry and witty as Duncan himself. Crucially, they all seem to like me too – it's not long before I totally relax and let my real self come out. Especially when we play Heads Up! and Duncan is shockingly bad at it. It's like Lucy and my grandad all over again.

'For god's sake!' I cry, frustrated that he's making us lose. 'How can such a clever bloke be so stupid?!'

His family found that *hilarious*. They even laugh when I'm not trying to be intentionally funny, which I don't mind *at all*. Makes me feel like part of the gang, to be honest.

'Your family is lovely,' I tell Duncan when we scurry off to make popcorn for everyone. I've just given him his 'Christmas present' – he said he can't wait to read it. Because the games have petered out a bit – we *have* been playing for ages – we're going to make popcorn and watch a movie.

'They're all right,' Duncan says, pulling a face that obviously means, *I know they are*. 'They like you,' he adds.

'I like them!' I say.

We sort out the popcorn, and I run it through to everyone and come back to help with drinks. Duncan is taking his time, noticeably so.

'My grandma would say you've not got a rush in you,' I comment as he makes up a jug of cordial.

'Slow and steady!' Duncan says. He loads up a tray and comes over to where I'm leaning against the big kitchen island.

'So …' he says.

'So …' I echo.

'How you feeling? You know, since you fell asleep in the woods.'

I cringe. 'I'm never going to live that down, am I?'

'It was weird!' Duncan insists. 'You're just so busy, you know? I don't want you exhausting yourself just for the column. Which, by the way, I still haven't seen any of yet …'

I wag a finger at him. 'I'm still working on them!' I say, which is true. 'I've got a bunch of first drafts, but it's been hard to find the time to polish them.'

'That's why we're doing this together,' Duncan points out. 'So I can help. Let me take a look. I love being your first reader!'

I nod. 'OK, I'll see what I've got for you.'

'Good. And we're FaceTiming with the girls tomorrow, about the launch? Ms K said she got her invitation – I didn't even know they'd gone out! Lucy and Star are doing a really good job of getting stuff done.'

'Oh, for sure,' I say. 'I didn't know the invitations had gone out either. But it doesn't surprise me. Lucy especially – she's so efficient!'

Duncan nods. 'About Lucy,' he says. 'Is she OK? I know Star has been worried and you said it was all OK, but … I know you, Taylor. There's more, isn't there? Is she in trouble? Has something happened?'

I look to the floor. Damn Duncan and his emotional intelligence!

'She's not in trouble …' I say, because that much is true.

'But you can't tell me the rest? Or won't?'

'Can't,' I say. 'Not yet. But I will.'

He nods slowly. 'Well. OK. You'll let me know if I can help or anything?'

'I will,' I say.

He scrunches up his nose, all cute and adorable. 'OK,' he says in a funny voice, and I push his shoulder playfully.

'You look like a gerbil!' I tell him.

'A gerbil?' he says, still creasing up his face. He puts on a funny voice. 'A gerbil?!'

He does a funny thing with his hands, like they're little gerbil claws, and pretends to come for my neck. I leap back, laughing.

'Stop!' I say. 'It's so creepy!'

'A creepy gerbil?' he says, stepping towards me again. I move back. He comes closer, and before I know it he's chasing me around the kitchen island, making me screech hysterically.

'You're so gross!' I say.

'Me? Creepy Gerbil Man?' he squawks.

'Yes!' I laugh. 'Ewwww!'

Duncan is laughing too, and even more so when he finally catches me.

'Aha!' he says, and I try to get out of his grip but can't, so end up dropping to the floor and pulling him with me so we roll around like wrestling lion cubs.

'OK!' he laughs. 'I surrender! You win! You win!'

I push him off me and he falls beside me. We both lie face down on the wooden floor, looking at each other, giggling.

'You're an idiot,' I say, and he smiles.

'Yup!' he says. 'But I guess that's why you love me!'

I stick my tongue out at him. 'Don't get too crazy,' I say, but inside I think to myself: *WAIT WHAT?! LOVE?!?!?!?!?!?!?!?!?!?!?!?!*

The next day, I report back to Lucy, who has asked me to meet up at Starbucks. It was on our side chat, so Star isn't here. Feels odd without her, actually. But I know Lucy just needs some advice on how to tell Star about her moving.

'That big house out past the supermarket? Is that where you mean?'

'Yes!' I say. 'Which, like my mum pointed out, means that every time Duncan has walked me home, he's gone *at least* two miles out of his way.'

'THAT is adorable,' sighs Lucy. 'Duncan!! He's just the dream, isn't he?'

I slurp on my mango and passionfruit Frappuccino. 'I need to lock it down,' I say. 'Figure out this grand romantic gesture and make it an official girlfriend-boyfriend situation …'

'I'm still on team flash mob,' says Lucy. 'After what we saw in London.'

'Oh yeah!' I say. 'I'll choreograph a whole routine in all that spare time I've got!'

'You're busy, I know, you *have* mentioned it …'

I open my mouth to give a sarky reply, but find I don't have one. Instead I say, 'Am I boring?'

Lucy laughs. 'No. But you do need to chill out a bit. Although I know being *unchill* is pretty much your personal brand, so perhaps that's bad advice.'

I act like I'm offended. 'I'll take that as a compliment, shall I!' I say, in a typically non-chill manner. 'Jeez!'

Lucy pulls a face. 'Anyway,' she says. 'Mum still isn't budging on the move. So.'

The mood immediately shifts. 'Oh, pants,' I say. 'Really?'

'Really.'

Lucy looks so sad, big eyes welling up. She swallows hard.

'I'm going to have to tell Star,' she says, voice wobbling. 'But … I'm actually quite worried. I don't think she'll take it well *at all*. She's … well, after everything that happened after her transition, she's not as outgoing as you and me, is she? I don't worry about you, because you're practically the mayor of Crickleton High. But Star …'

'I know what you mean,' I say. 'I really will try my best to look after her. But I think you're right. It will be hard on her.'

We sit, looking at each other. God, Lucy really is leaving? I can't believe it. We've been friends for so long. And I know moving doesn't mean we can't still be friends, but not seeing her every day? Not being able to come down to Starbucks and hang out like this, whenever we want? Lunchtimes will be weird, not having her clever mouth making a joke of everything. I think about what *How to Be Parisian When You're Not from Paris* says about friendship:

On Friendship

A Parisian woman knows that the real loves of her life will never be the typical romantic kind which can come and go, but will rather be her very best friends …

I don't think I understood that properly until now, but Lucy – and Star, of course! – really are like soulmates, like one-true-loves (except there's two of them). They're my everything. I suddenly feel like it's too hard to be strong for Lucy, like I want to cry too. I reach across the table and take her hand and we look at each other, words suddenly not enough to explain the way we feel.

'So, you two hang out without me now, do you?'

I look up. It's Star. And she looks ... furious.

'Star!' I say. 'Hi!'

She looks at Lucy.

'You're going to break up with me, aren't you?' she says. 'What's this? Some sort of brainstorming session on how to do it? Or have you been pushing me away so that eventually I'm the one to do it? Because I won't! I don't want to break up!'

Lucy bursts into tears then.

'I don't want to break up either!' she says, and Star looks from Lucy, to me, back to Lucy.

'Oh,' she says. 'So ... what? You just don't invite me sometimes?'

Star looks at me, betrayal etched into her face. 'No!' I say. 'It's just because ...' But I can't finish that sentence, because it isn't my news to tell. I take a breath. 'Look,' I say. 'Sit down. I'll go and buy you a drink.'

She seems reluctant, like she doesn't trust what's about to happen, which is fair enough: her instinct is right, it's just misplaced. Lucy and I aren't trying to hang out without her – Lucy and I are talking about how soon, it will be me and Star without Lucy!

I stand in line and pull out my phone to text Duncan as I wait. But he's already texted me!

Yesterday was great, **it says.** *Thanks for coming over!*

I text back, *Thanks for having me! Although, not thanks for your Heads Up! 'teamwork'. Think I'll partner with Melvin next time.*

Lol, **he says.** *What you'd gain in Heads Up!, you'd lose in Pictionary...*

True, **I type back.** *God, I hate that you're always right!*

He sends back a clown emoji and I order, slipping my phone into my back pocket as I head back to the girls.

Oh crap, Star is crying.

And Lucy is crying.

I sit down, look at them both, and as soon as Star says, 'She's going!' I burst into tears too.

We all sit there, tears streaming down our faces, distraught. It's probably the first time in my whole life I can't think of anything to say to lighten the mood. I don't want to lighten the mood. My best friend is leaving us!

'Are you girls OK?' a woman on the next table asks, holding a packet of tissues out. 'Take these.'

'Thank you,' I say sadly, and the woman cocks her head and says, 'Did somebody die?'

I look back at Star and Lucy, and thank goodness for this woman, because that does the trick: we're still crying, but suddenly we're all laughing, too.

This is just the pits.

I leave Star and Lucy to it – they deserve some time to talk alone, and I've got maths homework to do, and a few things to do for *The Instruction Manual*. I'm still laughing at the woman who asked us if somebody had died – I mean, we were being super dramatic, but if ever a moment called for drama this was it! It makes me think about Veronica Sellers, in a weird way. She obviously didn't die (thank god!) but she's still off school. I never did contribute to her care package. Eeeek, that's not cool of me. I wonder if she noticed. I hope other people sent stuff!

I let myself into the house, and since it's late afternoon Mum has started to make it all cosy, which she always does at weekends. There are lamps on and candles lit in the living room, wafting about a citrus-y smell that just makes me think: ahhhh, *home*. I slip my shoes off and go through to the kitchen, but Mum isn't there. Normally, at this point, if Mum wasn't around but I'd expect her to be, I'd shout out for her. But right before I do that, there's a giggle from her office. Some instinct sneaks in, where instead of making myself known I tiptoe towards the office door. I can't explain why, I just get a sense that making myself known would be worse than not, if that make sense.

I can't see who she's talking to, but it's on the screen of her computer. It lights up the room now it's getting dark outside. The person says something in French, in a low, gruff voice, and I think: *I know that voice.* Mum replies in French, sounding odd and coy, and it hits me that she's flirting. My mum! In FRENCH!

I move just enough to not make a noise, but to get a better look at the screen, and my growing suspicions are confirmed: it's Lucas, Axel's dad! Obviously Mum can be friends with whoever she likes but there's something about this that makes me feel ... odd. I don't have any other way to explain it. I just can't bring myself to knock and announce myself. I move away slowly and go back to the kitchen, where I grab a bag of Monster Munch and an apple.

Hmmmmm ... Axel's dad. I mean, I'd noticed they got on and had a nice time in London, but Mum has never said they've stayed in touch ... I'm 50 per cent freaked out and 50 per cent into this. Mum and Lucas? Mum ... and ... LUCAS?! On some level I so knew this was a thing, but on another level I've been so busy seizing the day I might have overlooked the hints. I just haven't had the brain space! Well. The bombshells just keep on exploding today, don't they!

17

I want to text Axel and ask if he knows our parents are talking this way, but if I do it feels like admitting something, and whatever that something is, I do *not* want to go there. Not yet. I can't fully explain why. I'm not saying Axel is *mine*, and so by extension Lucas is 'mine', but yeah ... not that Mum is stepping on my toes, exactly, but ... oh, for crying out loud, I don't know! I just feel some type of way, and it's a lot. I'm frowning without meaning to as I stare up at my bedroom ceiling, trying to figure this out. It's not good for me, ruminating this way, I know that. Grandma always says solutions are found in movement, i.e. get up off your butt and stay busy because that's better than sat around being grumpy. Maybe I should try to take my mind off it.

I know. I'll do some *Instruction Manual* stuff. The launch

is next week, and it really does have to be top notch. Ms K has asked how we're getting on, and so have a couple of kids I don't even really know at school, too – Calum Maggiore and even Horrid Anna in Year 10. How's that for our reputation preceding us?! Some of the editorial team from the *Register* have asked about it as well. I think they'll want to write for us when we're ready! It's a cool feeling, knowing people are interested. I never expected that random kids at school would care about what we're doing before it even launches. I guess I never really knew who was reading the school paper. But Duncan says that the website has ways to track how many hits we get, who is a recurring visitor, how long they spend on the site – loads of stuff! Ha, that will crush my soul if it turns out people only visit us once and stay for, like, ten seconds, but if they don't … if we do our job properly and they come back again and again and spend ages reading … I mean, talk about awesome!! I'll be headhunted by *Vogue* in no time.

I log on to the site, which is currently password protected. I type in 'DUNCAN.IS.AN.EDITING.GOD' and see the familiar landing page Duncan designed, the page that he first sent to me to propose this idea as a serious one. I click on the button to edit, and go through the articles I've already got to check they're reading well, and look good as a cohesive column. I'm happy with what I see: all my stories about staging a protest and forest bathing and London adventures. I was right about the mix of success stories and what Grandad would call 'learning curves' – stuff that hasn't worked out like I'd planned. Lucy is still moving, even though I tried to help her by talking to her mum, and trying to be fancy every single day isn't nearly as fun as embracing my chic side for special occasions. I managed to get a short piece about joining the netball squad up there the other day, too, because out of everything, I think netball has been the most unexpected pleasure. It wasn't until I sat down to write it that I realised OK, Josie's conditioning sessions might be a step too far for me, but the actual netball training is really fun. I feel like I'm learning a lot about teamwork, which makes playing matches really exciting. I know I do *The Instruction Manual* with Duncan, and the girls are helping with the launch, but the bulk of writing is just me, sat by myself, tap-tap-tapping away. You can't have a netball game without being totally switched on, but also really communicative with the people around you too. I feels useful, being on that team. I know for a fact that I contribute in a positive way – remember when I got player of the match? With writing, who knows how people feel once they've read it, if they even do at all. The immediacy of netball is cool to me. If I thought I'd only seize the day with netball for as long as I was working on the columns, well! I was wrong! I hope netball is something I can keep doing for as long as it keeps me so excited. Netball makes me feel like I've seized the day, and I hope reading about it makes other people want to seize the day too!

I get pulled out of my own little world when my phone rings for the start of a group FaceTime with the girls and Duncan. We have business to attend to …

'Oi, oi!' Duncan says, his usual effusive and enthusiastic self.

'Oi, oi!' Star says back, but it sounds funny coming from her. It makes me laugh.

'Oi, oi!' I say, and we wait for Lucy to accept the call so we're a four. She's a few minutes late, but when she logs on, she's totally professional. She barely blinks as me, Star and Duncan all say in unison, 'Oi, oi!'

'Right,' she says, ignoring us, and she's using her 'instructive' (aka bossy) voice. I know that means not to mess around, we don't want to get her frustrated. 'If I could start?'

'By all means …' says Duncan, handing her the floor. That's the thing about Duncan: he can read the mood of the room. He knows not to wind Lucy up without anybody having to explain it. I like that about him. It's mature. That's Duncan: mature, but not boring. He's mature *and* fun! A winning jackpot, if you ask me.

'Thank you,' Lucy replies. 'So. The party is six days away, and everything is shaping up nicely. The social club are giving us two hours in their space for free, and the local greengrocer's is sponsoring the decorations in exchange for six months' advertising on your site.'

'I didn't know we were accepting advertisers …' I say, stunned, because truly, this had never occurred to me.

'Same.' Duncan nods. 'I like the thought of small local businesses advertising on our site. Lucy, you're a wonder! I feel a bit stupid for not thinking of it. But it totally makes sense.'

'Do not judge yourself by my standards,' Lucy jokes. 'For you shall always fall short.'

Duncan shakes his head. 'You say that tongue-in-cheek, and yet why do I detect an element of truth to this?'

Star, ever the most reasonable one of us, interjects, 'We've all got our strengths! Lucy is very good at thinking outside the box! Duncan, you're very good at making sure the box is spelled properly! Now, what next, Lucy?'

'The gift shop on Blunder Road have provided one hundred small gift bags, which we've stuffed with sweets, from the old-fashioned sweet shop, a leaflet with some more info about you both and the site – Duncan signed off on that when you were at netball, Taylor – and we're just waiting to hear back from the last few local businesses as to their contributions. Basically to see who will give us free stuff.'

'One hundred?' I say. 'That's a lot …'

Lucy wags a finger. 'Probably not enough, actually. Your social stock has risen since the Period Protest.'

'That's what we're calling it officially, is it?' I say. 'The Period Protest?' I thought I only called it that in my head.

'Yes,' Lucy laughs. 'Basically, not only do half of Crickleton High want to come – they seem to be genuinely fascinated by what you're doing here, even you, Duncan—'

'Even me? Great,' Duncan says, deadpan.

'You know what I mean,' Lucy bats back.

'Unfortunately,' Duncan sighs, 'I do.'

'Aaaaaaanyway,' Lucy presses. 'Not only do half of Crickleton High want to come, but also local business owners and even some dignitaries as well. As in, the local mayor has said they're coming.'

'They are?!' I say in shock. 'Well, *that's* …'

'Big?' supplies Duncan. 'They're a *very* big deal. When they ran for the position we did some campaigning for them – me and my stepbrother. They're so progressive and inclusive and just *awesome*.'

'I second that,' I say.

'I third that,' says Star, who is an especially big fan.

'This is amazing, you two,' I say. 'You could run an events business!'

'Well, you just wait until the actual party,' Star says. 'Ms K is letting us bunk off last period with her to go set up early, and just like your grandparents said, we've got the projectors and everything! We just want people to walk in and have the wow factor. We've got some lovely decorations that Mrs Bates had left over from her wedding …'

'I'm not even there yet and I'm saying wow,' Duncan chuckles. Meanwhile, I'm distracted by the concept of Mrs Bates being *married*. I know the clue is in her name – *MRS* Bates – but I'd never considered that another human being would *like her*. But apparently they do. 'Seriously,' Duncan continues. 'How do we thank you? When we first set this up, I don't think either of us thought it could ever make a splash …'

'Speak for yourself!' I say. 'I'm the splash queen!'

'Correct.' Duncan nods. 'I should have seen this coming.'

'The three musketeers, Tay and two queers!' I cry gleefully, and the girls cheer along with me. 'There's *nothing* we can't do,' I say. 'And now you get to see it up close, Duncan.'

'And I'm loving every minute of it.' He grins. 'Really.'

The girls ring off and Duncan and I stay online chatting.

'They've knocked it out of the park,' he says. 'I guess it's just our job to make sure the site is strong enough to warrant the fuss. I'll go in and check everything, OK? And I think we launch with the basic site – the about page, my piece about what it's like to launch a website, and then your column, and use that to set the tone?'

'Agree,' I say. 'Maybe we can put a letter from the editors up there? Telling people what to expect?'

'Oh yes!' Duncan says. 'Let's draft that now, if you've got time?'

'I do,' I say, thinking of Mum downstairs, cooing to Lucas. I'd prefer to stay huddled up here than go down and bear witness to any more of that.

'OK,' says Duncan says, cracking his knuckles. 'A mission statement.'

I watch him walk to a room with a computer, where he opens up a Word document.

'Ready,' he says.

'OK,' I start. 'So I guess short and sweet is best?'

'Totally. How about: *A letter from the editors: a mission statement*, to open?'

'Yes,' I say. 'And then, The Instruction Manual *is a place where the only limit is your imagination. Opinion columns, local news, sports, culture and more ...*'

'Hold on!' Duncan says. 'You're talking too fast! I can't type quick enough to keep up!'

'It doesn't have to be this,' I explain. 'I'm just shooting out ideas ...'

'No,' he says. 'It's good. How about something like *there's room for everyone; we're an inclusive place with one goal: to represent what the teenagers of Crickleton really think ...*'

'Yes!' I say. 'Because that's exactly it! We want a place where we can say what we really want to say, instead of what school will *let* us say. Don't put that though – I don't want school to get mad.'

'We don't have to say it for people to get what we mean,' Duncan notes.

'OK, good.'

'So, *The Instruction Manual is a place where the only limit is your imagination. Opinion columns, local news, sports, culture and more, we're an inclusive place with one goal: to represent what the teenagers of Crickleton* **really think**.'

'That's it!' I say. 'Let's have that on the landing page. It will be awesome to see that projected on one of these screens. A real call to arms!'

Duncan holds his hands to his mouth like he's playing a trumpet. 'Duh-duh-duh!!!' he trills.

'That's actually very convincing,' I say. 'Do you practise your trumpet noises?'

'Only if there's time after practising my fart sounds.'

I roll my eyes. 'I'd rather not hear those, if it's all the same to you,' I say.

'It is,' Duncan replies. 'Because I'm really not getting on well with them at all. I just can't get the pitch of them right. Trickier than it would seem, convincing fart noises.'

'I wonder if there's an article in that,' I say. 'I'm sure if you're suffering, there must be many others too. You could start a support group.'

'Fart Noises Anonymous,' Duncan says.

'Hmmmm,' I say. 'I think with a name like that you could end up with people who make fart noises from their actual butts and want help and support. You need to clarify it is *fake* fart noise …'

'Fake Fart Noises Anonymous, then,' Duncan clarifies.

'You're so lame,' I say, laughing.

'This is not news to me,' Duncan replies.

'Ceeks forever?' I ask.

'Ceeks forever!' he sing-songs back.

I get loads done that night, and feel really confident about the launch. It's nice, seeing the columns together – I can trace the theme of them when I read them all at once. I've seized the day, and it's been … well, tiring, but fun! I just love living life to the max, as much as possible. I suppose I've had less time for Star and Lucy, and I wish I could see Duncan outside of school a bit more, and in school for that matter, and I am aware in the very back of my mind that I haven't spent as much time with Paul, Duncan's best friend, as he has with mine … and of course, getting up super early to fit it all in isn't my favourite thing ever … but the articles make me seem like I'm fearless and full of adventure. Anyone who reads them will surely think that I'm pretty badass! Not that it's about what people think, et cetera, but in terms of a brand as a journalist I'm really setting the tone.

'Taylor?'

Mum, outside my room. I've not even eaten tonight because I didn't want to go back down. I feel like I can't pretend to be normal, and if I go down and try I'll end up crying or something embarrassing like that – embarrassing because I don't even know what makes me want to cry! I don't know why I'm feeling the way I'm feeling, which is basically CONFUSED. When I was little we had a book about a colour monster, and different colours represented different emotions. Red was anger, blue was sad, green was calm, yellow was happy … Mum would ask me what colour I felt to figure out how I was feeling. Well. Right now all my colours are messed up in a big confusing bundle. I don't know if I'm blue or black or red or purple!

'Are you OK, honey? You've been working for hours.'

'I'm OK, Mum,' I shout through the door. Then I add: 'I'm going to bed soon! Night!'

Mum lingers at the other side of the bedroom door. Normally I'd tell her to come in – talking through a door is so weird – but I think we both notice how I don't, and how that feels 'off'. Mum pauses, like she's figuring out what to say.

'OK, darling,' she says. 'Sleep well.'

I think she's gone and turn back to my screen, but then I hear her say, 'I love you, Taylor.'

'I love you too, Mum,' I say, pushing back a rogue tear from my left eye. 'Night.'

I really don't get much done after that, and crawl back into bed to scowl at the ceiling some more. I must fall asleep, because it's light out when I open my eyes again, my blanket tucked all around me in the style Mum and I call 'Taylor Burrito', a glass of cordial and a covered cheese sandwich on my nightstand with a note from Mum that says, 'In case you wake up hungry.'

She's the best. I mustn't forget that.

18

*H*oly. Moly.

It's finally here! Launch day!

Duncan and I are holding hands as we walk into the social club, and it's like falling down the rabbit hole to Wonderland and ending up in a whole new world. What is normally a big brown box of a room is totally transformed.

Walking through a silver glitter curtain made up of loads of strips of sparkling shiny fabric should have been the first clue that Lucy and Star have gone above and beyond. The whole ceiling of the club is swathed in thin strips of rainbow-coloured see-through cloth, so that the lights shine through and make swirls of all different colours on the floor. Around the room are ten different projections on to the walls, and each one has a different page of my column on them. Somehow, they've got *The Instruction Manual* logo on the floor, and on a table in the corner there are rows and rows of paper bags with white cord handles that also have our logo on.

There's another table with rows of glasses so crystal clear they almost glow. Behind them are metal buckets the size of a small child, filled with ice and stuffed to overflowing with coloured bottles of lemonade and soda. The air is filled with the scent of pizza and chips, and sure enough the double doors to the kitchen open and we see two people I recognise from the Blunder Road café fussing about around the ovens. There are napkins with our logo, and the *very cool* sounds of some French rap that Axel introduced us all to echoing around.

'This is …' Duncan says, his voice full of wonder.

'I know,' I say. 'I'm … speechless.'

'Now there's a first.'

I spin around. Lucy is stood dressed all in black with a swipe of ruby lipstick across her lovely pout. She's holding a clipboard and a pen, and looks about thirty years old, like she runs a whole company on her own and makes millions of pounds.

'Whoa,' I say. 'You look amazing! And this room, everything …'

She breaks out into a big grin. 'I'm glad you like it,' she says. 'We worked really hard.'

'It paid off,' says Duncan, going in for a hug. I hug her too.

Star joins us and we stand as a four, taking it all in: this is by far the fanciest, most elegant thing that has ever happened to me.

And then the party begins.

Because I am not totally bonkers, I have never sat down and written a list of everyone I know in the world ever. If I did, I'd miss half the people in this room off the list, because my brain had no idea it knew most of Crickleton.

There's the mayor, Ms K and Mrs Bates, who is stood with a woman I assume is her wife. Loads of kids from school, people from the protest and French class and off the exchange. There's Year 9 kids, but some from Year 10 and 11, too, which is *mind-blowing*. Year 11s?! Like what?! I'm so busy saying hi to everyone that I lose Lucy, Star and Duncan in the buzz of people. Mum appears, all earrings and lip gloss, and throws her arms around me before handing me a tiny cupcake with acres of blue icing. On the very top is a square of white icing with the name of the website on it. It's the most professional thing I've ever seen!

'Bug! Look at this! I can't believe it!' she says, gesturing to both the cake and the party. I don't want to ruin my make-up, so pop the cake on the edge of a nearby table for later.

'You and me both,' I reply. 'I've even seen the journalist

that covered the period protest here. Can you imagine if she writes about the website?!'

'If she does, I have a feeling it won't be the first time your journalistic efforts are rewarded.' Mum smiles. 'Honestly, Taylor. I almost cannot believe my daughter is capable of such a success – but obviously I've met you, so I can!'

'There she is!' Grandma says, sneaking up behind me and giving me a hug. 'Woman of the hour!'

'Taylor, my love.' Grandad smiles. 'Look at all this! I feel like I'm at the Oscars!'

I would tell him to knock it off and not be so dramatic, but to be honest I know what he means. I'm in black jeans and black top – after failing to nail 'being fancy' I've gone back to my simplified French chic style of dressing, but I feel underdressed as the star of the hour. I should have worn my tutu! Star and Lucy have put so much effort into this that I hope they can tell I've given loads of thought to my outfit!

'Taylor?'

I turn around. Ms K is stood looking distinctly … mad. Huh.

'Hi, Ms K.'

'Ms K!' Grandad says gleefully. 'Oh, we've heard so much about you! You have such a great influence on our budding journo here. She really looks up to you. I still remember my English teacher. Mr O'Groat. He used to talk and talk and talk – loved the sound of his own voice – but to be fair, so did we all! He'd give these long winding lectures about what we were reading and the art of storytelling. Not that I'm much good at any of that stuff, you know, but a love of stories must run in our family somehow, considering Erica and Taylor have both gone on to write! Makes you wonder what else could have been, you know? If kids of my generation had been given more opportunities. Anyway. Listen to me, giving you a monologue of my own! All I mean is: it's a pleasure.'

He holds out a hand and Ms K shakes it.

'Nice to meet you,' she says, and she nods acknowledgement at Mum and Grandma too, before looking at me and saying, 'Taylor? A word, please?'

I follow her back through the streamers of the entrance and stand just off from the door. My tummy lurches and my palms clam up. My body seems to be warning me: *Beware, this is not good.*

'Taylor, I do not take any joy in saying this,' Ms K begins, a hand running over her stomach, her neck flushed pink and blotchy.

I furrow my brow, knitting my eyebrows together. *Uh-oh.*

But before Ms K can tell me what, exactly, she needs a word about, we suddenly hear a big *whoosh* noise, and then are plunged into darkness.

'What the … ?' I say, looking all around me for a clue. Half of me thinks this is like at a birthday party when you turn out the lights to bring out the candle-laden cake. The other half of me, though, knows that isn't right, and actually what we've got is a blackout.

'Everyone stay calm!' I hear Lucy say, in her bossy voice. I've never been so pleased to have a friend with such leadership skills. My voice has left my throat! I don't want to be the girl who throws a big launch party IN THE DARK!! 'This is a temporary glitch, please keep your senses of humour and bear with us!'

Nobody really talks, just murmurs amongst themselves and waits to see what will happen. Somebody moves back the streamers by the door and lets light spill in from outside. It doesn't totally light up the place, but it sheds enough light that we can see one another's faces. Oh! It was Ms K. Clever Ms K.

'You all right, Ms K?' I say, remembering we were on the verge of A Chat, capital A, capital C.

She steps off to the side, near the door, and I follow her.

'Taylor,' she says, voice low so nobody else can hear us. 'Of course I applaud your journalistic ambitions, and believe in the fourth estate, the freedom of the press, but, well, long story short, you've betrayed my privacy, and I am very upset about it.'

'Betrayed your privacy, miss?' I say. I don't understand what she means. It's not like I know some big secret about her and I've gone blabbing it all around. I honestly have no idea what she means!

'One of your articles, Taylor. You talk about how you walked in on me asleep at my desk? Nauseous? Those are private details that happened on a human level, not "colour" to add interest to one of your articles.'

Ohmygosh. Did I really put that in one of my pieces? I don't remember! If I did, I can understand why she's annoyed.

'Oh,' I say. 'I'm really sorry. I mustn't have thought it was a big deal, or that you wouldn't mind ... I would never deliberately write about somebody if they didn't want me to ...'

I trail off, because at the end of the day, I know that no matter what my intentions were or weren't, if Ms K says I've crossed a line? I've crossed a line. And the thought of that, of upsetting somebody as tremendous as Ms K, well, it makes me feel sick.

'I feel really embarrassed, Ms K. I'll take it down right away.'

She nods. 'I would appreciate that, Taylor,' she says. Then she adds: 'Look. You're talented and ambitious and really good at coming up with angles for stories, with ideas that connect with people. The whole premise of "Taylor Blake Seizes the Day" is smart, and a gold mine for showcasing what you're capable of. And I saw the mission statement for *The Instruction Manual* – I know how you essentially don't want to be constricted by the school newspaper, which I absolutely understand. But I need *you* to understand that the rules we have for the *Register* exist to maintain integrity, and you'll need some rules of your own if *The Instruction Manual* is going to succeed.'

Hot tears prick at my eyes. I can't believe I've upset her this much! I feel like a stupid little kid.

'Don't cry, Taylor,' she says, not unkindly. She reaches out a hand to my arm and gives it a pat. 'I don't want to upset you. Just be careful what you write, that's all.'

I try my very best to hold back the tears from spilling over.

'OK,' I say, my voice small.

'Oh, come here,' Ms K says, opening her arms out wide. I accept the hug, taking the opportunity to catch some deep breaths.

'There you are.'

I pull away. It's Lucy.

'Here I am,' I say, trying to sound bright and not mortified and chastised. Ms K puts a hand on my shoulder and says, 'Thank you for hearing me out, Taylor. Have a good night.' And then instead of going back into the party, she leaves.

I look at Lucy. 'Whoa,' I say to her. 'You'll never guess what just happened.'

But Lucy's face is serious and cross – it's not the face of somebody who wants to hear my tales. She looks … well. Furious.

'Taylor,' she says, and one part of my brain knows exactly what she's going to say before the other part of my brain can catch up. Very slowly, like my brain is underwater and so everything is blurry and slow, I know for a fact that she's mad at me too.

'You've written about my mum's new job,' she says, like she can't believe it. 'That's none of your business. She's not even told Mr Logan yet – you need to take it down. You're going to get me into trouble! We might not have power, but people are still passing the time by going on the website on their phones!'

Did I really write that? I mean, I must have if she's saying I did. I've been so tired, just trying to check all the boxes and get stuff done that half of the past few weeks doesn't even log in my head!

'Take it down now, Taylor! There are so many people here! And Mum is going to be here any minute!'

I blink, not quite processing the information.

She ushers me through a side door I hadn't even noticed before, where there's her laptop. There's also Star and Paul in the middle of what seems to be a really massive argument.

'What's going on?' Lucy asks, right as the lights come back on. It's really weird, but both Star and Paul have got blue lips, the blue smearing out on to their faces.

Star looks at Paul like she's so angry she could burst into flames. Paul looks away guiltily.

'Are you going to explain, or shall I?' Star says, and honestly it's kind of scary how mad she is. What could Paul possibly have done?

'I thought it would be romantic!' Paul says, like he might cry. 'I didn't know. I'm sorry!'

Star's face softens ever so slightly, and Lucy goes over to her and laces a hand through hers. 'What happened?' Lucy asks softly.

'It was me,' Paul offers. 'I turned off the lights at the fuse box because I wanted to …'

He trails off.

'You wanted to what?' I ask. Duncan comes in then.

'Oh, there you all are!' he says brightly. Then he seems to clock the mood of the room and lowers his voice to say, 'What's happened now?'

Paul looks at him, fear etched on his face.

Lucy looks at Paul's blue mouth, then Star's, and you can see a sort of realisation dawn on her face.

'Did you two kiss?!' she says, shocked. 'Star, did Paul *make* your mouth blue?'

'No!' shrieks Paul, his cheeks flaming red. 'I … I'm so sorry. It wasn't like that. I didn't know you were together!' he says, like he's begging for forgiveness. 'I'm sorry!'

Star says quietly, 'Paul tripped the lights so we could have some big romantic moment in the dark. The gifts … we've found the culprit.'

'It was you?' Lucy says in wonder. 'Oh my god.'

'Oh, mate,' Duncan says. 'You absolute pillock. And you've both been eating cupcakes, haven't you? It's the blue icing.' He gestures to his mouth, letting them know they both look ridiculous. 'Half the people out there have got blue mouths too!'

Paul wipes his mouth with the back of his hand, looking more embarrassed than I've ever seen any Year 9 boy be. 'You're always talking about these big romantic moments you and Taylor have, Duncan! I was trying to be like you!'

'He asked to kiss me, I said no, and then you lot all burst in,' Star says. She and Lucy look at each other, and I can tell they're making a silent pact not to berate the boy any further. He's absolutely mortified. Meanwhile all I can think is: Duncan talks about me! To his best friend! This is excellent!

'Paul, come on, mate,' Duncan says. 'Let's leave the girls to it, shall we? We can give out napkins – everyone needs them after those blue cakes.'

Duncan and Paul leave, and I'm left with the girls. I'm about to launch into a million questions about how Star ended up in here alone with Paul, how exactly he asked to kiss her, all of that – but Lucy spins her laptop towards me and says: 'Can you fix this, please?'

She's using her phone as a hotspot. I'm shaking as I log on to the site and 'unpublish' the article she means – 'Taylor Blake Does Something For Others'.

'OK,' I say, and it's the first time I've spoken in ages. My voice comes out all shaky and weak. 'It's gone.'

Lucy shakes her head. 'Good,' she says. 'Mum is gonna be sooooooo mad. I'm going to have to come clean about it. She hates lying.'

I nod.

'Sorry,' I say. 'I didn't think …'

'No,' she says. 'It's OK. People make mistakes. Thanks for fixing it so quick.'

This night has gone downhill fast. Lucy says she needs to go and check on the food and I take a moment to catch my breath, to do a couple of inhales and exhales to calm down. I think of Ms K, and so whilst I've got Lucy's laptop I decide to 'unpublish' the column that mentions her too. It's for the best.

I re-enter the party and try to keep smiling, saying hi to people as I pass, and it's not until I see him that I realise I'm looking for Duncan. He's stood with his back to me, reading one of the articles projected on to one of the screens. As I approach him, I can see it's the piece about pursuing a second kiss, and reaching out to touch his shoulder, I can tell by the way he tenses that he's upset about something.

'Hey,' he says neutrally.

'Hey,' I say, for a brief moment daring to believe that actually, he's the one person in this room *not* mad at me.

'This article,' he says, gesturing with his thumb. 'I haven't seen it before.'

I look at the screen, even though I know exactly what he's on about.

'Last-minute addition,' I say. 'Is it too … ?'

I don't know what I'm trying to ask.

'It's very personal,' Duncan says, frowning at the screen again, like he can't figure something out. I stand next to him and look at the screen too.

'Ms K is mad at me,' I say. 'For writing about her. And Lucy is too. I feel like I've scored the hat trick, now, with you.'

Duncan pulls a face, cocking his head.

'I'm not mad,' he says. 'But I do think it's interesting. You should be able to write whatever you want – that's what we said the point of the website was, right? But you've also written about me, and I don't know how I feel about that. It feels like you've told my secrets as well as your own. You've talked about *my* first kiss being with you, for example. That's …'

He doesn't get to conclude what it is, because I interrupt, frantic.

'I'll delete it!' I tell him, my heart breaking. Duncan is the best, loveliest, nicest person in the whole world – I don't want to tell his secrets! 'I really didn't mean to drag you into it, to betray your confidence or anything. That's what Ms K says I've done. I'm sorry, Duncan!'

He nods. 'I'm not about to scream and shout or anything,' he says. 'I'm mulling it over in an academic way. Like OK, what are the boundaries here? I just need some time to let it marinate. I wish you'd have run it by me, is all. You know? I feel … I don't know. I'm not very good at confrontation.' He gives a half-hearted *ha ha* after saying that, and he sounds so upset that when I nod, tears prickle hot and heavy at my eyes.

'OK,' I say, and in the space of half an hour this party has gone from the best thing ever to the worst.

'Duncan! I can't believe this! This is all so great, bro!'

We're interrupted by Duncan's stepbrother Melvin, and I issue him a weak smile before I excuse myself to go to the toilets and cry. I'm nearly there when Grandma intercepts me.

'Taylor!' she says. 'My love! Come here!' She opens her

arms out wide and I sink into her embrace. She doesn't even need me to tell her I'm upset: she knows, in a way only grandmas can.

The whole thing comes pouring out of me, about Ms K, about Lucy, and now about Duncan. I've majorly messed up! I thought I was writing honest truths but I wasn't! I was being a bad person!

'Shhhh,' Grandma says, stroking my hair and not caring that I'm making her blouse wet with my tears. 'I know if anyone asked you to change anything or take it down you would do in a heartbeat,' she says. 'That's just who you are. You're not a bad person who hurts people just for fun, are you?'

'No!' I wail. 'I'm not! But I have done! I *have* hurt people!'

'Everything is fixable,' Grandma soothes. 'I promise you. I do.'

We stand like that, Grandma comforting me, for I don't know how long. It's long enough that I find a way to breathe normally again.

When I finally pull away, Grandma looks me up and down, and then stares into my face hard, trying to figure out what she should do with me.

'It's a big thing you've done,' she says finally. 'Are you feeling like you've had enough? Do you want to go home?'

It's not until she says it that I realise that yes, I do. I can't do this any more: trying to write articles and be this big fancy opinions journalist and have a huge, 'special' life. I just want my *Toy Story* PJs, and my bed, and to sleep in in the morning without setting an alarm. I want to be in Star's bedroom with her and Lucy, not a care in the world, just us and our Tom Holland and Harry Styles fanfiction, writing stupid things to make each other laugh. I want to be Ms K's favourite, and to FaceTime Axel without worrying Mum is flirting with his dad, and I want beans beside toast at Grandma and Grandad's.

Basically, I just want everything to go back to being simple. And easy. And uncomplicated.

I look around the room at all these people, most of them touting an *Instruction Manual* goodie bag, and it all makes me feel so incredibly sleepy. I've had enough of it all. It's too hard, and I still get it wrong.

'Yes,' I tell Grandma. 'I want to go home.'

'Come on then, you,' she says, putting an arm around me. 'Let's get you off.'

Grandma leads me towards the exit, tugging on Grandad's sleeve on the way, and letting him know with a look that the evening is over. Mum follows, and in the cool night air I feel like I can finally breathe again.

'You OK?' Mum says, and I shake my head.

'Are you trying to hook up with Axel's dad?' I say, as a response.

Mum's mouth flops open, like a fish, and she briefly looks at Grandma before looking back at me.

'Let's talk about that later,' she says, pointing her keys at the car. 'Mum, Dad, you get yourselves off. I'll take Taylor home.'

Grandma and Grandad fuss about me, saying goodbye, and then I climb in the car with Mum and we drive home in silence.

19

I'm so ashamed. I've gone through all of the columns and decided to 'unpublish' most of them, leaving only my original column about why I want to seize the day, with an invitation for people to seize their own days and tell us how they're doing it. That's it. Ideally I'd like to delete that too, but we need *something* on the site. Now it's been pointed out to me, I can see how in trying to tell my own story, I've also revealed other people's. And that's none of my business – I've got no right to do that. It makes me sick to my stomach that I've screwed up this way, and even worse that it's with the people I care about. I texted Lucy and got nothing, and texted Duncan *I'm going to unpublish the columns* and just got *OK. It's up to you.* I don't go to form time in the morning because I can't bear the notion of Lucy ignoring me, but it turns out she's off today anyway.

Star says it will be OK, just give her time. I see Duncan once, from a distance down the corridor, but he's gone into the humanities block before I can catch him. I don't see him at lunch, either. I assume he's avoiding me.

The (only) good news is, we've got a netball tournament today, so I get to miss an afternoon of school and go on a coach with the squad to the leisure centre beside Lady Manners School and play a million netball matches one after the other, i.e. I get to be in my body, instead of my head. Once again I am thankful that seizing the day brought me netball, especially when it's caused me to lose so much more. I've never been part of a sports team before, and I have to admit it feels nice to be with a bunch of girls who almost certainly have no idea about *The Instruction Manual* and *Seizing the Day*. The netball team are all so sporty and focused on being fit that none of them ever wrote for the school mag unless it was a match report, and I've never talked to them about it because I just figured they wouldn't be that interested. I'm pleased though, because although they're all girls I'd probably never normally hang out with, united by netball, we get on. It's such a welcome escape. I can't believe I ever thought netball girls were snooty. I like them all!

'Right, girls,' Ms Perkins says from the front of the bus. 'Almost there. I'm super confident in our chances today, so I just want you to focus on great manners, representing the school well, and staying dignified and calm. No outward displays of victory that could rub other teams' noses in it or anything like that: same rule as always. Play well, encourage each other, thank the other team and the umpire at the end. Any questions?'

We're silent.

'OK, great. We've got a warm-up area where we can limber up and leave our stuff, and our first game is in half an hour. Let's do this!'

There's excitement in the air as we step off the coach, a sea of girls in joggers or netball shorts milling around, taking over every square inch of the leisure centre indoor courts: the floor, all available chairs, the toilets. There are players everywhere! Girls are stretching and running laps around the humongous row of courts (seriously, it's, like, eight netball courts all lined up side by side! Madness!). We find our area and start doing the same. My heart beats faster, adrenaline coursing through me.

'You good?' Josie asks me.

'Yeah,' I say. 'I mean, this is … a lot.'

Josie nods. 'Last year we came third. We played eight matches over six hours and afterwards I thought I'd never be able to walk again! But at the time I didn't feel it, you know? I was just high on playing. I love it! I love it so much!'

I must pull a face – I don't mean to – because Josie adds, 'It's addictive! Don't look at me like that! You'll see …'

I'm benched for the first game, because apparently it's against a 'C-level' squad and so Ms Perkins says for me to save my energy. Josie is benched too, and our goal defence Sabah. Despite playing netball now, I don't think I have ever sat and watched a match from beginning to end – it's actually amazing!

'Yes, Darcey!' I squeal to our wing defence as she intercepts a pass between the other team and immediately pivots to send the ball over to our goal shooter. Elegantly throwing the ball into the net, Joanne gets us our first point of the match. 'Come on, baby!' I yell, clapping madly. Ms Perkins gives me A Look. I remember what she said about decorum and grace. I purse my lips together and try to calm down.

The thing is, this is incredible. We win the first match, 4–1, and it sets us in good spirits. The girls all pat each other on the back and say good job and well done, and it feels good to be on a team being so nice to each other. I jump up and down on the spot as we assume positions for the second match, marked by a girl shorter than me from Lower Lane, who I decide before we play doesn't stand a chance. I might not be a good journalist or columnist or even a very good friend, but today I will be good at netball. I will be good at *something*!!

Josie passes me the ball and I leap through the air to catch it, breeze in my hair, smile on my face. I pivot, send it back to her as she fakes left and goes right, into a space, and then she sends it on the goal attack, who sends it to the goal ... but misses.

'That's OK!' I shout, even though I don't mean it. I want to WIN. I want this to be a success, when everything else in my sad old life feels so RUBBISH at the minute.

We go again, ball coming from the sideline from their side and frustratingly passed to their end of the court. They get a goal! URGH! This isn't how this is supposed to go.

'Keep your cool, ladies,' Ms Perkins shouts, and Josie claps her hands together to cheer, 'We're good, team! Eye on the ball!'

'Yeah,' says the girl marking me. 'Eye on the ball as it goes into our goal.' She snort laughs, and then the game restarts, her horrid smarmy laugh echoing in my head as I try to evade her.

'Here!' I shout after I've lost her, but right as Sabah sends me the ball my annoying little friend is back, and intercepts.

'Don't worry about it!' Ms Perkins coaches from the sideline. 'Stay focused, Blake!'

'Or don't,' my friend whispers to me as she stands *very* close.

I look at her. 'What's your problem?' I say, and to show that she doesn't scare me, I lean towards her so there's barely millimetres between us. She steps back, showing it's true what they say: bullies don't like displays of strength. I don't think she was expecting me to stand up for myself.

'You're *such* a wet cabbage,' she says, and I'm so shocked I miss the ball when it is thrown at me, watching it helplessly as it sails past and the other team get to throw it in.

I will *not* let this bully intimidate me! I decide to play like I have never played before, ignoring my marker like she doesn't even exist, and my plan actually works – we win! Only by one goal, which is closer than any of us would have liked, but still. TAKE THAT, RUDE WING DEFENCE!

And she really is rude – I do what Ms Perkins instructed and go to shake her hand at the end of the game, and she walks off! I look up to catch somebody's eye so they see it too, but everyone is busy being pied off by *their* player! THE WHOLE TEAM IS RUDE!

'Rise above it,' Ms Perkins says, after their coach refused to shake her hand too. 'Like Michelle Obama, when they go low, we go high. OK?'

We agree that yes, of course, let's just focus on our next match. But Lower Lane have a break then, so come and stand quite menacingly around our court, loudly cheering for the other team.

'Can you believe this lot?' I say to Josie, loud enough for them to hear. 'Pathetic.'

I know that's not exactly taking the high road, but god! You'd think even if they were mannerless, they'd still be reined in by their teacher!

'Who are you calling pathetic?' the wing defence from before says, but I pretend not to hear her.

Turns out, that's a mistake. We make it into the semi-final and win, which is so amazing that we end up flinging ourselves into one another's arms and celebrating like we're the champions already – it's exhausting, playing so many games one after the other, but in that moment I think the word is *exhilarating*. Like oh! You work really hard and then get a good result! YES! THAT IS HOW IT IS SUPPOSED TO WORK!

Lower Lane have got faces like thunder. I'm not sure where they came in proceedings, but they haven't played in the quarter-finals so it can't have been a very good day for them. No need to take Crickleton's win so personally, though, is there? Is not our fault they're not very good.

Our team gather in our changing room for a pep talk where Ms Perkins runs over strategy and tells us she's proud of us no matter what – that today has been some of the best netball she's seen from us. She even singles me out, says I'm on the right track for her player of the matches again! How about that!! Player of the TOURNAMENT!!

Ms Perkins leaves, and we take a minute to refuel: we've got those blue drinks with electrolytes in, and some peanut butter protein balls that Sabah's older brother makes. It barely registers that other people have joined us in the changing room until the other girls all fall silent. I look up. It's the Lower Lane lot, my wing defence stood in front with a ball, throwing it up and catching it like invading the personal space of another team is totally normal.

Nobody speaks. Wing Defence just tosses up the ball and catches it, tosses up the ball and catches it. She looks right at me. I raise an eyebrow and pull a face, like: *What?* I'm not going to speak first! She's stood there like we should be afraid of her or something. Like *I* should be afraid of her.

'This changing room is just for Crickleton High,' Darcey says. 'Do you need something?'

'Yeah, actually,' Wing Defence says. 'SHE owes us an apology.'

She points at me.

'Me?' I say, not even bothering to get up. This is all so ridiculous.

'You were the one who called us pathetic, weren't you?' Wing Defence says. 'So yeah, *you.*'

I look around at my teammates, trying to communicate with my face that these girls are *crazy*. But most of them look legitimately afraid something bad is about to happen. Not even Josie is saying anything, she's just looking around like she's establishing where the emergency exit is, like this might all descend into one big mass brawl. I've never been in a fight in my life! But suddenly this feels ... sinister. The changing room feels claustrophobic and dangerous. Maybe I've played this wrong. Maybe I should just say sorry.

'I didn't call *you* pathetic,' I say with a shrug. 'I meant when you were all cheering for the other team it was pathetic. Like, not very sportsman-like.'

'We can cheer for whoever we want,' Wing Defence says, stepping towards me. Then she says, 'Think fast!' and lobs the ball at me so it hits me square in the nose.

'OUCH!' I shriek, dropping the last of my protein ball to the ground and grabbing my face. Blood is pouring out of me and on to my white trainers in big globs.

'OHMYGOD!' I hear somebody cry, and then the girls are all stood up and there's a hive of activity and Lower Lane must run off because all I can see is our team colours and wads of tissue, my eyes watering like they never have before. I think I'm in shock – I can't speak. But the others are doing plenty of that for me. They're all saying variations of *I can't believe it* and *What a cow!* and *I knew something was going to happen, Lower Lane are known for being vicious.*

'Ms Perkins!' somebody shouts, and then Ms Perkins is there, kneeling in front of me – I must have sat down at some point. I'm on the bench, a wad of blue roll at my face, just ... dazed, I guess.

'Taylor, can you see how many fingers I'm holding up?' Ms Perkins asks, and I say, my voice sounding very far away, 'Three, miss.'

'Good, OK. Just keep holding your head forward and swapping the tissue every few minutes. Now, can somebody tell me what the hell happened here? And, Josie – get the girl some ice, would you please?!'

Ice is found and it hurts to put it to my face, which feels like it's been punched by a giant rather than had a ball thrown at it. Who knew a ball could hurt so much! It's tender all around my nose, across my eyes, on my forehead ... god. What if it bruises? Am I going to have a bruise? I don't even know if I have enough make-up to cover a bruise!

I can't believe that player did that! That stupid, horrible, girl!

'We have to win!' I say to the girls, who have fallen into an eerie silence as Ms Perkins stands outside the changing rooms yelling at the coach from Lower Lane. It's hard to make out every word she's saying because of the cheers coming from the games in session, but I catch *despicable* and *forfeit* and *outrageous*.

'Taylor, you know you can't play now, don't you?' Sabah asks gently. 'We can go out there and win for you but ...'

'Your face,' Josie supplies. 'You need to rest.'

I nod. 'Go and win then,' I say, and what do you know? They do!

It's not long before the buzz of our victory wears off. By the time the coach brings us home I am sore and emotional. My high from the day has gone, and reality has set in: now, not only am I back in a world where everyone is upset with me, I'm back looking like I've had a disagreement with a lamp-post.

'Taylor, darling, what the hell happened?!' Mum asks, when I get in the car. I'm about to tell her when Ms Perkins comes and knocks on Mum's car window, and explains that the girl who did this is disqualified from area competitions forever, and her coach has suspended her from the team for the rest of the year.

'I should think so,' Mum says. 'Thanks, Ms Perkins. I'll get her home, now, thanks.'

Mum tries to make conversation, but it hurts to talk so I'm not really up for chatting. I ache, and just want to lie in a nice hot bath with loads of bubbles from my Body Shop collection. I think about texting Members Only to let the girls know what happened, but we haven't talked as a threesome today. Duncan too – it's not like him to be so distant, a bit off. I suppose I could call Axel, but I don't want to risk having to say hello to his dad or even *thinking* about my mum and him. Mum could walk in and start flirting and that would do the opposite of cheering me up. I decide to drop everyone a *Hey! How was your day?* message, just in case anyone feels like they do actually want to talk to me.

Lying there in the semi-dark, letting myself float in the water, I feel ... lonely. I've been working so hard lately to seize the day, and yet right now is probably the loneliest I've ever felt. Hurting people you love is the worst feeling *ever, ever, ever.*

Mum lets me have a cheese toastie in my room, in bed, where I sit with my iPad. I scroll through Netflix but don't really fancy anything, and look at my news app but nothing is going in. I'm opening and closing apps half-heartedly, and don't even realise I'm logging into *The Instruction Manual* inbox until I'm blinking hard, trying to figure out what I'm seeing.

There's almost a hundred emails!

Most of them have the subject line 'Seize the Day' or similar, which makes my tummy flip because at first I assume they're telling me off. But as I open the first one with only one eye open – the other squeezed shut like that might protect me – it becomes clear: people have sent in their own ways of seizing the day, just like we asked them for. And they've been nice about the launch and the columns they read back when they were still up!

OMG!

One email says:

Dear Taylor,

Your Seize the Day articles have really inspired me, and I just wanted to write and let you know to keep it up! It's made me think of one of my older sister's favourite films, where one of the characters says, 'You're supposed be the leading lady in your own life!' It's sort of like, if we seize the day, we get to become the leading characters in our own stories, don't we? That's how I think of it, anyway.

From,
Hallie Stones

Another:

Hello. I've never written to anyone I don't know before, so this feels really strange! But I really like your Seize the Day piece! It has made me think about how I can seize the day too! Like just trying new stuff, maybe, because what have we got to lose! So thanks!!

And:

> *I can't find your Seize the Day columns on the website any more, but I LOVED THEM at the launch party. You're a good writer! I like to seize the day by being nice to people. Some people might think that's wet but I just think when you're nice to people, every day is nicer. Try it! You might think so too! From, Lawrence Parker*

A big wet dollop of something lands on my hand as I scroll: I'm crying. I'm sobbing, in fact! This is the best thing that has ever happened to me! All I've ever wanted is people to like what I write! AND THEY DO! Praise be!!!! What a marvellous ray of sunshine when everything else feels so dark and grey!! Nobody has texted me back and it is weighing on me, but these emails are a comfort – and that is not nothing.

20

Right. I've made a decision. This is Operation Be a Superb Human – I need to sort out my life, person by person, until I like it again – starting with myself. What have I become, racing from one thing to another? I'm tired, neglectful, and far from making me *more* engaged with life, I'm so knackered I just want to be in bed! Well, no more. I've woken up feeling like I've had a big revelation, like things are quite a bit clearer to me. Those emails last night … they've made me feel like I *can* contribute something to the world. But, actually, my contributions don't have to be these big sweeping adventures that are tiring and manic, just so I can I distil them into stories. My contributions can be small, intimate moments and gestures to the people I love, so I can make them feel as seen and appreciated as those emails have made me feel.

Maybe it's not about doing more for the sake of more, but doing less and making sure it's only the meaningful stuff I keep?

Anyway. I can't lie, I did consult my Bible for inspiration. *How to Be Parisian When You're Not from Paris* says:

On Apologies
When a life is lived with passion and vim, it makes sense that on occasion the Parisian woman can inadvertently upset or offend. When this happens, she is quick and heartfelt in making amends, owning her mistakes and taking steps to ensure it will not happen again. She gives flowers, hand-delivers thoughtful notes, and makes time for the people she loves.

First up, an easy win: Grandma and Grandad. I haven't upset them and so obviously I have nothing to make amends for, but I want to create special moments for everyone I love and I know they'll be receptive to my efforts. They love me no matter what, and I don't think I've ever annoyed them or upset them in my whole fourteen years of being alive, which is more than I can say for literally *anybody* else. I decide to stop at the bakery and spend some of the birthday money I have saved on their favourite cakes: an 'elephant's foot' for Grandma (it's a chocolate bun with cream in the middle, all misshapen like a big elephant's foot, hence the name) and a jam-and-cream doughnut for Grandad. I wasn't going to get myself anything, because this is all about them – but when I see the cupcakes I decide it would be bad manners to sit and watch them eat without having anything myself, so add one to my order.

I walk up there. I know my face is a mess from netball, because 1) I have a mirror, 2) the woman who served me asked who won the fight (literally, does she know it actually was a fight!) (well, kind of) (gosh, would I have hurt that girl back if I'd had the chance?! I can't even imagine throwing a punch!!) and 3) it hurts. A few people I pass do a double take at the strange girl with the black-and-blue face, but what can I do? Explain to every single person as I go by? I don't think so!

Anyway. Reason number 4 I know my face is bad? When I let myself into Grandma and Grandad's, Grandad looks up from where he's sat doing his crossword and drinking his tea, and literally spits it all out over himself and then has a coughing fit.

'David?' Grandma yells from the kitchen. I hear the clatter of pots that comes with her unloading the dishwasher. 'David!' she says, louder, when his coughing fit doesn't stop.

'Hello to you too,' I say, patting him on the back. 'Thanks for making me feel like a leper. I appreciate that.'

Grandma comes through and *shrieks* when she sees me.

'Taylor!' she says. 'What the … ? Is this from yesterday?!'

'Yes,' I admit. 'Not my finest hour. Is it really horrible to look at?'

Grandma opens her arms to hug me, and I let her hold on for longer than is strictly necessary.

'I'm OK!' I say, into the fabric of her jumper. She's squishing tight. 'I'm alive! It was just a ball to the face! It could have happened to anybody!'

'That's not the way Erica tells the story,' Grandma says. 'She says another player off a *very bad team* singled you out.'

'Well, when you put it like that …' I say sheepishly. Singled out? That makes it sound so bad!

'Taylor,' Grandma says seriously. 'You know this is pretty major, don't you? You understand that? This was *assault*, and that girl needs real, serious consequences.'

'She got them,' I say. 'I promise. Can we talk about something else now, please? I know you're just worried, but …' I hold up the box from the bakery. 'I've bought cake! I thought we could sit in the garden and eat it? With a cup of tea?'

Grandma's face goes from concerned, to puzzled, to something softer. 'Well,' she says, evidently deciding to let the conversation move on. 'That's unexpected. What's the occasion?'

'No occasion,' I say, going into the kitchen to get plates

and cake forks. 'I just wanted to spend some proper time with you.'

Grandad gets up and opens the patio door, letting in the fresh air. 'Well,' he says. 'Beautiful day for it. I'd never turn down cake and my best girl.'

'The question is,' I tease. 'Which comes top? Me or the cake?'

'Oh,' says Grandad. 'The cake, of course.' He comes to the kitchen and kisses me on the head. 'But you are a *very* close second, poppet.'

We have a really nice morning, just sitting and looking at the garden and chatting and laughing. Grandad tells me about some drama at the Northern Soul night they were at last night, and Grandma says we should plan a day out again soon, because she loved going to London with us all so much.

'I'd like that,' I say. And then I think about my new pledge, my new-found desire to have smaller moments like this. 'But can we do more of this, too?' I say. 'I don't need some big city adventure to have fun with you both. This is my idea of a brilliant time.'

Grandma hits my arm. 'You tease,' she says, with a giggle.

'No!' I say. 'I'm not! I promise! I mean it!'

'Oh, Taylor,' she says, like she might cry. 'You're such a

good girl. Come here. You're going to make an old woman get emotional!'

She loops an arm over my shoulder and pulls me in tight, and then Grandad leans in too.

'Well, aren't we just a bunch of feelings today!' he chuckles. 'I love it! You two are nuts! And nuts are my favourite.'

Next on my list is Duncan. Keeping on my cake theme, I decide to make him one like he had on his birthday. I know he likes chocolate cake, and Grandad makes a great one, so I figure why not leave one on his doorstep as a way to remind him I pay attention to him, care about him? He said he needs some space, so this feels like the best solution: he doesn't have to see me, but I can still remind him I exist and that I'm not *all* bad and I really am sorry. I get it now: what happens between me and Duncan is strictly personal, strictly private.

'So it's going well then, with Duncan?' Grandad asks as he melts some butter and measures out some milk.

'Kind of,' I say, putting a coffee pod in their fancy machine to make a small espresso. It's Grandad's secret chocolate cake ingredient – it doesn't make the cake taste like coffee, it makes the chocolate taste more chocolatey? I know. It doesn't make sense to me either, but trust me! It works.

'Kind of?' Grandad clarifies. He hands me the baking tin. 'Just grease these, would you? We should have started with that.'

'I sort of wrote about him,' I admit, putting the butter on some kitchen roll and getting to work. 'And he said he didn't mind, but …' I can feel myself blushing, 'Well, I've come to understand that it's not OK, including other people's stories in my work. Like, people deserve privacy, so I need to write in a way that gives my point of view, without speaking for anybody else.'

Grandad absorbs this, adding the cake mix to the bowl and gently folding everything in.

'This needs the electric whisk now,' he says, and for two minutes I watch him make the mixture into a fluffy batter that can go into the greased tins. Once they're in the oven he says, 'You know. Your maturity astounds me.'

'Mine?' I ask.

'Yes,' he presses, leaning against the kitchen counter. 'Saying you've learned what is appropriate to write about and what isn't – that's a big thing for anybody, let alone a fourteen-year-old. And I don't mean to sound patronising when I say that. Honestly. You're so intelligent, so insightful. I'm so proud of you.'

'Grandad!' I say, welling up once again. I am forever on the edge of tears lately!

'Taylor!' Grandad mimics. I laugh.

'You're always so kind to me,' I say. 'I'm the luckiest granddaughter ever.'

'I'm the lucky one, kid,' he says, ruffling my hair. 'I really am. Just don't be too hard on yourself, OK? Believe it or not, even I still get things wrong sometimes, or make a wee misstep.'

Grandma comes in then, just in time to say, 'Oh, that's right. I've got a list of his mistakes, with dates and times noted, if anyone would care to see it?'

'Hey, you!' Grandad chuckles. 'Your poop stinks too, you know!'

'Yeah, yeah,' Grandma says. 'I'm not perfect either. But then who is?'

I pull a face. 'I think Duncan might be,' I say, and I actually mean it. He is!

Grandad drives me home, and on the way we stop at Duncan's massive mansion to deliver the cake. Ronnie answers the door, her smile as big and friendly as ever.

'Taylor!' she says. 'Oh, I'm so sorry, he's not here! He's away for the weekend with his mum and stepdad! Bit of a last-minute thing.'

'I made him this,' I say, offering up the cake. 'It should keep, so, just give it him when he's back?' I add. 'I didn't know he was away.'

'He didn't tell you?'

I shrug. 'I've been a bit out of it,' I say, and Ronnie looks at me sympathetically.

'Your face …' she says. 'Are you all right?'

'Netball accident,' I tell her. 'And with the website launch and everything, it's all been a bit mad. Duncan probably didn't get chance to tell me he'd changed his birthday weekend plans …'

'Well, he'll be so thrilled with this. Chocolate cake is his favourite.'

'I know.' I smile, glad to have got something right. 'Well, I'd better go. Tell him happy birthday from me?'

'He's got his phone, you know, if you wanted to text …'

I don't mention he's ignoring me.

'OK,' I say. 'Thanks.'

When I get back in the car Grandad says, 'You OK?'

'Yeah,' I lie. 'I'm OK.'

It's been at the back of my mind all day that somebody else I need to pay some attention to is Mum. Ever since overhearing her phone call with Lucas, I've not really been myself around her, and of course she's noticed. In *Raising Empowered Teens*, Mum's second-favourite book after *How to Be Parisian* …, I know it says teenagers need space, and I think both me and Mum have been surprised by how well we get on and how much time we genuinely like spending together. So it's been obvious, my weirdness, and I think I owe her an explanation.

'Mum?' I say, when I get home.

'Hey, bug,' she says. She's on the sofa reading and listening to some chilled-out jazz music. 'Good day?'

'Yeah,' I say.

'And how's your face?'

'Sore,' I tell her. 'But all right. It's more everyone else's reaction that reminds me of it.'

'I get that,' she says. 'I hope it heals quickly for you.'

I wander over and sit at the far end of the sofa, where her feet are.

'Mum?' I say, and she closes her book, folding the corner of a page down and giving me her full attention.

'Taylor?' she says back. I smile, mockingly rolling my eyes. 'Sorry,' she says.

'Shall we go for a Starbucks?' I ask.

'Now?' she says, surprised.

'Why not?' I ask.

'So what's the occasion?' Mum asks, once we've got our drinks and we've found a table in the corner by the window overlooking the high street. 'Or is this a "just because" kind of a thing?'

I use my straw to stir my drink, not quite able to meet her eye.

'Well,' I begin. 'I just wanted to say that I know I've been a bit ...' I trail off, and let the silence hang between us.

'Moody?' Mum supplies eventually.

I dare to look at her. She's amused, her lips upturned into a smile.

'Yes,' I say back in a funny voice, and she smiles at me.

'You don't always have to be a Smiling Sally for me to love you, you know,' Mum says. 'You're a teenager. Being a bit sullen sometimes is forgivable.'

'Did you read that in your book?' I tease.

She chuckles. 'I did, actually,' she replies. 'But having been a teenager myself, many moons ago, I do remember the drill.'

I nod. It's a fair point.

'What were you like as a teenager?' I ask. 'Were you horrible?'

'Me?' she clarifies. 'Horrible?! No! Never.' I can tell she's over-egging it, pulling my leg a bit. 'OK, well ... sometimes,' she admits. 'I did find everything overwhelming, and I had all these *feelings*, about everything! All the time! I was a walking, talking *feeling*, with my battered and bruised heart on my sleeve. Everything felt so personal. Mum and Dad – Grandma and Grandad – were saints, really. They taught me a lot. You don't realise until you become a parent yourself. I try to do as much of their good stuff as possible, and wing the rest.'

'You're a good mum,' I tell her. 'I don't think I say it often enough. You're the best mum ever, really.'

'Oh, bug!' she says. 'I wasn't fishing!'

'I know,' I say. 'It's just ... you didn't deserve me being moody this week. I understand what you mean about having so many feelings, because that's me.'

'I have spotted that, yes ...' Mum says.

I pull a face. It's one thing for her to notice, but she doesn't need to say it out loud! Not everything needs to be spoken!!

'Anyway,' I press. I take a deep breath. 'Basically I saw you on FaceTime with Axel's dad.'

I had planned to say more than that, to explain it was an accident and she seemed happy when she was chatting to him and to clarify if that's why she's been practising her French, reading her French novels and whatnot. But the rest doesn't come out. The air hangs between us with a heavy pause.

'Yes.' Mum nods slowly. 'I had thought that might be it. After what you said at the launch party about him.'

She doesn't look guilty, or caught out. Nothing like that. She looks ... normal. Maybe a bit relieved?

'You know,' she says. 'It's been interesting, this "Taylor

Blake Seizes the Day" thing. These past few weeks, I've watched you really try to grapple with living your best life. You've been so deliberate, thinking about what you want, how you want to live, what makes sense to wring the most out of life. You've inspired me, really. You have, Taylor. I think you inspire a lot of people around you. I'd like to think you get it from me, but how can you when I haven't been seizing my own days? I've been in a bit of a rut. Teaching, writing, and yes, I have friends, but we go to the same pubs and restaurants, never really try anything new. So when we all went to London, it was as exciting for me as it was for you. And Lucas was this breath of fresh air – handsome, funny, a real gentleman. We just seemed to have so much to talk about! And I think it became apparent very quickly that it could be romantic between us. I can't explain it, really – it was ... magnetic? I just felt really *pulled* to him. I told him I wanted to be careful, because we couldn't ruin the friendship between you and Axel, but at the same time I just thought: I'm in my forties, and I know feeling this way is so rare. So I jumped in, Taylor, with both feet, and ...'

'Do you love him?' I ask. I feel like I'm watching a movie as she talks. No way did I expect some sweeping Hollywood epic like this!

She sighs. 'I'm definitely falling fast,' she says. 'And I don't know how that looks: he lives there, I live here. At our age, we have these vastly different lives. I've wanted to tell you, but I wasn't sure what I'd be telling you *exactly* …' Mum reaches out a hand and slips it into mine. 'I love you so much,' she says. 'And if you really don't want me to pursue things with Lucas, I won't. Just say the word.'

I think about it. 'Sounds like it's too late,' I say. 'Can't get the genie back in the bottle once he's out, can you?'

'I don't know about that,' says Mum. 'I'd never want to upset you. If you really didn't like it, I wouldn't pursue it. I mean that.'

'It's OK,' I say. 'Really. In fact … I guess it's kind of awesome of you.'

Mum looks at me with her crinkly-eyed face, the one she does when she's having lots of feelings.

'I really do love you, you know,' she says.

'I love you too, Mum.'

By the time we get home, I've had an idea. Because, you see, I can't stop thinking about how Mum said she was inspired by me to seize the day. And then all those other people – they wrote and said they were inspired too! But the person who inspired me is Veronica Sellers. I've barely thought of her at all lately, and that's just not right. I can't imagine how awful it must be to get really poorly and then have to miss loads of school to recover. She must be so bored! And maybe even a bit lonely. And so, if I think of how nice it felt for other people to say *I* inspired *them*, imagine how nice it will make Vee feel if she knows it's actually all because of her! What a thing Veronica has taught all of us. I'm going to put all the emails together in a big scrapbook and give it to her, so she can see the effect she's had on us all. If I was her, I'd LOVE it!

My phone beeps. Duncan!!

Thanks for the cake, it says. *Ronnie texted a picture. Looks delicious!*

You're welcome! I say. *Happy birthday!*

Thanks, he replies.

I see him start to type something else, but then he stops and nothing comes through. Urgh! Duncan! Say it! Say what you're thinking!

Can we hang out soon? I type, sending it before I can talk myself out of it.

He doesn't reply, and it gives me an ominous, heavy feeling in my stomach. I don't think this is going to turn out well.

21

I desperately try to push thoughts about Duncan aside. I've started to spiral, because if things go sour between us, will we still talk? Will we still work on the website? I feel like there's so much I want to say to him, but it feels easier to just stick my head in the sand. I almost don't want to know the truth, if that makes sense.

I've decided to focus on an act of service instead – namely Veronica's scrapbook. It's a bigger project than I thought, making it, so I'm well occupied. For some reason Mum had a spare A3 book of coloured sugar paper in her office, so I'm using that and have printed off the nice emails and cut them into different shapes, just to keep it interesting. But OMG my hand aches so much! I have to keep stopping and taking a break to walk around the house and do funny arm stretches.

I've got cloud-shaped emails, stars, ovals, rectangles ... and then on each page where I've glued them I've drawn fun coloured borders and annotated it with things like *This is so cute!* and *You did this! You inspired this!* I think Veronica will like it! Although I wish I'd got Star and Lucy involved, to spread the workload a bit, ha.

On one of my leg stretches I grab my phone and text them photos of my progress.

Members Only

Star: *That's so cool!*

She's gonna love it. Trust!

Lucy: *Guys, Mum wants to take me out to Pizza Express later*

'for a chat'

I'm so nervous

I think she's going to try and make me feel better about moving

Star: *Any more news on that?*

Dates, etc?

Lucy: *Guess I'll find out over my dough balls ...*

Me: *We're here for you*

No matter what she says or what the plan is

We love you!!

Lucy: *I love you both too!!*

Right as I have my phone in my hand, Axel FaceTimes.

'*Bonsoir!*' I say, swiping to answer. I do it in a silly, dramatic voice that I know will make him laugh. It works.

'Taylor! *Mon cherie!*' he laughs. '*Ça va?*'

'Yeah,' I say, and it hits me that I should probably take this opportunity to discuss … *things*. Parents. Their … relationship? I didn't even ask Mum if they're boyfriend and girlfriend! Oh my gosh! What if Mum has a boyfriend before even I do! If things with Duncan are as bad as I think they might be, that he really has gone off me after the launch, they'll be G&G, Axel and Pierre, Mum and Lucas, not to mention Star and Lucy (even long-distance) … and then me, a big fat gooseberry because even the boy I've had my first kiss with thinks I'm unbearable.

'Taylor? Helloooooo?'

I focus back to my phone.

'Were you … *how do you say*? Away with the fairies?'

I take a breath.

'I was,' I say. 'As usual, lol.'

'My best thing about you,' Axel tells me, 'is your imagination. I love it!'

'Awwww,' I say. 'Axel! You always know the perfect thing to say!'

'Not always,' he says. 'But I think it is nice, no, to make people feel happy to be themselves?'

'J'agree!' I say, only realising too late that I actually think that's made-up French, and not real French. Axel doesn't correct me though.

'So,' he says slowly, changing the subject. 'I have some information.'

I can tell, simply by the look on his face, that he knows what I know.

'Is it about your dad, and my mum?' I say.

He nods. 'You already know?'

'I saw them on the phone,' I say. 'But also, now I've had time to think, they did get on *very* well in London. And I'm pretty sure they met up in London again too …'

'Yes,' says Axel. 'My father, I think … it's love?'

'Well, Mum is pretty great,' I joke.

'She is!' Axel says. 'It's fine for you? If they are in love?'

I shrug, pushing my lips into a thin line.

'I asked my father, but how does a romance work, when you live here and she lives there? I do not understand! They are in different countries!'

'I thought the same,' I say. 'I guess they can travel or whatever. But they won't see each other very often.'

'You're OK with this, then?' Axel asks.

I nod slowly. Reluctantly. 'I just want Mum to be happy,' I say. 'As long as it doesn't ruin our friendship, of course!'

'Of course!' Axel agrees. 'Let us promise, we will be friends no matter what.'

'Friends no matter what,' I nod. 'BFFs!'

'BFF?' Axel asks.

'Best Friends Forever,' I explain.

'I'm glad,' Axel says. 'I would like to be your friend forever!'

The next day, we go for lunch at Grandma and Grandad's. They do a big roast, with Yorkshire puddings as big as our heads, and loads of gravy that Grandad makes properly, from scratch, and that tastes rich and creamy and meaty and fresh all at the same time? I can't properly explain, it's got to be tasted to be believed.

'I've been invited to Paris next month,' Mum tells us as we eat. 'How would everyone feel about a Taylor-and-Grandparents weekend adventure, if I go and do that?'

Grandma spears a carrot baton with her fork and looks between Mum and Grandad from under her lashes.

'To see Lucas?' I ask, and Grandma gives a wee nod of the head, as if confirming to herself that yes, Taylor knows what's happening. But then I doubt myself, and maybe Grandma and Grandad *don't* know what's happening, and this is the first they're hearing of it!

'Wait,' I say. 'Do they know?' I use my knife to gesture across the table.

'They do,' Mum says.

'Anyone with eyes *knows*,' Grandma says with a smirk. 'Honestly. It was like watching a film in London, how Lucas mooned over your mother right from the very moment he laid eyes on her.'

'Mum!' shrieks *my* mum. 'He didn't *moon* over me!'

'He blinkin' did,' says Grandad. 'And so he should. You're as good as they get, Erica. The man is lucky to know you.'

'You're all totally biased,' Mums says, and it's not often Mum gets coy or shy, but right now she's so shy she could be a coconut. 'But on this occasion, I'll let you be. It's nice to hear! You're not all normally this nice to me!'

'We are!' I say. 'We're always nice to you!'

'Except when you try to make custard,' Grandma says solemnly. 'You never get it right, and I just don't understand – custard is such a simple thing to make!'

'It's so hard to get the proportions right!' Mum says defensively. 'And Tesco sell perfectly fine ready-made custard, so it all works out in the end.'

'That's the trouble with everything today though,' Grandad points out. 'Everything can come in a packet if you want. Do you know, I recently saw ready-made beef burgers – bun and all – that you are supposed to put in the microwave. I mean, honestly, I can't think of anything more rancid!'

'I can,' I say. 'Cucumber.'

'You and your cucumber!' Mum says, shaking her head. 'How can anyone not like cucumber? It doesn't even taste of anything. It's ninety-nine per cent water!'

'Can't be,' I say. 'Water doesn't smell like monkey butt.'

'How do you know how a monkey's butt smells?' Grandma asks, laughing, and I reply: 'Because I've met his uncle!' and point at Grandad.

'Me?!' he says. 'You cheeky sod!'

He throws his napkin at me and I squeal. It almost goes in my gravy.

'If he's the monkey's uncle,' Grandma laughs, 'then who am I?!'

'I wouldn't like to say,' Mum laughs.

We're all talking nonsense, but it's just so nice. This is what we do best, sit and chat rubbish together, and tease each other. It makes me think that everything will be OK, even if Mum is dating Axel's dad. Who lives in another country. I wonder if that means one day we'll end up moving to France?! Whoa. That would be wild. But then, if Lucy moves, and I move, Star will be left behind on her own.

That's the thing about emotions, isn't it? You never just feel one at once. All my colours are mixed up again …

'To confirm,' Mum says. 'Everyone is all right with me going to meet Lucas in Paris for a weekend?'

'Fine by me,' Grandad says.

'And me,' Grandma says.

Everyone turns and looks at me expectantly.

'Urm,' I falter, and Mum says: 'You can tell me the truth, darling. Say anything, ask anything.'

'Well,' I start. 'It's just … do you think … I don't know, like … are we going to end up moving to France or something?' I ask.

Grandma faintly says, '*Oh.*' I know she hated it when Mum lived away before – it must have occurred to her too. If it hasn't, I've just made it a possibility, I suppose.

Mum considers this. 'We're not moving to France,' she says. 'I mean. At least not yet, bug. It's early days! And I would never do anything you wouldn't want to do.'

'I love France,' I say, 'and want to live there one day. But I don't want to leave Crickleton High. I know everyone, and have the website and my favourite teachers and my friends and … with Lucy moving, it's made me realise how much I *like* Crickleton High, and our life here. For now. It feels safe. But not boring safe. Safe in a good way. Like I can be myself and try new things. Does that make sense?'

What I don't say is that there's Duncan here too – although if he bins me off maybe I *will* move to Paris ASAP, because that will be awkward and sad and horrible.

'You make perfect sense.' Grandad winks at me, and

maybe it's a trick of the light, but he seems to have a bit of a tear in his eye.

'My lovely girl,' Mum says. 'I wouldn't want to disrupt your education anyway, and your life – not after it happened to me. I never recovered!'

'Here we go …' Grandma says, but she's teasing. We all know Mum hated moving as a teenager.

'Is Lucy really going then?' Mum asks. 'Saoirse accepted the job?'

I look at the table, staring hard at my empty plate.

'Looks like it,' I say. 'She's going out with her mum today to talk about it. Pizza Express. Everyone knows that Pizza Express is for birthday parties or bad news …'

'That's a shame,' Grandma says. 'Lucy's a good friend to you. You've got such a lovely little gang, haven't you?'

'Yeah,' I say. 'I do. Or did. It won't be the same if she goes. When she goes …'

I find myself getting emotional, but I don't want to cry. They'll be plenty of time for that!

'Pudding!' Mum says, lightly banging the table with a hand. 'Pudding will make us all feel better. Taylor, you clear the table. Mum and Dad, you stay sat – I'll sort it. You've done enough.'

In the kitchen Mum rubs my back as I scrape leftovers into the bin.

'You OK?' she asks quietly.

'Yeah,' I say. 'Probably got PMT. My period is due again soon. I'm always crying before my period is due, aren't I.'

She moves her hand up to my shoulder so she can spin me around.

'Come here,' she says, pulling me in for a hug. I sink into the softness of her top, listening to the thump of her heartbeat. All I can think is, *I don't want Lucy to go. I don't want Lucy to go. I don't want Lucy to go.*

'I don't want Lucy to go,' I finally say out loud.

'I know, darling. I don't either. It's not fair.'

I sigh.

'But, darling, she's a good friend, and won't be *too* far away, and I promise you, I'll drive you or give you train fare whenever you need it or want it, all right? Friendships are so important, and I'll do everything in my power as your mother to remove any obstacles you might encounter trying to keep it alive. All right?'

I practically squeeze Mum's head off as I hug her tight in gratitude.

'I won the mum lottery with you,' I whisper, and I mean it.

22

The next morning I'm an absolute bag of nerves. Lucy has called an emergency Members Only meeting, and I know it's to confirm what we've been so worried about, and it really makes me want to cry, but I know that I can cry on my own, later, and right now I should be strong for Lucy, who would probably like the monopoly on *not* being strong on account of this awful thing happening to her.

Anyway, the walk down to the high street feels like it takes ages, mostly because I'm not walking very quickly. The slower I walk, the less fast I'll get there, and if I'm not there I can't hear the bad news, can I?

But then I turn the corner and there Starbucks is, and to make matters worse I'm the first one there – Lucy and Star must have had the same idea about getting here slowly. I have to sit for an agonising five minutes, with my drink, just waiting. Star comes then, looking ashen and like she hasn't slept. Her eyes are red-rimmed, like she's been crying.

'Hi,' I say, hugging her.

'Hi,' she says back, and we're both so … quiet. Down. This isn't like us at all. It's horrible!

Star gets a drink, and by the time she joins me again it's everything I've got in me not to text the chat saying BLINKIN' HECK LUCY GET HERE NOWWWWWWWW!!!! But it's nice to get a moment with Star, to prep.

'I just want to say,' I tell her, 'that I'm here for you, OK? We're still besties, and Lucy is still one of the gang whether she's around the corner or an hour away. I know in terms of, like, being a couple, it's going to be trickier …'

Star nods. Softly she says, 'I think she'll break up with me.'

'What?!' I say. 'No! Surely not!'

'I think she will,' she says. 'She won't want to make moving harder by having to think of me back here, will she?'

I look at her. She's distraught.

'Come here,' I say, motioning for her to come and sit at my side of the table. I pull her in close and she rests her head on my shoulder. We sit like that, being in our feelings, until Lucy appears the other side of the glass, outside on the road.

'She's here,' I say. 'Let's be strong for her, OK? I'm here for *both* of you.'

Star swallows, rubs under her eyes (which only makes them look more red, but she's trying!) and sits up straighter. Lucy skips past the counter without getting a drink and comes straight to us.

'I have news,' she says, instead of hello. Star and I look at her. I hear Star take a breath, readying herself.

'Mum has formally accepted the job,' she says, and I feel Star stiffen. 'And ...' she says. She looks between us, and I don't get it. She doesn't actually seem that sad. Her mum got the job and it's like Lucy is about to tell us that she has access to Tom Holland's personal phone number and he wants to know when we're all free to hang out. Is there a way she could actually have decided moving is a good thing?!

'She accepted?' Star clarifies. 'Nooooo!!'

'But!' Lucy says, and I'm not imagining this – she really does sound excited, I'm sure of it.

'But?' I say.

'I'm not moving!' she shrieks, throwing her arms out and giving us jazz hands.

'What?!' I say, loudly enough that the barista looks over to see what the fuss is. But let them look, I don't care! Lucy isn't moving?!

'Mum is going to commute!'

I look at her, shaking my head. I'm vaguely aware that tears are streaming down Star's face, but she hasn't moved – she's frozen to the spot.

'Explain!' I say, waving a hand. 'Quickly! I don't understand!'

Lucy nods, like, *Yeah, this is a lot to take in.*

'The job is just over sixty minutes away, and she's going to drive there and back every morning and every night. When I'm in Year 10, she might stay away one night a week, but she basically says she's going to do the job, to get into a leadership position, and keep looking for something closer to home in the meantime too. I might have to sometimes ask to sleep over with one of you two, but it's a private school, so it works out because their holidays are longer, so she only has to commute crazy hours six weeks at a time, and then gets two or three weeks off … I have to help with dinner more, help with the housework … but crucially, THAT HOUSEWORK WILL BE AT MY HOUSE THAT IS HERE, NOT A MILLION MILES AWAY!!!'

I get up and practically launch myself at her.

'Taylor! OMG!' she shrieks.

'This is the best news ever!' I tell her. 'I am so, SO happy!'

An old man on the next table tuts loudly and says, 'You could *please* rein it in a bit?'

I pull myself off Star and say, without even thinking

about it first, 'She nearly had to move away! And now she doesn't! Excuse *me* for having friends I care about!'

And then my hand flies to my mouth, trying to keep the words I've already said from tumbling out between my lips.

'Sorry,' I say, suddenly sheepish. 'I shouldn't have said that. We'll go somewhere else.'

I look at the girls, about to say we should leave, but the man interrupts my mortification to say: 'No. *I'm* sorry. It's the anniversary of my wife's passing, and I'm feeling grumpy and sad, and I miss her and I feel angry and wanted to shout at somebody. So I shouted at you. Just ignore me. Honestly. Ignore me.' He looks at Lucy, who has gone bright pink at my rudeness – or maybe because she's so happy. I'm not sure. 'I'm pleased you don't have to move, love,' he adds.

'Thanks,' Lucy says, and then nobody knows what to say after that.

The man gets up.

'Enjoy your day, girls,' he says. We watch him go.

'Well, that got sad very quickly,' Star says. 'Poor man.'

'Yeah,' I say. I think about what Grandad would be like without Grandma, but quickly try to think of somebody else because it's just too, too sad. 'Let's go to my house,' I say. 'Mum will be so happy you're staying, Lucy.'

23

It's only been a week of limited Duncan Higginbottom communications, but it's a week that's felt like two years – and so when I bump into him, literally, because he's coming around the corner from PE and I'm coming around the same corner but in the opposite direction from French, I feel twenty emotions at once. I'm happy, nervous, frustrated, and everything in between.

'Oh!' I say, looking up into those fantastic cheeky eyes of his.

'Taylor!' he says, and he sounds ... pleased. He coughs, rearranges his face, and lowers his octave to add, 'Long time no see.'

'Yeah.' I nod. 'It's been ages.'

There's a pause, which I hate, because normally with

Duncan there are no awkward pauses. But then, he said he needed a minute, so I gave him a minute, and since then he's the one who has been avoiding *me*, soooooo …

'You coming from French?' he presses.

'*Oui*,' I say simply. If this is Duncan's way of saying we can go back to normal now, maybe I should play along. I add, 'You coming from PE?'

'I am,' he replies.

Another pause. I can't figure this out. Does he hate this? Does he hate talking to me because he still doesn't trust me? I can't stand it. I wish I knew where I stood.

But then …

'Wanna do something soon?' Duncan asks, and I swear he sounds nervous asking. Like I could ever turn him down!

I blink. 'Does this mean I'm forgiven?' I say hopefully.

'Forgiven?' he repeats.

'You said you needed space,' I say. 'Which, for the record, I have respected. But also for the record, I really am sorry for crossing the line and writing about us. I promise I won't do anything like that again.'

'I know you won't,' he says. 'Thanks.'

'Sure.'

We look at each other, and Duncan gives me his cute smile. It makes me melt.

'Text me, then?' he says. 'When you're ready?'

'How about you text me?' I counter. 'And I promise I'll say yes to whatever it is you suggest.'

'Cool,' Duncan says. 'Bungee-jumping it is.'

Before I can give him a sarcastic eye roll, Paul walks up the corridor, shouting Duncan's name as he spots him.

'Mate, we'll be late for English!' he says, adding, to be polite, 'Hey, Taylor.'

'Hey,' I say, and then Duncan is walking away.

OK. So. He wants to hang out again. I heard that correctly? This is good! This is very good!!

'I keep thinking about Mum and Lucas,' I tell the girls the next day. We've met up at the marketplace to walk to school together, because LUCY ISN'T MOVING! And we still get to be Tay and Two Queers! At Crickleton High! We're all giddy with it, all aware of what could have changed and so relieved it won't. We've been spending *loads* of time together in celebration. It's like a big exhale.

I add: 'If Mum can leap into love with both feet, I want to feel brave enough to do the same …'

Yes. I'm still thinking about Duncan. I need to make this official, so he knows I like him and I know he likes me.

'But you *do* leap,' Lucy says as we pass the Co-op with toilets. 'You're the queen of leaping.'

'Hmmmm,' I muse. 'I don't know. I think I need to do

what you said all along, and ask him outright to be my boyfriend.'

'Do it!' says Star. 'In fact, let's help you make a plan for it at the sleepover!'

We're planning the *ultimate* sleepover this weekend. We've got a list of things to do and *everything*. Don't worry, it's not a challenging and dramatic list like my seize the day stuff! It's all pure and good fun. So far we've got:

- Watch *To All the Boys I've Loved Before*
- Karaoke
- Acting out our Tom Holland and Harry Styles fanfiction (I'm Harry)
- Handstand challenge
- Blindfolded make-up challenge
- Group photo shoot in said make-up
- Make friendship bracelets
- Invent a secret Members Only handshake (we've been meaning to do this for ages, even if it is a bit babyish. SOMETIMES BABYISH THINGS CAN BE MADE COOL BY THE RIGHT PEOPLE, OK?!)
- Face masks

And now I suppose we've also got PLAN HOW TO ASK DUNCAN TO BE MY BOYFRIEND. It's way overdue – I really like him, and I feel like with everything that's been going on I've not made that as clear as I should. So. I will! And I can't wait!

When we arrive today, school is a hive of activity. Apparently Veronica Sellers is here! I passed along my scrapbook for her last week, through her form tutor, Madame Jones, but nobody had mentioned that she'd be back in action so soon. Nobody really seems sure if she's *back* back or just visiting, but as we file into assembly and she's sat on the stage, I get the impression she's just visiting. She looks like herself, with her hair done and nice clothes, but she's got a walking stick beside her and she looks smaller, somehow, like she's shrunk a bit while she spent a lot of time in bed. She smiles at people as we all take a seat – she must feel like an animal in a zoo with us all gawping. I try to do my most encouraging and kind smile, even when she's not looking in my direction. It feels like the right thing to do. Dotted around are the teachers, apparently all doing the same thing. Ms K clocks me and comes over to where I'm sitting at the end of a row.

'I heard about your scrapbook, about the seize the day emails,' she says, smiling. 'Just wanted to say good job. You're back to being my superstar pupil.'

She gives me a thumbs up and a wink, and before I can reply walks back to her chair by the wall. Thank goodness we're OK again! The world doesn't feel right if I'm not Ms K's favourite!

'Year 9,' Mr Logan bellows. As he talks, I'm aware of a dull ache in my lower back, and a growing sense of cramp in my stomach. My period is about to come at any moment. Gosh, what a month it's been since my last one! Still, looking at Mr Logan as he drones on with some 'housekeeping announcement', at least I know if I need a day off, it will be authorised. Out of everything that's happened recently and feeling so out of control of so much, at least there was that: I made a change for the better. I did a good thing.

'And now,' Mr Logan continues. 'As you might have gathered, we have a guest with us today. A very special, brave and resilient guest, our very own Veronica Sellers.'

He pauses, and we all applaud – politely at first, but it gives way to something louder and more raucous, until we're whooping and hollering and cheering, and Veronica has her face in her hands, pretending to be embarrassed.

'Veronica?' Mr Logan says, when we've halfway quietened down. Kudos to him he doesn't tell us to pack it in or anything: he seems to accept that yeah, Veronica being here is indeed something to go crazy over.

Vee uses the walking stick to help her stand, accepting the help of Mr Logan to walk to the lectern, where there's the microphone.

'Hi,' she says, her voice shaky, and it's sweet enough and lovely enough that we all burst into applause again. She scrunches up her face and laughs. It's really cute!

'Thank you!' she says. 'You've all been really kind since I got sick, and Mr Logan said I could come in and talk to you all about what happened, and share some thoughts I've been having. I've basically been in bed for five weeks, you see, first at the hospital and then at home, and I always thought that sounded so fun and relaxing. But, spoiler alert: staying in bed is only fun when it feels like you're breaking the rules. When you actually *have* to stay in bed and cannot physically get up, it sucks. I think I've been unwell enough that I can say *it sucks butt* without Mr Logan giving me detention, so let me say that. Being bedridden sucks *butt*.'

Mr Logan waves a hand as if to agree that of course he won't give her detention, and it makes us all laugh. Veronica is funny! Who knew! Not to mention that apparently Mr Logan is capable of humour. Will wonders never cease?

'Anyway. When I was in bed, loads of you sent cards and games and messages and it was really nice of you. So, thanks. It made me so determined to get well and get back to school, and I told myself that when I did, I'd do things a bit differently.

'I've always been quite shy, and I think that's OK. Not everyone can be star of the show, and nor should they be. But for me, I think I used being shy as an excuse not to try new things, and not to take chances. And if you don't get out there and try new stuff, what's the point, you know? Taylor – Taylor Blake – filled me in on her column for her new website, about seizing the day, and how loads of people wrote to her about how *they* seize the day.'

I'm surprised to hear my own name mentioned, and literally every single person in the hall cranes their neck to find where I am and give me a good gawp. I spot Duncan though who smiles at me, and suddenly that doesn't make me feel as exposed. Star knocks into my shoulder supportively, and I give Veronica a wee thumbs up. She gives me a thumbs up back. I see Mr Logan frown slightly. That man really does not like me. Obviously I don't care.

'I've seen all the letters you wrote her, and she was kind enough to give me some credit. I don't know if I deserve it, but I do know that she's right: we should be seizing the day. We should be taking chances and giving things a go and not hiding ourselves. And Mr Logan agreed to let me come and talk to you all because I thought asking everyone together like this was the best way to make sure everybody says yes.

'My question to you all is: If we all start taking more chances and trying new things, could we all promise not to laugh at each other? To maybe even support one another? I, for one, know I would feel so much more confident to take a leap of faith if I knew you'd cheer me on whether I fly or fall. So. What do you say? Can you do that?'

Nobody says anything. The hall is deathly silent. You know that saying, you could hear a pin drop? Literally, I think I do. We all look at each other uncomfortably, out the window, at the floor. Suddenly, nobody wants to looks at the stage any more. And you can see it on Veronica's face, the worry that she's tried to make a big rousing speech and … nobody is biting.

Then there's a slow clap. Duncan stands up, his hands in front of him in applause, and he stops only to shout, 'I'm in!'

Oh god. There's another beat, and for a second I think it's just going to be Duncan and Veronica in cahoots together. So I do it. I stand up as well, right as Bilious Billy, who I see on the bus sometimes, does, and Jason Clementine, and Lucy.

Somehow, we start chanting, *TAKE A CHANCE! TAKE A CHANCE!*

More people stand up, until there are more stood than sitting, and then we're all on our feet, stomping and clapping and yelling, yelling, yelling.

TAKE!
A!
CHANCE!
TAKE!

A!
CHANCE!
TAKE!
A!
CHANCE!

'Honestly,' I tell Grandma and Grandad later, 'it was *amazing*. Like something out of a movie! It went on for ages and ages, everyone just screaming that they'd take a chance, until Mr Logan switched out all the hall lights and we got confused enough to get quiet and he could tell us he admired our spirit, but that was –' I put on my Mr Logan voice here – 'QUITE ENOUGH, THANK YOU!'

'That sounds so marvellous!' Grandma explains. 'Gosh, kids today, eh, David? Can you imagine doing that in our day?'

'I can't,' Grandad concedes. 'I was too busy twagging it off school to go to the woods and blow stuff up.'

'David!' Grandma says, right as I exclaim, 'Blow stuff up?!'

Grandad looks at Grandma.

'I'd like to strike that comment from the record,' he says sheepishly. Grandma looks furiously at him.

'I should think so,' she tuts, but she winks at me to let me know she's laying it on thick for him.

My phone beeps then, a text from Duncan.

Milkshakes tomorrow? it says. *Ceeks reunited?*

Ceeks reunited, I text back, grinning like an idiot. Squee!! I get another date with Duncan!!

'Anyway,' Grandma presses, and I look at my screen just in time to see Duncan's smiley face emoji. I put my phone down to focus on my grandparents again. 'Now it's got me thinking about how I need to take a chance, Taylor! Because there's life in this old dog yet!'

'I've seen the video of you dancing at your last Northern Soul night,' I say. 'I think it's safe to say you're full of life …'

Grandma gives us a little twirl on the spot to show off.

'See!' I say. 'Incredible.'

'Thank you, bubs,' she replies. 'But seriously. David, don't you think we should do something out of the blue? Something fun just because?'

'Well, I do keep on about finally going on that backpacking trip for over-sixties, the one in Brazil,' Grandad says. 'It's not like we're short of a bob or two.'

That's Grandad's way of saying 'we've got spare cash'. I go to say he can buy me a new iPad then, if he wants, but he spots me trying to make a joke before I even do it.

'No,' he says, holding up a finger. 'I will not buy you a new iPad.'

'How did you know what I was going to say!' I laugh, and Grandad laughs too.

'Because I'm clever,' he replies.

I leave them to it – they're suddenly on Grandma's desktop computer actually looking at trips, as if they might do it! – and I busy myself on my perfectly functional older iPad, because I've got an article brewing in me …

Taylor Blake Seizes the Day … by Not Seizing Anything at All

Once upon a time, I thought I wanted to be special. I thought I wanted people to know my name, all across the world, and I thought I wanted to have a big, magical fancy life, and I thought the way to do this was to Seize the Day.

To me, seizing the day meant being the 'best' at life.

I know, crazy, right?

How can anyone be the best at life?!

I'm not sure what I was on. For a moment, I suppose I thought that maybe in the same way we get graded at school, there was some sort of committee who grade us at 'life'.

And that if you get up early, and wear the best, nicest outfits, and take funny cool pictures at fun places you have to travel to, like London, or Paris, that it gave you more 'points'.

But (spoiler alert!) it doesn't.

You can't 'win' at life.

You can't do life better or worse than anybody else.

That's what I know now.

It's not about how your life looks from the outside. It's not even about impressing yourself with how fabulous you are. The best things in life are quiet and leave you with a huge sense of peace – and that can feel boring. But peace isn't boring.

I get peace from baking birthday cakes and visiting my grandparents.

I get peace from remembering to be kind to my mum.

I get peace from going to Starbucks with my best pals.

And hanging out with the boy I like.

That's how to seize the day.
Chase peace.
Be calm.
Show kindness.
Embody love.

That's what I think, anyway.

24

Right then. Today is the day. I'm doing it. I am asking Duncan Higginbottom TO BE MY BOYFRIEND!! It's also the day I am quitting Josie's conditioning club too. Once was enough for me! I'm too scared to do it in person, so I send a text. It says: *Josie, just to let you know I've loved doing your conditioning club, but I won't be coming any more. I can't fit it in as well as schoolwork, writing for my website, and netball practice and matches. I hope that's OK.* She texts back right away. *That's fine,* she says. Huzzah!

'He'll say yes,' Star says as we linger by the school gates, where Duncan said he'd meet me.

'Obviously.' Lucy nods. 'But also, it's still a scary moment. There's always that small voice in the back of your head that's like: What if they say no?!'

I look at her and blink.

'Sorry,' she says, biting down on her lip. 'Not that you should have that tiny thought or anything. I honestly meant, it's an irrational thought! Be gone, stupid thought!!'

'I think you're making this worse,' Star stage-whispers to her, pulling her in for a hug. 'Come here, you fool.'

They stand there hugging, Star telling Lucy to shut up, and I see Duncan walking down the main path with Paul, listening intently like he does. He's such a good listener, so good at paying attention and then asking super intelligent and smart questions. Oh, Duncan. Lovely, lovely, Duncan!

'Right, we'll make like a banana and split,' Star says. 'Come on, you,' she adds to Lucy.

The girls wave at Duncan and peel off (whoops, accidental banana joke there), and Duncan says bye to Paul too, who spots Lucy and Star walking hand in hand and hesitates – but then Lucy sees and waves him over. He looks to Star for permission, who nods. I guess the girls have forgiven him for that ridiculous episode at the launch party, then.

'Hello, you,' Duncan says, standing in front of me.

'Hello,' I say, and whoa. It's like a whole zoo is in my belly, not just the butterflies. My palms are sweaty, and I'm sure I am irrationally blushing. Gah!!

'Milkshakes at the fancy café?' he says. 'My treat? I've got some birthday money.'

'That sounds nice,' I say, and I think, *OK, he doesn't hate me, he's being nice, this is all very normal.*

'Are you all right?' he asks, frowning. 'You seem ... I don't know. Not yourself.'

'Yes!' I say, a bit too brightly. 'Yes, yes!'

'OK ...' says Duncan. 'Shall we go then?'

He holds out an arm for me to take, but I realise I cannot walk a single step without knowing what we are, if he really will be my boyfriend. I can't make up conversation and do a bad job at listening or even come close to cool and funny and nice to be around if this is all lingering in the back of my mind. So. I don't take his arm. Instead I say:

'Duncan? There's something I've been meaning to ask you. Urm ...'

He gives me his listening face, his paying me attention face, and I must not let myself get sidetracked by his nice eyes.

'Basically ...' I continue.

God, why is this so hard to say?!

'Duncan Higginbottom: Will you be my boyfriend?'

He looks stunned. I must say it a bit too loud because a pair of passing Year 12s look over and I hear one of them say, '*Awwwwww!*' So patronising. Urgh.

Silence.

He doesn't say anything.

Literally twenty years pass, both of us frozen and looking at each other, and it's horrible, horrible! And then Duncan crinkles his eyes all soft and says, 'Taylor?'

Oh god. The way he says it … I know what's going to happen here. He's going to say no, and ask what I'm on about, and laugh in my face and run away and I shall have to emigrate to Greenland or similar because I'll never be able to show my face at Crickleton High again.

'It's OK,' I say, back-pedalling madly. 'You don't have to say it. It's OK. I should never have asked. I'm sorry.'

And then, guess what Duncan goes ahead and does? Laughs! He blinkin' laughs at me!

I WANT THE GROUND TO SWALLOW ME WHOLE.

'Taylor!' Duncan says, and he's playing games with me, really, because even though he's telling me to get stuffed, he's reached out and laced his hand through mine, his lovely warm skin making mine tingle with delight. (Which is annoying, since now I'm going to have to vow to hate this charming warm-skinned boy forever.)

He's still chuckling, but less so now. He must have seen how utterly bright red I've gone. I wish I could run away but I feel glued to the spot.

'I was going to say,' Duncan presses, 'that the reason it's so funny you're asking me to be your boyfriend is because I thought I already was your boyfriend!'

I look up at him in shock.

'You did?' I ask, my voice coming out all wibbly-wobbly.

'Of course I did,' Duncan says. 'You're the only girl for me. You know that. I thought we'd been official ever since our first date.'

'Really?' I say.

'I mean, I don't know how this works!' Duncan says. 'I've never done this before! I didn't know we had to, like, have a whole big conversation about it. On reflection, it makes sense that we'd have a whole big conversation about it, but ... it just felt natural with you!'

'So, it's a yes,' I clarify. 'You'd like to be my boyfriend? Because I haven't seen you properly since the launch. I thought you were trying to ditch me or whatever.'

'It's a yes! A million times yes!' Duncan says, and he does it with so much passion that it makes me laugh now, because I HAVE A BOYFRIEND! AND IT IS DUNCAN HIGGINBOTTOM! NICEST BOY IN THE WHOLE SCHOOL!

'I was just giving you space. I know how overwhelming it's been doing the column and seizing the day and just *being Taylor Bluke*. I didn't mean to make you worry. Sorry! Come here,' he says, leaning in and rubbing his nose against mine. 'I think I'd like to kiss my GIRLFRIEND.'

'OK,' I whisper, smiling so much it will probably get in

the way of a kiss. But who cares! 'I'd like to kiss my *boyfriend* too,' I add.

And our lips meet, even though we're outside of school and anyone could see. It's sweet and gentle and the best ever, and I think, yes, this. This is what it's all about. *This* is how you seize the day: slowly, thoughtfully, and with your whole, whole heart.

Publishing Credits

A heartfelt thanks to everyone involved in getting this book from its first messy draft written at my kitchen table, to this incredible finished book of which I am so proud:

Literary Agent: Ella Kahn
Commissioning Editor: Alex Antscherl
Desk Editor: Jessica Bellman
Copy-Editor: Jess White
Proofreader: Sarah Taylor-Fergusson
Art Director: Laura Bird
Design Assistant: Grace Barnes
Illustrator: Lucia Picerno
Production: Nicholas Church
Marketing: Tim Hardy
Publicity: Emily Marples
UK Sales: Sally Wilks, Frances Sleigh and team
Export Sales: Sarah McLean, Hattie Castelberg and team
Audio Editor: Ashleigh James
Translation Rights Sales: Barney Duly, Jo Blaquiere, Lucy Gibbs, Yas Langley

… and a huge thank you to you, too, for reading. Please don't forget to leave a review on whatever website you use and like!

About the Author

Laura Jane Williams (she/her) is known as the queen of the meet-cute. She is the author of eight romance novels for adults, several non-fiction titles, and her work has been translated into languages around the world. When she's not telling stories, Laura likes movie marathons, parenting, and throwing weights around at the gym.